"If we must part, give me this hour."

She began to weep. "If I had known we'd have so little time—"

He tightened his arms around her. "No, Adeline. Don't think that. We'll be together again."

"Swear it."

"There will come a time—"

"In this life?"

"My lady—" His voice was hoarse with passion.

She clung to him with trembling, desperate force. "Stay with me," she said. "This place. This hour. It is all we will have."

"No. Stay here. Live for me, Adeline."

She turned her face to rest upon his chest, and looked out across the winter meadow and the trees beyond. "There is no one near," she said. "Even the hawks have gone. Give me this hour, Simon. Give me your child."

He shuddered as if she had struck him. "Would you have me forget all caution? You know what you would suffer, bearing the child of a man damned by his deeds."

"Do you know what I would suffer, if I never saw you more, and had no child of yours to comfort me? If we must part, give me this hour. Just this hour—"

BOOK YOUR PLACE ON OUR WEBSITE AND MAKE THE READING CONNECTION!

We've created a customized website just for our very special readers, where you can get the inside scoop on everything that's going on with Zebra, Pinnacle and Kensington books.

When you come online, you'll have the exciting opportunity to:

- View covers of upcoming books
- Read sample chapters
- Learn about our future publishing schedule (listed by publication month *and author*)
- Find out when your favorite authors will be visiting a city near you
- Search for and order backlist books from our online catalog
- Check out author bios and background information
- Send e-mail to your favorite authors
- Meet the Kensington staff online
- Join us in weekly chats with authors, readers and other guests
- Get writing guidelines
- AND MUCH MORE!

Visit our website at
http://www.zebrabooks.com

SILVER WIND

LINDA COOK

ZEBRA BOOKS

KENSINGTON PUBLISHING CORP.

http://www.zebrabooks.com

For Stephen, Gordon, and James

CHAPTER ONE

Early October, 1190; Kent

Mathilde did not stay to watch her betrothal broken. Her brothers had sent her from the great hall before Simon's arrival; only the flicker of bright cloth at the turning of the stair betrayed that she tarried close by. Simon drew his gaze from the trembling hint of green surcoat and faced Mathilde's brothers.

"You will give her up," Eustace Bouteville said again.

"I can do nothing else." Simon looked across the ancient hall and saw the sunlight upon old Eudo Bouteville's shield, high on the timbered wall.

Eustace let out a long breath. "Then we are agreed. It must be so; even if she would go into exile with you—"

From the stair came the sound of slipper upon stone, and a small cry of dismay. Simon looked back to the passageway and saw, in the light from the Boutevilles' extravagantly glazed windows, a glimpse of Mathilde's white and distant face. In that moment, Simon saw terror in the lady's prominent, staring eyes. He had not noticed, during negotiations in happier times, that she had the small, soft chin of a rabbit in winter.

Simon turned back to the lady's brothers. "You would not give her to me," he said. "Not now. And I am not so far damned that I would take her from you."

He saw relief in Eustace Bouteville's eyes and imagined that he heard a grateful sigh in the distance. Renouncing his claim to Mathilde Bouteville had proved easier than he had foreseen. It was but one among many hasty farewells he had made; he had managed far more harrowing tasks in the past two days.

Simon drew a long breath. "I would have Mathilde know that I regret losing her. If this trouble had not come upon me, I would have taken her to wife in all honor, and counted myself fortunate to have her."

"If one day—" Eustace Bouteville's words died before his brother's warning frown.

Simon drew a stern breath. "There may be no mercy for me," he said. " Not in these next years. Perhaps never."

Eustace muttered a low oath and reached toward Simon in a small gesture of regret, a cautious move that would not bring him within a sword's length of

Simon's arm. Behind Eustace, Simon saw Rannald Bouteville glance to the end of the long chamber, to the men-at-arms standing in silence against the wall. The sun was low, streaming cold and crimson through the open door, casting a narrow path that Simon must follow.

It was time to go, before the coming night forced the Bouteville brothers to deny him lodging. Before fear moved them to violence. "Give her my farewell," Simon said, "and wed her to another." He took a last look at the passageway and saw that Mathilde's rich hem had vanished. Alone, he walked into the shaft of sunlight from the door.

"Where—"

"How—"

The words rose to echo among the soot-darkened beams of the hall, sending a sparrow in frantic beating from its perch. Simon halted, and turned back to Mathilde's kin. "I go to Wales," he told Eustace. "To serve the Marshal in the black mountains, and to keep the peace."

Simon looked to Rannald and saw a different question in his eyes. "I cannot tell you how it happened," he said.

Rannald's face darkened. "That you, of all men, should take naked steel into the abbey and—"

"Leave it." Beyond the ragged silence, Simon heard the distant voices of drovers on the hillside. "The dark is coming," he said, "and I should be far along the road when the sun goes down."

The stableboy was standing where Simon had left him, still holding the reins of Simon's mount. There had been no need to tell him that the lord of Taillebroc would not seek shelter here.

Even the ostlers of Bouteville knew that Simon of Taillebroc was in disgrace, and that only the wealth and the honor of his ancestors had kept the mad and dangerous lord from banishment beyond Christian realms.

The devil himself could not have won Taillebroc a place at Boutevilles' hearth this night.

Savare was waiting beyond the river, sitting near the great, twisted oak above the fording place. He rose to his feet and led his horse forward. "It's done?"

Simon nodded.

Savare mounted and turned south. "There's no harm in a last look. We should take the high road above the abbey."

The high road was the shorter way to Maidstone; the easier path, out of sight of the abbey and Taillebroc's distant tower, would take them miles out of their way. Simon gave another brief nod of assent. "The high road."

For the last time, they rode in the golden autumn light along the ridge road. Below them, the abbey lay quiet, the smoke of its kitchens rising straight in the cold and windless sky. The faint odor of windfallen apples drifted from the orchard.

"No trouble there," Savare said.

Simon turned from the sight of Taillebroc's far walls. "The Marshal promised there would be no violence done to the grave."

"And the abbot has enough of our gold to keep him true to his oath, and pray for our sire."

Simon placed his hand upon Savare's shoulder. "Come, brother. There's nothing to be done but meet the Marshal's men and ride on to our posts."

Savare drew a long breath. "Old Harald waits there. Said your armor will rust in the foul weather if he doesn't follow you to Wales to care for it. I would go with you both—"

His brother smiled. "Go your own way, Savare, as the Marshal has ordered. We'll meet again at Taillebroc, in better times." Simon turned back for a last view of his lands. "We'll have it back one day, when God wills Longchamp and his creatures from the land."

"Aye. And if God should need a good sword arm to do his will—"

"—You will not offer yours. We swore an oath; we will honor it and keep the Marshal's trust."

Savare shrugged. "He left you with little enough. You lost the land, a rich heiress—" He took up his reins and turned in the saddle. "Tell me, Simon. Did you weep to give up Mathilde Bouteville? Did you mourn her dowry?"

Simon shook his head. "I didn't come close to weeping."

"You smile? Was your speech with the Boutevilles so amusing? Simon, there are times I would swear you find a jest where only madmen would look."

"No, brother. There was no jesting, but as I left Boutevilles' manor—"

"Well?"

Simon's smile broadened. "I saw a rabbit. It was easier, at the sight of it, to take my leave of the Boutevilles."

"Our trouble has turned your mind strange. Do me a kindness and forget the Boutevilles—and the rabbit—before we come upon the Marshal's men."

Together, they turned west and rode into the setting sun. A wind rose behind them, bringing the scent of rain. William the Marshal was camped somewhere ahead on the Maidstone road; nowhere else would the Taillebroc men find shelter this night.

Late October, 1190; Normandy

To a hostage, even a young female hostage tolerated with kindness by her guardians, the sudden arrival of a royal advisor could bring bad tidings or death. The unheralded appearance of William Longchamp was such an omen: bishop of Ely and chancellor to Richard Plantagenet, Longchamp held the power of life and death in his hand. Adeline, daughter of the unreliable chieftain Caerdoc, had heard the tales of Longchamp's ruthless ambition; she uttered a prayer that her father had not crossed the king's dangerous favorite.

Her guardians had not expected Longchamp's visit; the stableboys and kitchen maids, from whom Adeline had learned the identity and number of the other Plantagenet emissaries who appeared with increasing frequency in these unsettled times, had not known that the hunched and haggard rider followed by a score of mud-showered guards was the chancellor himself.

Only when the lady Maude had summoned her to the solar had Adeline learned that she must have immediate and unrehearsed speech with King Richard's chancellor. Maude had sent her women from the long chamber and followed them, leaving Adeline quite alone with the cloaked and sullen man who had announced himself as William Longchamp and demanded Adeline's presence.

Her lady's vielle lay where Maude had set it down, and the broderie cloth intended for the chapel's altar was rumpled, pushed aside in haste to clear a place for the chancellor to sit upon the settle bench. Beyond it, young Alice's loom sat idle; a shuttle of polished bone dangled from a length of wool, twisting slowly in the draft.

Beneath the familiar scent of roses and dried lavender brought from the south, Adeline caught the smell of wet wool and hot wax. At the chancellor's ungainly boots, mud flowed into the rushes.

The flat gaze slid to focus upon her. "You will understand, child, that an act against my person is a strike aimed at our king. Violence done to the king's chancellor is treason." Longchamp folded long, narrow hands upon his knee. "Treason—plain and simple."

With difficulty, Adeline remembered to keep her voice soft and her words timid. "Has my father—"

Longchamp's bearded mouth contorted in surprise that she had spoken unasked. Adeline lowered her gaze from those black brows and narrowed eyes, and held a demure silence beneath the chancellor's long, offended stare.

"No," he said at last. "Your father, though foolish enough to allow raiders to ride free at his borders, has not yet turned traitor."

Adeline sat quiet and willed her body not to tremble as Longchamp rose and approached her. A narrow, chill hand drifted to touch her cheek, then closed upon the pulse of her neck. "Your father remains loyal," the chancellor breathed, "to save this little neck from hanging. He has seen what becomes of Plantagenet hostages when their sires turn to treason."

It was nausea, not fear, that threatened Adeline's fragile control. None of the tales surrounding King Richard's new chancellor had prepared Adeline for the loathing she felt at his touch.

The fingers loosened. Adeline looked up to find the chancellor settled once again upon the bench, his features bland and expectant. He had placed those deadly hands beneath the folds of his cloak.

"Now, child, you may speak."

Adeline's throat had closed in fear. She forced a rasping breath, and then another. "Have I—Does my lord bishop believe I have offended him?"

A smile rippled above the tilted, shaggy jaw. "I know of no offense. Is there something on your conscience, child?"

Adeline raised her chin and looked into Longchamp's eyes, seeking a hint of the man's purpose in this dangerous game of fear and wits.

"I am King Richard's loyal subject," she said, "and honor you, my lord bishop, as his chancellor. My father's loyalty to the throne has been clear and unchallenged these five years past."

"Before winter comes, your father may find himself tempted to act against me."

Adeline held the chancellor's stare without flinching. "I cannot imagine it," she said.

He sat back and drew the cloak closer about his shoulders. "A traitor has been exiled to Caerdoc's lands—to be warden for the Marshal's fortress above the valley."

Adeline managed not to frown. How could a traitor escape the king's justice and live to take charge of a Norman fortress and lead a garrison of soldiers? Why had William the Marshal taken a dishonored man into his service? No traitor, however wellborn, could achieve what Longchamp had described.

The chancellor was watching her with eyes narrowed to black slits. Adeline slowed her breathing and found the words that should follow Longchamp's declaration. "My father will be doomed to fight this man," Adeline said, "for he will have naught to do with a traitor."

The cold smile spread wider. "Of course he will resist, child, but he will need help." Longchamp leaned forward. "And I will need information—a warning if Taillebroc moves against me."

With a flicker of pleasure, Adeline recognized that the traitor in question must have frightened Longchamp. Badly.

"You wish me to send letters to my father and bring you news of the traitor's plans?"

"You can write?"

Adeline nodded.

"You will write nothing of our dealings. You will tell no one of our speech. I will send my man to hear your words and bring them back to me."

"Then how—"

The chancellor stood and walked to the lady Maude's table to stare down into his reflection in a polished bronze mirror. He began to stroke the uneven beard, frowning as it flattened against his cheek. "The negotiations for your betrothal to young Nevers must end," he said.

In this hour, she had forgotten her guardians' talk of a marriage. The image of Nevers's pocked face and young, loose mouth rose within Adeline's mind; she managed not to smile at the prospect of ruining the betrothal plans.

"We will send Nevers home with a purse of gold to sweeten his regret. Then you will return to your father."

Home.

She was to go home. Longchamp's face blurred beyond Adeline's vision. She was going home—

The chancellor was watching her struggle not to weep. "Your father's sins will cause him no more grief, and you will remain with him as long as he wishes to keep you. All this in return for your promise that you will send me word of Simon Taillebroc's dealings with both Normans and Welsh of all stations.

You will warn me should he begin again to speak treason of me—or of his king."

Freedom. Longchamp had offered her freedom—"Come here to me," the chancellor whispered.

His hand snaked out to seize her arm. "I know what you imagine—that you will have your freedom at a trifling price. But know this, Adeline of Caerdoc: Simon Taillebroc has bought his own freedom with wealth, influence and the devil's help. He's a traitor and a priestkiller. A priestkiller left unpunished through the Marshal's foolishness."

Adeline stood silent before the chancellor's rage. The fingers upon her arm tightened into a hurtful claw. "Simon Taillebroc drove his sword through the heart of a holy man before the altar of Hodmersham Abbey. Above the resting place of his kin, in sight of his own father's tomb. This is no rebel baron, girl. It is the devil's creature you will watch for my sake, and you will send me warning if he rides forth to do more violence to the land, and to Christ's anointed servants." He released her arm and began to force his hands into heavy gauntlets. "You will earn your freedom, child; if you fail me, you will see your father damned and hanged with Simon Taillebroc."

The lady Maude gave her a small chest and warm clothes for the journey, and promised a maid and five men-at-arms to escort her to the coast and across to Dover. Though she tried to learn what Longchamp had told her guardians of his purpose and his destination, Adeline could discover nothing.

No one spoke of the chancellor's sudden appearance and abrupt departure that same night. Only the mud upon the rushes and the lingering odors of sealing wax and fear remained.

CHAPTER TWO

On the last day of the journey, the hills lay dark before the track, and the wind held the cold promise of snow. The Hereford guardsmen had fallen silent; they rode with gazes fixed upon the narrowing road, watching the forest that would soon close about them.

As they neared the woods, the riders formed a single line with Adeline and Petronilla in the middle of the armed train. A last glance at the form and folds of the hills above the tree line revealed no familiar sight for Adeline, no sign of homecoming.

The passage through the trees was narrow, and the wind strong; with each new gust, ice-laden branches bowed and brushed near the path, scraping near the riders' faces. Aspen leaves swirled beneath naked trunks, rattling half-frozen in the northern gusts. An army of Welsh brigands could pass unnoticed and unheard behind the clatter and pulse of this wind.

"This is a savage place," Petronilla shouted. "They should have summoned your father to come down and bring us from Hereford."

Adeline looked back and nodded her head. Petronilla would expect no reply to the complaints she had renewed each hour past Hereford. Both women had heard the soldiers speak of Caerdoc: None would invite that battle-scarred wolf from his lair, now that the old beast had begun to keep to his valley and raid close to home.

At last, in the deep of the forest, the tangle of hazel scrub and bare, clustered trunks gave shelter from the wind. Adeline pulled her mantle close about her shoulders and kept her nervous palfrey in place behind the first riders; she smiled to see that the small bundle she had tied to the saddlebows had not shifted.

Petronilla's voice broke the quiet. "If that man Caerdoc doesn't recognize his daughter when he comes upon us, what will happen then? Adeline, go up and ride before us all. Take your hood from your face."

"Quiet back there. She'll stay where she is."

At the guardsman's words, Petronilla lowered her voice to a muttered lament. Unused to indifference from healthy young men, Petronilla had discovered the grim side of riding with seasoned soldiers through dangerous ground.

Adeline sat straight in the saddle and closed her eyes to conjure the image of her father's face; after

their years apart, would she recognize him, and would
he know her for his long-absent daughter? The
thought had troubled her since Hereford. More troublesome still were the questions that would come
later. A dozen sleepless nights had not yielded an
easy way to answer them.

Behind her, Petronilla sneezed. "Is there no place
to stop and warm ourselves?"

Adeline shook her head. "Not here."

"No manor, no farm?"

Adeline extended her arm toward the lonely view
just beyond the naked trees. "As you see, this is a
remote place." She glanced again at Petronilla and
drew a silken square from her sleeve. "Here," she
said. "Your eyes are watering."

Petronilla daubed at her streaming eyes and car-
mined nose, and turned a poisonous look upon the
guards. "The lady Maude's men were more courteous. They would have found us shelter long before
now. We should not have let those men turn back at
Hereford. This is the wilderness, and we are lost."

Adeline looked ahead, then back to Petronilla; the
woman's face was settling into ominous lines.

The soldier beyond her rolled his eyes.

Adeline pointed to the guards at the front of the
train. "These men know the way. We'll reach the
valley, safe enough."

"Safe? I gave up safety when we crossed the sea.
And now the lady Maude's servants are gone, and we
might be lost. And your father may kill us all for
intruders before he sees you."

"My father doesn't kill travelers." She hoped. The

dangers of catching Caerdoc by surprise would increase as the day went on.

"Still, if you rode ahead, where your father would see you—"

Petronilla's words trailed off into the wind, lamenting the day she had set sail from Normandy to see the lady Maude's hostage guest safely to her home. Adeline looked back once again at the unhappy woman. "If you don't want to stay for the winter, I'll send you back to Hereford," Adeline said. "My father will give you silver to pay your passage home."

"Alone? I think not." Petronilla huddled deeper into her cape. "We're too far gone. I'd not make it back to Hantune. The lady Maude didn't understand that it would be so far. Or so cold." Her words trailed into a resonant sniff.

Adeline sighed and drew breath to renew the discussion that had sustained Petronilla since they had embarked at Caen. "Lady Maude will reward you next spring when you return," she said. "She told me you are the bravest of her maids, the most practical. Of all her household, she chose you."

Petronilla's thin mouth turned down in displeasure. "The lady Maude had her reasons to send me, I vow."

"There was a problem?"

"Nothing for your ears, Adeline."

Petronilla's hints of a household scandal had begun in Caen, and become a daily ritual during three long weeks of travel. Adeline had begun to enjoy the small challenge of piecing together the scraps of gossip in which Petronilla took such pride. Today, she sensed a darker cast to Petronilla's hints. "Surely the lady Maude's reasons were to your credit," Adeline said.

Petronilla lifted her chin. "Of course. She had to choose one of her women to go with you, and turned first to me."

"Thank you for agreeing," said Adeline.

"You couldn't go alone into a nest of thieves and bandits. Not when you've had years among gentle-folk." Petronilla glanced up the track. "Why did they not send word ahead to your father, to keep him from attacking us?"

The young guards behind them drew closer. "The woman is right," said the taller of the two. "Caerdoc's archers are as deadly as his temper."

The second soldier laughed. "Then ride ahead, as the woman said, to tell the old bandit we're coming."

"I'll not do it."

"Then shut your mouth and keep your eyes open."

The two young soldiers seemed at the point of blows.

Adeline looked back over her shoulder. "He will see me among you," she said. "And even if my father doesn't notice me, he'll not attack. There is a treaty. He keeps the peace and pays tribute to the king."

So far.

The guards fell silent; Petronilla's long sigh echoed Adeline's unspoken fears. In her five years abroad as a hostage to Caerdoc's peace, only two letters had reached her from home: a cautious message from Father Cuthbert, asking for details of her mother's death in Normandy; and a brusque greeting, also penned by Father Cuthbert, from Caerdoc himself. Her father had bid Adeline not to despair in her time among Henry Plantagenet's vassals. The Normans, Caerdoc had reminded her, were her mother's people, and would not strike down one of their own; that advice, now four years stale, had been Caerdoc's last word to her.

Adeline turned her gaze back to the road ahead. In the past two years, that single message from her father had given her many sleepless nights. Would Caerdoc abandon the terms of his treaty with the Normans and leave Adeline's fate to the kindness of his dead wife's people? Waking fears had shadowed Adeline's dealings with her keepers; she had come to dread the arrival of every messenger, and had ceased to resist the lady Maude's schemes to betroth her to the landless but well-connected young Nevers. From Wales, from her father's people, there had been no further word.

The first riders cleared the forest and regained the clear, long views of the foothills above the tree line.

Of a sudden, the wind stopped. Across the high meadows, there was a strange silence broken only by the soft whickering of horses and the creak of saddles. Adeline's party was not alone.

There was a muttered curse and some fumbling among the guards. The bishop's standard rose upon its staff to sudden, trembling prominence above the sergeant's shoulder. Behind Adeline, there came the subtle scrape of hard, gloved fists upon stiff leather scabbards. At the sergeant's side, a restive horse shied from the sight of the Hereford banner.

Caerdoc and his men were on the road ahead, ranged across the meadow track. Behind the mounted band, ten clean-limbed horses on leading halters had lowered their heads and begun to graze.

"Who are they," Petronilla cried out. "What are they?"

"It's my father," said Adeline. She pulled the hood from her head and nudged her mount forward to the front of the guard.

A dozen sleepless nights spent rehearsing the words she would speak had not prepared Adeline for this moment. Struck dumb and near foolish, she looked across to her father's astonished face and waited for him to speak. And wondered where he had bought— or stolen—the fine Norman horses his men rode.

The sergeant of the guard hoisted the bishop's banner higher and drew breath to break the silence. "We bring your daughter back to you," he bellowed.

Caerdoc did not move. Behind him, his men began to mutter. Adeline looked from one scowling face to the next, but could find no familiar soul among them. The sound of her heartbeat began to pound in her ears.

The sergeant glanced back at her, then drew breath again and faced Caerdoc. "Your daughter," he called out. "She's here. With us."

"The devil you say."

Ten more men emerged from the woods and crowded the road behind Adeline's party. Caerdoc spoke to the rider at his side, a tall youth with a hint of red beard below his spotty face, and waved him down the track; to the men who had come up to surround Adeline's party, he made a single, wide-armed gesture.

The sergeant turned again to Adeline. "What did he say to them?"

"I don't know."

"Lady, you may be as much at risk as we are."

"In truth, I didn't understand what he said." Adeline's own voice sounded weak to her ears. She straightened in the saddle and drew a deep breath.

"Daughter?" Caerdoc had chosen a single Frankish word to address his half-Norman child.

The guards drew aside as Adeline rode forward. "Father, I'm here."

They met halfway between the parties, out of the hearing of the bishop's men and Caerdoc's band.

"It is you," Caerdoc said. It might have been the late-autumn cold that had tightened the lines about his eyes and sharpened the thrust of his jaw. Someone had trimmed his blade grey hair to precision.

"Yes." Adeline drew a deep breath. In a throat constricted with emotion, words were an effort.

"They set you free?"

"They did." Her father's big Norman mount was restive. Adeline saw him calm the beast with a single touch of his hand to the cropped mane. She took heart: It seemed that Caerdoc was not riding a newly stolen mount.

Her father's expression did not change. Once, his brows had been thick black slashes above mottled hazel eyes, and had given clear warning of his mood. Now, they had paled to silver; his face was harder to read.

The grey brows merged in an unmistakable scowl. "Why? Why did they give you up?"

She had not expected tears or an embrace in this open place, before the eyes of her father's men. Nor had she expected her father's suspicions to send all other emotion from his speech.

Adeline had words to answer him. Words taught to her by Longchamp three weeks ago, in Normandy. "They told me that you have a Norman garrison above you in the old fortress now, and that there is no more need to hold me as a hostage to keep the peace."

Caerdoc's mouth twisted in a grim smile. "And they think to add these men to the garrison? I'll not feed more Norman mouths this winter."

Her father had not grown softhearted in her absence; even in this day of homecoming, his valley and its provisions were his first concern. Adeline looked away, back to Petronilla and the men who had brought her home.

The sergeant came forward. "We are members of the bishop's guard, sent from Hereford as your daughter's escort."

"Then go back to Hereford now."

The sergeant's face had turned an angry red. Adeline nudged her horse closer to her father and pointed back to Petronilla. "The lady Maude sent that woman with me from Normandy. I have told her she may stay for the winter as our guest, and start home in the springtime. Will you permit this?"

Caerdoc frowned. "They set a spy to watch me through the winter?" He stood in the saddle and looked down the file to point to the silent, pale

Petronilla. "Go fetch her to me," he called out in clear, Norman words. "No, not you—let Howyll do it."

The spotty, red-bearded youth turned his horse and trotted past the small guard to Petronilla.

Behind Caerdoc, his men waited without expression.

"Father—"

"Adeline." He took a long look about him and waved the Hereford sergeant back to his men. They were once again alone between the two bands. Caerdoc placed a hand upon Adeline's shoulder. "Your mother— Tell me how it happened."

The question she had dreaded was before her. Here, in the open, with strangers' eyes watching.

"Tell me now. How did she die?"

Adeline looked down at the saddlebow and curled the reins about her hands. And then, remembering lessons learned in childhood, unwound the leather reins and placed them across her palm. Beside her, Caerdoc cleared his throat. "Tell me," he said again.

In five years among the Normans, she had imagined words she might use on this day. And had thought that she had no more tears to shed in her mother's memory. Beyond Caerdoc's shoulders, she saw the curious faces of the men who followed her father, and lost the image as it blurred with the onset of tears. She raised a hand to pull her hood back over her head.

She heard her father's saddle creaking, and saw a wide gauntlet cover the reins upon her saddlebow.

"You weep? Look at me, Adeline. They killed her, then? Don't fear to speak; I need to know this."

Would he strike down the bishop's guard? Attack the Norman garrison? This was no time to show weakness. Adeline raised her face. "The tears," she said, "are from the cold."

Caerdoc made a gesture of impatience. "The Norman swine taught you to cover the truth." Adeline's palfrey shied away from Caerdoc's sharp words.

Petronilla's cry rang out, shrill and sudden. The tall youth had seized the reins of her palfrey and was attempting to lead her from the small band of Hereford men. Petronilla had turned in the saddle and jerked the reins back from the lad's hands. "The packhorse," she cried. "We go nowhere without that packhorse." A second shriek followed.

At the sound, Adeline's mount tossed her head and sidled away from Caerdoc's large horse. From the red-bearded youth, a single outraged shout rose above the shrillness of Petronilla's complaints. Caerdoc looked up and cursed.

"Don't touch her again."

The words came from a distance behind Adeline. From the looks upon the faces of Caerdoc's men, she saw that the deep Norman voice was known to them.

She turned in the saddle. A rider had appeared before the tree line, not far from the track. Behind him, a company of mounted men waited within the wood, their swords bright among the ice-covered branches.

The stranger drew the helmet from his head and placed it beneath his arm, moving with deliberation as if there were no need for haste; his hair, trimmed short for that helmet, curled dark above a long, impassive face. With his free hand, the knight beckoned to Adeline. "Come to me," he called. "Don't be afraid."

Behind the knight, the woods began to move with the wind's return. Some gesture, some small motion of compliance Adeline had not intended, must have caused her palfrey to move farther from the track and turn her rider to face the stranger. Behind her, Adeline heard her father's exasperated growl.

The stranger's mouth had curved with a slight smile. "Move away from him; come to me."

"There is no need."

"Are you sure? There was a scream. A woman's scream."

His voice held the promise of warmth and shelter; in the hard-featured face, his eyes shone dark with the same promise. Adeline could not look away from that gaze. All else—Caerdoc's muttered curses, the confusion among the bishop's guard, the wind-bowed branches shattering their delicate skins of sleet—all else seemed to diminish, muffled beneath the deep pounding of Adeline's heart.

"You had better come to me," he said again. "I'll see you safe this day."

Caerdoc gave a curt order to his men and turned back to face the rider. "She's my daughter, Norman fool. Set one hand upon her, and I'll see you in hell."

The steady smile did not falter. "Lady, is this true?"

"Yes."

He glanced down the track, and back to Adeline. "And the other woman?"

"She travels with me. We are bound for Caerdoc's valley."

Somewhere behind her, a voice began to speak in rapid Welsh. The Norman made a small gesture to the silent men behind him, then turned to Adeline once again. "Why did the other woman scream?"

"She was surprised. Nothing more. The men with her are the bishop's guard from Hereford, bringing me home. There is no problem. Sir, I—"

"Yes?"

"—I thank you."

The smile deepened, then vanished as the knight turned his gaze back to Caerdoc and pointed beyond him. "Tell me about those horses."

"They're mine," said Caerdoc. "Bought from my cousin Madoc yesterday. Go to him and ask him, if you wish. He will tell you."

The rider shrugged. "I believe you bought them from Madoc. Where did your cousin get them?"

"I didn't ask him."

The knight looked back to Adeline. "I'll follow you to the valley."

"It's not necessary—"

Caerdoc rode forward to block Adeline's view of the rider. "He'll follow us in any case; our old fortress is now in his command. This is Simon Taillebroc, daughter. Do you know the name?"

Her face must have shown recognition. The Norman knight looked away from her regard.

Caerdoc raised his voice so that the bishop's guard would hear. "Do you see what the Normans have sent to plague us this winter? He is the priestkiller

Taillebroc—so beloved of the Plantagenet that he lost only his lands for his crime. Rather than kill him, as justice demanded, the Marshal set him to watch over my valley."

The man called Taillebroc looked across the meadows to the sky, then turned his gaze back to Caerdoc. "The eyes of a priestkiller see as much as any other man's. They see that those horses were not bred in these mountains. They will see, Caerdoc, if you go out raiding again to break the peace." Taillebroc raised his hand to bring his men forward, out from the aspen trees. There were twenty of them, well mounted and armed against both violence and the cold. Within moments, they had passed Caerdoc's party and begun the long journey up the meadow track.

The bishop's guard said hasty farewells and turned east to begin the journey back to Hereford. Soon, only Petronilla, the packhorse, and the red-faced Howyll remained upon the path.

Caerdoc rode back to his men and issued a swift succession of orders that left them in two groups. He returned to Adeline and pointed to the larger of the two. "Go with them—you and the other woman and that packhorse. I'll go ahead and see that all is well."

"Is there trouble?"

Her father shook his head. "No more than before," he said.

Then he was gone, riding west without a backward glance.

CHAPTER THREE

Harald the armorer spread his hands wide in frustration. "I lost Caerdoc's trail. He didn't stay with the women, but took half his men and rode ahead. When the girl and her maid reached the manor, the uproar was done, and the old fox was gone from the place. We didn't see him leave."

Simon Taillebroc turned from the watchtower rail and beckoned Harald forward. "What have you learned of the daughter?"

"Caerdoc's folk wouldn't say much, but the priest talked a little." Harald leaned his burly form against the timber battlement. "It cost me a shilling and the promise of a dozen tapers to get him to speak."

Simon raised a brow. "He should have told you all he knew, for fear of offending Simon the Priestkiller."

Harald shrugged. "The shilling was faster."

"I'll give you a purse of shillings. You should go back and see the priest again. Get him to talk about the raiding if you can; he may know how Caerdoc disappears without riding through the pass."

Harald nodded. "He might. He has an eye for the silver, that one."

"What did he tell you for the first shilling?"

"As little as he dared. Five, maybe six years ago the old king took the daughter as a hostage for Caerdoc's peace and sent the girl to Normandy. The mother went with her to see her settled in a Norman household, but didn't come back."

"Is the daughter a bastard child?"

"No, the mother was wed to Caerdoc. The priest Cuthbert spoke of it."

"But didn't return to her husband?"

"Could not. She died on the way. Caerdoc thought her murdered, and almost started a rebellion in these parts. Then he went to earth here and has kept the peace ever since. The rest you know: He raids close to home, has never been proved to attack a Plantagenet force, and hides all else from the king's justiciars." Harald sighed. "It's a fool's errand to keep watch over the old fox."

"Is the daughter wed?"

Harald shook his head. "The priest said nothing of a husband. And he said there's little talk of the daughter's years in Normandy among Caerdoc's folk. They're tight-mouthed as ever, even with each other."

"The girl—"

"Her name's Adeline, they say."

Simon looked across to the single, narrow pass into

Caerdoc's valley. "The girl—Adeline—seemed to have no joy in coming back to this place. I thought her a captive, taken in a raid."

"Then give thanks to sweet Saint Hrothswitha that you challenged Caerdoc before you struck. We might have lost the peace out there, with Caerdoc's men armed and ready to fight."

Simon placed his fist upon the rail. "I saw his face when I came upon them. He should have spoken sooner to warn me away—to say that the woman was his daughter. Instead, he held back until the last moment, as if he hoped I'd attack him. He let her deal with me, though she had been weeping, and looked as if she had been riding hard."

"She should have spoken."

"The woman said a little—not enough. I saw her hesitate before she told me who she was. The daughter is as close-mouthed as the rest of Caerdoc's people, for all her years away."

"Well, she won't change her ways among these people. She was down there in the great hall with the woman who traveled with her, the two of them sitting beside the fire pit. The Caerdoc folk had brought food to them and left them alone."

"Alone?"

"As if she were a Norman born, sent to plague them."

Simon turned from the rail. "They treat her as a stranger?"

"Not as a stranger. As if they knew her, and were afraid."

"Damned Welsh. Do they think she brings a contagion with her from Normandy?"

"She brought a maidservant who burns their ears with complaints." Harald stretched his arms and sighed. "We'll be cold and draft-ridden up here this winter, but I wouldn't change it for the manor hall, with that Norman maid setting the Welsh women into a temper."

Simon looked across the valley; storm clouds had formed high above the far ridge. Before long, there would be ice on the ground. He placed a hand on Harald's shoulder. "You could be in a better place, before the snows come. Go back to Taillebroc, Harald. Up here, it will be too cold for your old bones."

Harald gave Simon a good-natured blow to the arm. "Young lord, look to your own bones this winter. I have enough flesh on me to keep the damned Welsh wind from freezing my gut. And no better winter pastime than to watch you deal with the mad folk down in Caerdoc's hall."

"You could go down to Hereford and work at the sheriff's garrison."

"For Longchamp's brother? I'll not forge the sword he'll use to attack you."

"You could warn me if Longchamp himself comes to Hereford." Simon forced a smile. "Come, Harald. Before he died, my father told me that your trade was never more than a ruse to listen to the talk of those who brought their weapons to you. The old king's spies would have paid in gold to listen beneath your forge."

Harald flexed broad, misshapen fingers. "My days

at the forge are over, Taillebroc. I'll not forget that
your father took me in when I lost my skill, and could
scarce hold a common soldier's sword. I'll not repay
his act by leaving his son to Longchamp's killers.''

Simon shook his head. ''Then stay another fortnight, until you tire of these games of chase and
follow. It won't be easy up here, watching the pass
while Caerdoc plays us for fools.'' He drew a leathern
bag from his hauberk. ''If you're bound to stay, then
wait a few days, and take another shilling to the priest
to see what you can learn about Caerdoc's travels.
Tell him that Simon the Priestkiller grows impatient
of this game.''

Harald shook his head. ''Why do you remind him
of the killing at Hodmersham? If you have to strike
at Caerdoc this winter, the people will claim that you
acted once again in haste, in error. No justiciar in
the land would spare you, if trouble comes again.''
Harald growled an oath and placed a contorted hand
upon Simon's shoulder. ''If you must be exiled so
far from Taillebroc, then turn it to the good, and
keep these folk from remembering why some might
call you Priestkiller.''

''I live at the Marshal's mercy as it is.'' Simon looked
into Harald's red-circled eyes. ''My time may be short.
We both know it. Look to your own safety; my father
would say the same, if he lived.''

Harald brought his fist down upon the rail. ''If
this priest—if Caerdoc's people could know how it
happened, back at Hodmersham—''

''They cannot know. And they will not know. Do
not imagine, old friend, that I will spare you if you

tell them." Simon gave a last glance to the valley pass and turned from the sentry's walk. "When you go down, send up the first watch. I'm weary unto death."

The wind died before sunset, leaving dark clouds just beyond the far ridge of the valley. As the sun left the sky, yellow hearth light shone from the narrow windows of Caerdoc's hall, and embers soared with the column of grey that rose through the smoke hole in that broad slate roof.

Upon the far slope, shepherds' campfires burned bright. Nearer to the valley floor, torches bobbed above those who climbed up the hill from Caerdoc's manor.

The sound of distant voices rose through the stillness and reached the sentry in the high fortress above the valley, mingling with the thin notes of his whistle-flute.

Simon found the sentry pacing across the walkway. "Any sign of trouble?"

Luke halted and lowered the flute. "None. I counted the torches leaving Caerdoc's hall just now. Only ten of them climbing the hill to the shepherds' huts, just as before."

"There could be as many as five men sharing each torch. Tomorrow, I'll post a man to watch them as they pass."

Luke nodded. "As before, most of them go up past the brewhouse first. They say Caerdoc is generous with his board and his mead."

It would be a long, cold night in the fortress. If

Caerdoc and his shepherd-warriors would offer a place at their hearth to Simon's soldiers, the Norman outpost would soon be deserted. It was Simon's good fortune that the old fox Caerdoc had not yet offered that strategic welcome.

Simon descended the ladder on the tower wall and crossed the small bailey yard to the guardhouse. "Harald," he called. "Come with me. We'll go down to see how Caerdoc is passing the night."

A moment later, Harald stepped out of the warm garrison house and pulled a second cloak about him. "Why now?"

"Caerdoc won't expect us after dark. And the household will be in some confusion with the arrival of the daughter. It's a good time to appear."

"And if he doesn't admit us?"

Simon threw his cloak across his shoulders. "He has to. It's our right to enter the byre to fetch our horses."

"He knows we keep twenty mounts up here."

"And he must continue to shelter and feed the others, and give us access to them, or break his treaty with the Marshal. I have decided, Harald, that I want two more mounts up here at the fortress. You and I will fetch them tonight. It's as simple as that."

Harald sighed and turned to the long stable built against the far bailey wall.

"We'll walk down," said Simon, "and ride the horses back."

Harald shook his head. "A cold walk down the hill, a scuffle with Caerdoc's sentries, and a cold ride home? This is a ploy, Simon, to send me scuttling back to Kent before winter comes."

"You might think of it again." Simon took a burning brand from the bracket at the gates. "We'll warm ourselves in Caerdoc's hall for an hour before we take the horses. How can he refuse us a place at his hearth?"

"With a simple sign to his household," said Harald. He drew a swift hand across his throat.

"I think not. He won't know whether we have a company of twenty men waiting outside the stockade. Caerdoc won't risk a fight, not with his daughter in the hall."

Harald's laugh echoed in the darkness as they began their descent. "The daughter. Of course it's the daughter. I shouldn't have told you she looked forlorn. But if she pleases you, Simon, it's worth the trouble of a cold walk down the hill."

Simon shrugged. "She pleases me, but I'll do no more than look upon her, and speak with her if I can. I'll not go beyond that. Our purpose is to count the men in Caerdoc's hall this night, and see how many ride out with him at dawn. It's time we began to learn how many he slips past us."

"Caerdoc would have your head if you touched his daughter."

Simon stopped and looked down at Caerdoc's stockade. "I'll not snare her in my life. I'd not do that to any woman. Not now."

High above them, in the sentry tower, the notes of Luke's whistle rose from the polished bone to float upon the night.

* * *

There were no sentries outside the stockade, or upon the walls—an unthinkable lack of concern for the manor's defenses. Simon cast a long look about him before walking through the unsecured gate; from above him on the hillside there came the blaze of torches and the sound of drunken voices in the nearest croft. Mingled with that distant noise, Simon heard smaller, closer sounds of footsteps moving through the bracken.

Harald took the torch and made his way through the gates. "He has sentries, I'll vow, but not where we expect them. Wherever they are, they chose not to stop us."

Simon took a last look into the darkness and followed Harald through the gates. "They watched us come down the hillside, and followed us. By now, Caerdoc will know we're here."

"He will have hidden his daughter away."

He had not.

She was seated beside the fire pit, eyes half-closed in the warmth of the hearth. The woman's hands rested upon the skirts of her fine green surcoat; her unbound hair seemed a river of palest amber as the firelight shone through it. At her side, the troublesome Norman maid nodded in restless sleep.

On the other side of the long pit, Caerdoc sat at his board with six men; their cold-chapped faces and short cloaks were signs that they were fresh from the road. Simon frowned. There had been no sign of travelers in the hour since the sun had set. Once again, the fortress sentries had been blind to the movements of the valley men.

Caerdoc looked up and smiled at Simon's obvious consternation. "Welcome, Simon of Taillebroc. It's a cold night. Have you come to warm yourself at my hearth?"

Caerdoc's daughter opened her eyes and gave a small nod in Simon's direction. Beyond that small gesture, she did not move. Simon had seen a hart remain that still as the hounds had passed nearby in pursuit of another. He bowed his head and smiled.

"Have we not brought enough firewood up to the fort? I keep my promises to William the Marshal, and would not have you go short."

Simon turned back to Caerdoc. "We must speak, before winter, about the firewood. All other things are sufficient: We are well supplied with food and with drink, and our horses sheltered, as you promised the Marshal they would be."

Caerdoc had remained seated at his board; he did not ask Simon to join him. "Then you have come for your horses?"

Beside him, Simon heard a rustle of linen and silk; Adeline rose to her feet with slow, fluid grace. "There is hot mead on the board," she said.

Simon turned to Harald, then back to Adeline. "We thank you."

Caerdoc looked from Simon to his daughter, then spoke to his men in rapid Welsh. They moved aside to make room for Simon and Harald at the long table. Adeline approached with two earthen cups of steaming drink, then retreated to her place beside the snoring maid.

Simon raised his cup to Adeline. "Your health, my lady. And may your homecoming be happy."

She gave a small smile in response, then looked back to the fire. In that brief moment she had resumed the same serene posture: eyes half-shut, slender back straight as a rosemary sprig, hands curled upon her skirts.

The five men at Caerdoc's board had shed their cloaks and filled their cups again. "A cold night," said Simon in halting Welsh.

A hoarse giggle came from the end of the table. The spotty youth who had earlier braved the displeasure of Adeline's maid was sputtering red-faced into his tankard. Two small lads emerged from beneath the board and began to caper about the fire pit, echoing Simon's awkward words.

Caerdoc silenced the lads with a single barked word; a servant woman appeared and shooed them from the hall. He turned to Simon. "A drunken raven speaks better Welsh than you. We know your Norman tongue. With old Henry Plantagenet at our doors, we learned it well."

Adeline raised her head. Caerdoc grimaced. "Yes, daughter. It matters not that you lost your Welsh among the Normans."

The shadow in her eyes was painful to see—almost as hurtful as the courtesy with which she nodded in reply. How did Caerdoc's daughter maintain her mask of contentment in the face of this prickly homecoming? Simon fought the urge to obliterate Caerdoc's cold scowl with a few well-placed blows. "I have English as well," blurted Simon.

"Speak whatever you like." Caerdoc thrust his cup into the mead bucket and raised it again. "But in all things touching the treaty, speak to me in your Norman tongue. We don't waste good Welsh words on such matters."

Simon drank of the warm, herbed mead. "Then when we meet tomorrow to discuss the firewood you must bring to the garrison, we'll speak Norman words."

"And in Norman words, I'll tell you that I have seen the great pile of wood you have upon your northern wall. We'll bring more when you need it."

"The woodpile is for a beacon fire." Simon saw Adeline shift upon her bench and turn to watch him with undisguised curiosity. He smiled to himself. It was clear the lady found military matters of greater interest than his own earlier attempts to speak with her.

"We have no beacon fire," Caerdoc growled.

"You do now."

"None would watch for it. The line of beacons passes far from here."

"The Norman garrison in the hills above your kinsman Rhys keeps a bonfire in readiness. It will be easy, if raiders come, to summon help."

Caerdoc did not attempt to hide his contempt. "We need no help to keep raiders from the valley," he said.

Simon did not attempt to hide his amusement. "I believe you, Caerdoc. I'll vow no one remembers the last time a party of raiders came to your walls. It's your good fortune, but must be damned hard to explain."

At his side, Simon heard Harald set his cup down and mutter an oath.

For a long moment, Caerdoc regarded Simon with a puzzled frown. Of a sudden, his features formed a cautious smile. "Damned hard," he repeated. "So none have attempted it." The smile broadened. "Your old king Henry was satisfied that his rich Norman barons might pass by my valley unharmed. The new king Richard must be content with that same treaty."

Adeline had not taken her gaze from his face. Simon glanced at her, then back to Caerdoc. "You and I will keep the peace, God willing. And to do that, I will have a beacon fire ready." He set down his cup and beckoned Harald. "I thank you for the mead."

Caerdoc nodded and made a slight gesture to the end of the board. "Young Howyll will light you to the byre, and see you past the gates."

The lanky youth rose to bask in responsibility. He picked up a horn lantern and lit a stub of candle within it. Simon bid the impassive Adeline good night and took a curt farewell from her father. As he neared the door, the small lads reappeared from the kitchen passageway, spouting shrill questions to those who remained at the board. There was a smile on Caerdoc's face as he waved them silent with a small gesture.

Simon followed Harald from the hall. Caerdoc seemed fond of the raucous boys from the kitchen;

they might be bastard sons. Had he no smiles to spare for his daughter, after her years away?

The garrison's horses were sheltering just inside the door of the byre. Beyond them, at the far end of the great barn, the new beasts Caerdoc had brought into the valley were confined behind a wooden rail. Howyll stepped before Simon and blocked his view of Caerdoc's new mounts. "Your horses are here, beside us. Which of them will you take?" Simon pointed to the two smallest geldings and led one to the mounting step outside the byre.

Harald groaned. "No saddles?"

"It's not far."

Together they rode out through the gates by the light of a single torch. "You chose well, taking the smallest of the lot. The garrison stables will be sore crowded this night."

"In the morning, we'll bring down two others for Caerdoc to feed. I won't spare him from any part of the Marshal's treaty terms."

"I heard that lad Howyll offer to come up and fetch them. Why did you refuse?"

"We need to enter the manor stockade as often as we have good reason to do so."

"A duty you neglected before Caerdoc's fine daughter appeared."

Simon ignored Harald's amusement. "Did you watch her? She sat aside, quiet as a cat watching a bird, listening to the talk. The old man bristled when I spoke to her, but seemed not to care that I stared at her beauty. But when the children—Caerdoc's bastard sons, they might be—came out to mock me, Caerdoc and the servingwoman sent them from sight. They didn't seem a household eager to welcome a daughter back—or even to notice her."

Harald sighed. "Simon, they might be wary of your reputation, and afraid that you'd strike the lads in anger if provoked."

He looked back at Harald's sorrowful face in the torchlight. Of course. That must have been the reason. The truth was that he had, in that brief hour watching Adeline's hair in the firelight, forgotten his sin. And had not remembered, in all that time, that they called him Priestkiller.

CHAPTER FOUR

It was not the homecoming Adeline had imagined. Her father was a stranger of few words, and those few spoken with obvious caution. Adeline had waited for Caerdoc to speak again of her mother, to repeat his terrible question when they found themselves alone. But when his men had left the trestle in the great hall to seek their pallets, and Petronilla had dragged her saddlebag into the sleeping chamber, her father had said nothing more than to bid Adeline a good night. Caerdoc himself would sleep somewhere outside the great hall, in one of the longhouses built against the stockade walls.

"I saw him through the arrow loop," said Petronilla. "Your father went into the servingwomen's house and came out again with one of them."

Adeline sat down upon the wide, plain pallet in the

place where once her parents' great bed had stood. "He left his own chamber to us."

Petronilla lifted a small bowl of oil and held the flickering light high above her head. "Look about you. There's nothing here but woolen coverlets and dried herbs. This is not your father's sleeping chamber."

"Years ago, it was."

Petronilla set down the small lamp and lifted the coverlet from the bed. "Not as much dust as I had expected. It will do." She began to fold her surcoat. "Did you hear what I said? Your father went to the servingwomen, in that row of storage huts against the stockade."

Adeline shrugged.

"Don't you want to know which of them came out with him?"

"Be grateful he didn't see you spying on him. Petronilla, it would be best not to appear curious to the people here. They are nervous of us as it is. They—" Adeline turned to the darkness of the far wall and brushed a sudden tear from her face.

Petronilla was spreading a second coverlet over the pallet. "Nervous? Surly, I'd say."

Adeline turned back to help Petronilla. "They seem not to trust me now. My speech seems strange to them, I think."

"They answered back well enough when I asked for a brazier to warm this chamber. They have Norman words and the will to use them when they refuse the necessities to their lord's daughter."

"He isn't their lord."

"Their chieftain then. Whatever. The one gentle-woman, the weaver Maida, spoke up for me, but the others laughed and turned away. So we'll suffer from the cold."

"It's not so cold. My parents slept here, and warmed it with a brazier only in the worst winters. The door isn't far from the fire pit."

Petronilla sighed. "These folk may be your family, Adeline, but they show no great kindness to you. And you do seem a stranger to them."

Maida, the soft-spoken woman who had charge of the manor's looms, had looked upon Adeline with wistfulness and a little kindness, but showed no willingness to speak of the changes Adeline had found in Caerdoc's household. Though Maida watched over the two young lads who had inherited Caerdoc's brow and steady gaze, neither Caerdoc nor the woman herself would speak of the boys' parentage.

Her father had given her the good sleeping chamber beside the great hall, but he had ignored Adeline's surprise at the unfamiliar look of the chamber and refused to hear her questions. The great bed, the carved chest, and the tapestry hangings—all the treasures Adeline's mother had prized—were gone, and in their place were simple furnishings Adeline had not seen before. In the morning, she vowed, she would find what was left of her mother's things and begin to restore them to their places.

Petronilla wedged the door shut, snuffed out the lamp's small flame, and wrapped four layers of woolen bedding about her shivering body. "If I die of the cold, tell the lady Maude that your father and his servingwomen are my murderers."

Adeline caught up another blanket and threw it across Petronilla's huddled form. "We'll survive, somehow. It won't get much colder than this."

Petronilla's teeth ceased to chatter. "We did well today to survive an encounter with Taillebroc the Priestkiller," she muttered.

Adeline took her cloak from its peg and brought it to serve as a blanket. "He thought us in distress."

"Well, I was in distress. When that great lout of boy took my reins and pulled my horse from the track, it was all I could do to beat him off. If he had spoken a single word of courtesy, and promised not to ravage us, I would have kept quiet."

Adeline smiled to herself. "Ravage us? Both of us, before my father's eyes?"

"Well, one of us. You should have seen the way that young bull calf looked at me. I had to cuff him twice before he'd give back the reins."

Adeline closed her eyes. "I'm sorry he frightened you."

"I was sore afraid, and the guardsmen did nothing—gaped at us as if they were simpletons. Which they were."

"You dealt with him well enough."

"That I did. You had troubles of your own, with that Taillebroc man threatening to take you from us. There's a dangerous one. He killed a priest and lost his lands in Kent, so they say."

"So they say."

"Still, he has a fine look about him, as if he hasn't

forgotten his noble birth." Petronilla sighed. "He might have suffered a spell of madness, as did Sir Launcelot in the wilderness."

"He's not mad. William the Marshal trusts him with the garrison." Adeline pulled the coverlet close about her shoulders.

"I'd not trust him within an arm's length of you, Adeline." Petronilla sighed in the darkness. "He's not for maidens, that one."

At dawn, Caerdoc called to them through the door. Maida appeared soon after, carrying an urn of warm water and offering to help the women dress.

"Your father waits to speak to you," she said to Adeline. "And to you also," she told Petronilla.

They found him with the two children sitting at his great chair before the trestle board. Caerdoc tossed an apple into each child's hands. "Now go out to the byre and help Howyll with the horses."

He pushed the bowl across to Adeline and Petronilla. "The last of the summer's fruit," he said.

Adeline bit into the hard, tart apple and recognized a taste from the past. "Mother would save them dry for the winter. Hundreds of them."

Caerdoc looked away. "The women still do."

"I'll help in the storerooms, as Mother used to do."

Her father frowned. After a moment, Adeline sought to fill the awkward silence. "You have built a few more storehouses, since I left."

Caerdoc cleared his throat. "I have decided, Ade-

line, to send you west. To winter with my cousin Rhys
for your greater safety."

She put down the apple. "Father, I want to stay.
After five years—"

"—You'll go to Rhys, where the Normans cannot
find you and take you hostage again."

In the four weeks of her journey, Adeline had imagined the barriers she might find, and the dangers she
might risk in spying upon Taillebroc. Never, in all
her worries, had she considered that her father would
not allow her to stay.

Longchamp had not anticipated this move. Or had
he, and expected her to counter it? The chancellor
would not forgive failure; if Adeline failed to send
reports of Taillebroc's doings, Longchamp would see
Caerdoc's treaty broken.

Caerdoc reached for her hand and gave it an awkward caress. "Don't look so grief-stricken," he said.
"After the winter, when I see where the Marshal next
sends his troops, I'll know whether it's safe for you
to return."

Adeline drew a swift breath. "Father, please let me
stay. Why should the Normans want a hostage again?
They have a full garrison to watch the valley. If the
worst happens, and the Marshal needs a hostage once
again, I'll go willingly. I promise."

"I'll not give you to them again. Trust me, I won't."

"I didn't suffer in Normandy. You were right when
you wrote to me and told me not to fear my mother's
people. They treated me well—"

"That they did," said Petronilla. "My mistress, the
lady Maude, even offered her youngest nephew as

husband for your Adeline. A fine young man he was, and most taken with your daughter. What could be better proof of Adeline's good treatment? The young man was of good family, and could have had—"

Caerdoc's face had darkened to solid purple. "They betrothed my daughter? They offered my daughter in marriage without so much as a word to me?"

Adeline closed her eyes. Had she not warned Petronilla not to mention the lady Maude's marriage scheme? "Father," she said. "It was an idea, nothing more. The lady Maude was at the point of writing to you to suggest a betrothal when word came that I was to go home. There was no betrothal. There was no contract."

Caerdoc's eyes narrowed. "Is this true? Tell me, Adeline. Was there some—disrespect? Some—"

"Nothing. There was nothing save an idea that the lady Maude might have suggested to you, had I stayed." Adeline turned to Petronilla. "It was but gossip you heard. Nothing more."

Petronilla looked from father to daughter, then down to her lap. "I was mistaken," she said. "Must have been—"

"So," said Adeline, "you see there was no problem." She rose from the bench.

Her father rose to face her. "You will go to Rhys before the snows come. You and this woman. I'll send word to him today."

Adeline bowed her head. A messenger might reach her father's cousin by tomorrow at nightfall. And by the second night, Caerdoc would have his answer. Somehow, in the next two days, she must change her father's mind. And keep him from guessing that she had her own desperate reasons to remain in the valley.

Caerdoc rose from the table.

The woman Maida appeared in the doorway. "Would the ladies come sit with my weavers? We have attempted a long tapestry in the Norman style."

Caerdoc smiled. "Yes. Of course. That would be a good place for them."

Adeline followed Maida from the hall. As they passed the byre, she whispered a word to Petronilla. Within the hour, Petronilla was instructing six lady weavers in the methods of Norman broderie. And Adeline was riding with the easily duped young Howyll to fetch the extra horses from Simon Taille-broc's fortress.

Viewed from the valley floor, the watchtower seemed taller than before and less crooked than she remembered it. Both were true, Howyll said. The lord Simon Taillebroc had pulled down the stump of the ruined platform and commandeered enough timber to build another tower and a second longhouse for his troops. Then Taillebroc had taken over the ruins of the old garrison hall for himself and walled off the solid part that remained as his own lair.

Taillebroc had taken for his own use the ancient hall where Caerdoc's fathers had kept watch over the valley; he must have done it to annoy Caerdoc, Howyll told her. Who else, asked Howyll, but a man destined for strife and damnation would wish to spend the long winter nights separate from his fellows, sleeping alone with the ghosts who must watch over that ancient hearth pit?

Adeline imagined that long, powerful body asleep beside the fire, and the dark, unruly hair upon a soldier's pallet. "Is he alone?" she asked. "Or does he have visitors he doesn't share with the others?"

Howyll turned a sudden, intense pink. "No, he doesn't bring women to the fort. Once or twice he rode across the hills with his men to the widow Nesta's house and asked for a very clean whore."

"I didn't mean that—"

"—Not that I saw it myself," Howyll stumbled on. "One of your father's men heard him speaking to Nesta. And told me. Much later, I mean."

"I understand."

"Look there. They see us."

The gatekeepers were well trained. They left Adeline and Howyll waiting in the high, cutting wind that whistled across the promontory where Taillebroc had rebuilt his fortress. After a time, the men had returned to swing the heavy gates out upon their new leathern hinges.

The low morning sunlight shone through the mist rising from the bailey ground, casting subtle shadows upon timber walls and packed earth. Simon Taillebroc stepped from the door of the old hall and stood waiting as they approached. The richness of his black tunic and the crispness of his black hair gave him a hard-edged presence as the ground mist curled about him.

His strong, graceful hands had offered her protection in the near-lethal confusion of her homecoming;

those same hands had slain a priest—a simple priest from the abbey at Hodmersham, on Taillebroc's own lands. The dark gaze that only yesterday had given Adeline uneasy courage had, not long ago, looked upon a holy man to whom Taillebroc had offered only death.

He made a small gesture. "You are well come, Adeline of Caerdoc."

In the short ride up to the fortress, she had made a plan. Adeline nodded a greeting, then pointed to the small timber hall from which Taillebroc had emerged. "My father is bound by treaty to bring firewood for the garrison. I am to bring woolen hangings to keep the wind from the old hall; you will not need a large fire then."

In Taillebroc's black gaze, there was no sign that he believed her. Adeline kicked a foot free from the single stirrup she had used in her ascent to the fortress and slid from the back of her palfrey. Taillebroc waited still where he stood; he had not moved to help her.

She gave the reins to Howyll and brushed her mantle straight as she approached Taillebroc. "I'll look now to see what is necessary."

He put out a hand to stop her. "We need nothing from Caerdoc's weavers. Tell him I thank him, but cannot accept."

"My father might see this as part of the treaty," she said. Adeline's gaze went to the old hall.

Taillebroc shook his head. "Measure out the guardhouse, if you wish." He inclined his head toward the old hall. "You need not see it. No one lives there."

Through the half-closed door of the hall, Adeline saw the faint glow of embers against the darkness within. "No one?"

Taillebroc still held her arm. His touch was gentle; though he kept her from going where she wished, he was as soft-spoken as a courtier leading the lady Maude into her great hall in Normandy. "My men sleep in the guardhouse. As you see, it is large, too long to measure save by pacing its length." He hesitated. "I think you may do that by walking outside the walls."

"I will count my paces, out here."

"Of course." He walked with her to the garrison's longhouse. "As you see, it is new, and well built. There will be little wind through the walls. You should keep your hangings for Caerdoc's hall."

The weak sunlight fell upon raw yellow timber. The resin beaded upon the planks cast a heavy scent, and shone bright as scattered gold. Taillebroc walked beside Adeline, slowing his long stride to match her own steps as she walked along the wall.

It was a longhouse, and Caerdoc would be angry if forced to send half the year's wool to hang upon the walls. Adeline put the thought from her mind; she would be long gone from the valley before the snows came, and Taillebroc might never ask what had become of Adeline's false offer.

This might be her only chance to see the fortress; if she could find something of interest to Longchamp, he might forgive her early departure. She looked up at the watchtower. "You built a tower as well, since you came here."

"Yes. On the old foundation."

"When I was a child, it was nothing more than a falling ruin."

Taillebroc glanced at the tower and back to her. "Why did Caerdoc let the fortress decay? The manor is unprotected now. Did he not fear that one day it would be overrun?"

"He said—" Adeline hesitated.

"What did he say?"

"He said that the only way into the valley is through the pass. From the manor gates, he sees who comes through."

"And then? He would see them come, and keep them from the manor walls?"

"Of course. We would have good warning. His men ride out often."

"And when his enemy comes though the pass, where does your father expect his women and children, and his livestock to wait out the battle? Inside the stockade? With a few fire-arrows, his enemies could kill you all."

Adeline did not answer.

Taillebroc reached as if to touch her face, then drew back. "Caerdoc should take better care of his treasures."

That suggestion of a caress, and his hesitation, caused her face to flame with sudden heat. Adeline raised her hand to touch her blazing cheek.

Taillebroc stepped back. "I have frightened you."

"No. I'm not afraid."

He looked beyond her to the stable. "The lad looks ready to leave. You should not stay."

She glanced behind her and saw Howyll mounted once again, with two horses on leading lines behind him. Beside the stable door, a thin-faced man-at-arms slouched watching her. He pulled a small flute from his tunic and began to play.

"Go now," said Taillebroc. "And do not come here again. This is a rough place. It's not for you."

Once again, Adeline felt that he would touch her, perhaps walk with her to her palfrey and lift her into the saddle. And once again, he turned away.

Simon Taillebroc walked to the old hall and through the narrow door.

He did not look back.

The soldier with the flute stopped his slow tune and helped her mount her palfrey. Howyll guided his horse and led the others behind him as he passed through the fortress gates. Adeline waited until he was clear, then saw the soldier's hand come up to close about her reins.

"I am a messenger," he said.

The blood stilled within Adeline's veins. "You are Taillebroc's man?"

"I am with the garrison. Once, not long ago, I was William Longchamp's man. He trusts me still."

Howyll had stopped beyond the gate; he looked back and frowned. With effort, she ignored the numbness of fear that had come over her arm; she raised her hand to Howyll and waved him on.

The soldier watched Howyll turn to ride down the hill. "If you have a message for Longchamp, tell it to me. Send for me if you need to. Send for Luke."

She looked down at the soldier's narrow face and

quelled a gasp of astonishment. "You are Long-champ's spy? Why did he send me as well?"

Luke moved to the off side of her palfrey and began to check the saddle girth. To any who saw them, Luke was offering a small courtesy to Caerdoc's daughter. "Longchamp never gives his reasons," he said. "Nor would I ask them."

His thin mouth twisted into a smile. "You may go where I cannot. Be sure, lady, that you do all that is possible to give our master what he needs."

He released the reins. "The chancellor is not a patient man. Very soon, he will expect some word from you."

Adeline shook her head. "There's nothing yet."

Longchamp would not care to know that Simon Taillebroc lived apart from his garrison in the ancient hall. Longchamp must never know that Simon Taille-broc had looked at Adeline with a mingling of warmth and desire that had left her trembling—

"Do not think to cheat Longchamp. Laziness will earn you pain. Disloyalty rouses the killer in him."

"Have you trouble?" Taillebroc's voice sounded across the bailey yard. He stepped from the old hall and began to walk toward Adeline.

The man called Luke stepped back from her pal-frey.

"No, no trouble," she said, and rode out from the gates of Taillebroc's garrison. She looked back once to see Simon Taillebroc watching her retreat; Long-champ's messenger had vanished from sight.

CHAPTER FIVE

Adeline rode down to Caerdoc's manor as slowly as she dared, letting her palfrey pick its way down the steep fortress hill at its own pace. At the bottom of the slope, she turned from the rutted track and took a narrow path through the fields to the small lake beyond. She slackened the reins and allowed her horse to graze upon the frost-withered grass along the shore.

There would be trouble when she returned to Caerdoc's hall. Her father would have long since discovered that she had not spent the morning safe within the manor walls with Maida's weavers.

As a child, she had learned that Caerdoc's daughter must never disappear from sight, must never go alone beyond the stockade walls for any reason. She had obeyed her parents' rule, and survived those first years only to lose everything—home and kin—as a hostage to the Plantagenets, in a world a child could only begin to comprehend.

When he discovered her absence, Caerdoc would be swift to anger; his anger would grow to fury when he learned that she had gone up to Taillebroc's lair. Adeline shivered in the thin sunlight. Her father had already decided to send her away; her ride to the fortress and back could not worsen her predicament.

After tomorrow, she would be exiled once more from Caerdoc's valley. She would not see Simon Taillebroc again; Longchamp would find another to watch the dark knight and discover his secrets. When she returned—if she returned—she might find that Taillebroc had not survived the winter.

Longchamp's enmity toward Taillebroc must be even greater than Adeline had imagined. He had sent two spies to watch the man, and no doubt had a plan to use them to bring Taillebroc low.

It was foolish to weep over the fate of a man she had met only yesterday and would never see again. Longchamp had enemies along the width and breadth of the Plantagenet empire; Taillebroc was not alone in his troubles.

Her own father might be next on the chancellor's list of troublesome subjects to be brought to doom and dishonor. In these times, with a man like Longchamp holding Britain and Normandy within his power, there could be no certainty of peace for any man.

Adeline drew a long breath and raised her face to the sky.

A small hawk circled high above the lake, soaring in unhurried grace. Adeline dropped her reins and took a long, careful look at the valley walls above the manor and its fields. If her father did not change his decision, she would leave the valley before she had revisited the half-remembered haunts of her childhood. The hawk flying far above her had seen more of Caerdoc's valley this day than Adeline would see in the long year to come.

The fields were bigger than her recollections of them. They lay blackened from stubble-burning, rising from the small lake to the lower slopes of Caerdoc's valley. Above the burnt land, sheep moved upon the steep meadows; about the three small rivers descending to the lake, swaths of dark forest cut through the high pastures.

Adeline gathered the reins and turned her horse toward the manor. Close beside the stockade, nestled between the chapel and the wall, the herb plot seemed scarce withered by the frosts. There were herbs for every purpose; if a woman had learned the skill, she might cure a sickness, or feign it. Adeline slipped from her palfrey's back and walked past the squares of herbs, and wondered which of them could be used to bring a day's fever to a healthy young woman and leave her too ill to travel.

"We have been lucky with the frosts, so far."

Maida had led a bay packhorse around the corner of the stockade. Cloaked in fine dark wool, she stood smiling at the far side of the garden.

Adeline smiled back. "Where do you go?"

"Up to the shepherds' hut."

The panniers were heavy with cloth-wrapped bundles. "Are they not coming down to winter near the hall?"

Maida shrugged. "The flocks have grown, these past few years. Some must winter up on the south wall of the valley."

Adeline looked up at the rutted track that snaked through the pasture. "Are you going far?"

Maida followed her gaze. "Not far. One day, you should go up with me."

"I'm to leave in two days. My father will send me to Rhys for the winter." Adeline watched Maida as she spoke. The woman's features showed a little regret, but no surprise at Adeline's words.

Maida nodded once. "In the spring, then. When you return, there will be time." She smiled again, and led the packhorse past the frost-thinned herbs to the beginning of the narrow track.

"Maida—"

The woman hesitated and looked back.

"How long have you lived here?"

She made a small gesture. "Four years. Four years and a summer, now. Rhys had more weavers than wool, back then. Three of us left and came here." Maida looked beyond Adeline to the stockade walls. "Your kinsman Rhys has a great hall of his own, with earthworks around it. You'll be safe there."

"Of course." Adeline caught her palfrey's reins and walked back to the manor gates. If her father sent her from this valley, none of her kin—not Caerdoc, nor his cousin Rhys—would be safe from Longchamp's anger.

* * *

No one challenged her as she rode back into the stockade. Petronilla was at the stable door, hands upon her hips, confronting a terrified Howyll.

"You knave—you young idiot—you lost one of the pannier bags. Don't deny it."

Howyll tried to edge through the stable door, but shrank back before Petronilla's angry gesture. "I told you, I did no more than lead the packhorse here. To the stable. You watched me unload the panniers." He rolled his eyes. "You watched every move I made."

"Then if you tell the truth, the bag must be miles away, back where you and your pack of brigands came upon us and nearly started a battle with your clumsiness."

"Clumsiness? There was no clumsiness before you shrieked at my horse and frightened it."

"I was telling you, young knave, to keep your hands off our packhorse. And if you had, we'd not be missing the bag. Go back and get it."

"I have work to do."

"You're running away without finding the bag."

Howyll made a calming gesture and peered into Petronilla's flushed face. "I was to help Maida take food up to the shepherds. As it is, she left without me. I'll look for your bag tomorrow."

Petronilla seized Howyll's muscled arm. "You'll look for it today." An expression of cunning came over her features. "I don't believe you. If you're following Maida, take me with you."

He shook his arm free. "I'm late as it is." He

glanced beyond her and sighed. "Your lady is waiting to pass."

Adeline looked from Howyll's crimson face to Petronilla's high color. She handed the reins to Petronilla and offered her the cloak from her shoulders. "Take my horse," she said. "It's a fine day for a ride."

Adeline turned from the sight of Howyll's confusion and walked into the warmth of the great hall. Caerdoc was gone; a servingwoman scrubbing the trestle board would tell her nothing.

From the brusque answers of the woman at the trestle, Adeline learned that some folk whom she remembered well but had not seen at the manor had moved on to western lands, far from the ranging patrols of the Norman border lords. Of those who had remained with Caerdoc, Adeline remembered some faces and even fewer names. A heaviness grew in her heart as Adeline imagined what she might find when she returned to the valley next year. By then, would she find even fewer faces from the past?

Night came too soon.

Adeline could not sleep. Petronilla, exhausted by her ride and disgusted by the squalor she had found at the shepherds' hut on the valley wall, had described each detail of her trials before falling asleep. Only at the end of her ramblings had the drowsy Petronilla told Adeline a thing that had robbed her of her night's rest.

There were men-at-arms living in the shepherds'

hut. At least six of them. None of them helping the
shepherds. All of them weather-burnt, hard-eyed men
more dangerous than the manor guards who rode
with Caerdoc. They sat about in the clearing before
the hut, Petronilla said, and warned her away with
their fierce looks.

Howyll seemed to know them, but had refused to
answer Petronilla's questions about the surly men
who must surely be fugitives.

Only Maida had entered the hut, and to Maida
alone had the brigands shown respect. Maida had
been as deaf as Howyll to Petronilla's questions, and
had scolded Howyll in rapid Welsh on the way back
down to the manor. With a touch of pride, Petronilla
had said that Howyll defied Caerdoc's wishes by bringing a stranger up to the hut.

Petronilla had fallen silent then, leaving Adeline
to stare into the darkness and consider these tidings.
Six former rebels living among the shepherds offered
no great surprise. Caerdoc had always sheltered fugitives from Norman justice in the valley, and he had
managed to keep these particular ruffians out of sight
of the fortress.

It was ominous that the men had gathered in one
place, living as a small army might do. Was Caerdoc
planning a rebellion? Would her father and Simon
Taillebroc one day lead their men into war in this
valley? At Rhys's stronghold, she would be a day's
ride from the conflict, and would be the last to know
the tidings, if strife took lives of those she had known.

Adeline turned to face the far wall; through the
arrow loop, she saw the far watchtower washed by the

half-moon's light. Did Taillebroc sleep alone in the
ancient hall beside that tower, or did he lie wakeful?
Adeline closed her eyes and tried to put thoughts of
Taillebroc from her mind.

Still, sleep did not come. A fitful, waking dream
moved just beyond her tight-shut eyes and cast flickering images of a firelit chamber and the face of
Simon Taillebroc beyond the fire.

Adeline sat up. The distant crimson flames were
no dream: High on the valley's northern wall,
Taillebroc's beacon fire blazed into the night. One
of the border fortresses must have given the alarm
that rebels or brigands had struck, sending Norman
soldiers to hunt for brigands in the night. Her
thoughts went to the men at the shepherds' hut, and
she prayed that they were gathered around their own
campfire, far from the raiding that had caused the
alarm.

It was impossible to sleep. In her imaginings, Adeline heard the sound of riders passing the manor
walls and the distant rattle of weapons held ready.

It was too real. Too close.

She was half-dressed in her shift and mantle when
she heard the heavy voices begin to quarrel beyond
the walls, and had her cloak at the ready. She placed
a hand over Petronilla's mouth and whispered a
warning.

In that moment, a single blow fell upon the chamber door. "Caerdoc. Show yourself, and we'll leave
you in peace."

It was Taillebroc's voice. Louder than she had
known it, and pitched to a savage growl.

"Caerdoc. Answer me."

Petronilla sobbed.

There was a silence beyond the door, then the murmur of other voices.

"Caerdoc, there are raiders outside the valley. Speak to me and prove that you're still abed. We'll not harm you or your woman."

Adeline approached the door. Where was her father? Was it possible that he was abroad in the night, pursued by Norman patrols?

She stood as close as she dared to the door. "He's here. Leave us in peace." Her voice, hoarse with fear, was not her own.

Again, there was silence. And once again, a blow to the door. "Damn you, Caerdoc. Don't send your woman to speak for you. If you're there, show yourself. There will be no mistake about this night. Show yourself now, or you're an outlaw."

The hammering began soon after.

"Tell them," Petronilla cried. "Make them stop."

Adeline pulled Petronilla from the bed and fumbled in the darkness to find a second cloak. "We delay them," she whispered. "Every moment they spend here, my father might be saving himself." Together, they dragged the mattress from the bed and shrank behind it into the far corner.

The door burst open in a flood of torchlight and voices. Adeline's fingers clawed into the mattress so hard that when Taillebroc seized it and flung it to the floor, she fell with it. Above her, Taillebroc's sword flashed crimson in the light of the torches.

Petronilla began to scream.

Taillebroc uttered a swift, violent curse. "Where is he?"

Adeline shook her head.

Taillebroc pulled her to her feet and set her against the wall. "Idiot women. You both could have died. This is Caerdoc's sleeping chamber. You said he was here. We came in ready to—"

Adeline gasped. Taillebroc followed her gaze to the sword he still held above him, ready to strike. He took his hand from her shoulder and stepped back.

He lowered the sword. "Tell me," he said. "Tell me where to find him. If he's abed, or barricaded somewhere to defend himself, I'll leave him in peace. Prove to me he's not out raiding tonight."

Adeline pushed away from the wall and pointed to Taillebroc's sword. "Prove to me you speak the truth. I think you will murder him, wherever you find him."

Taillebroc rammed his sword into its scabbard and reached for her arm. "You mean to delay me. I speak the truth, madam. Tell me where to find Caerdoc in this manor, in this hour, and I'll leave you both in peace."

From the doorway came the sound of angry voices, and the splintering of wood.

"Tell him. Tell him now," Petronilla cried.

"Tell me what?"

Petronilla covered her face with her hands. "He's in the women's house. He sleeps with the serving-women."

Behind them, someone laughed. Taillebroc spat an order over his shoulder, and there was silence once again.

The hand upon Adeline's arm moved down to her wrist. "Come," said Taillebroc. "Show me where your father sleeps."

Petronilla ran beside her as Adeline kept pace with Taillebroc's long strides. The hearth was deserted; beside it, empty pallets and overturned benches lay strewn upon the rushes.

At the door of the great hall, Taillebroc cast an arm about Adeline's waist and carried her against his side, to keep her bare feet from touching the mud of the bailey yard. Behind them, Adeline saw the men of Caerdoc's hall, disarmed and silent, crowded against the stockade wall and under guard by Taillebroc's men.

He set her down upon the stoop and gestured for the others to follow. Petronilla slapped away an offer of help and pulled on her boots. "It's there," she said, and pointed to the last of the new huts against the southern wall of the enclosure.

Taillebroc drew Adeline to the narrow door. "Call to him," he said. "Tell him what we want. Tell him we'll harm no one, but need to see that he's here."

Adeline struck the door with her fist. "Father, hear me. Speak to Taillebroc. Show him you're not out with the raiders."

There was a dragging noise inside the hut, and fierce whispers. Then Caerdoc's voice rang out. "Adeline, what has he done?"

She looked down at Taillebroc's hand upon her arm. "He broke a door, nothing more. He wants to see you, to prove that you're not with the raiders."

"He hears me. Tell him to get out."

Taillebroc uttered a savage oath. "Come out. Show yourself. Do you leave your daughter out here to deal with me?"

"There are women in here."

"I'll not harm them. I'll not harm you. You have my oath on that. Show your face, and I'll believe it's you, and not some foul-voiced kinsman."

"Do you know what your oath is worth to me, Priestkiller?"

Taillebroc's hand upon her arm did not waver. Only his voice showed the strain of Caerdoc's insult. "Open the door, and let your daughter and her woman go in with the others. Then come out to face me. Do it, or I'll call you less than a man. Do it, and I'll leave you in peace."

To the right of Caerdoc's door, in a windowless storage hut, came the high, frightened voice of a woman, and the murmur of others to comfort her. Taillebroc heard it, too; he drew Adeline back and made her stand behind him. "The women aren't with him. He's alone, and ready to strike. Speak to him, if you wish. But don't go near the door again."

"Leave us. He's in there. That's my father's voice. Don't provoke him. Please—"

Caerdoc's door slammed open. Behind him, within the simple walls of a common house, was the taper-lit chamber of a Welsh lord—the rich sleeping chamber of Adeline's memory. Her mother's bed. Her mother's clothing chest. The smell of sweet herbs and the still-rich colors of familiar tapestries.

And Maida standing tall and pale behind Caerdoc. Beyond Maida, standing against the wall hangings, was a servingwoman holding the hands of two small children—Caerdoc's sons.

Despite the splendor of the room, there had been no place to hide. No way of escape. Caerdoc had hidden his woman and his sons from the eyes of outsiders, but they had been helpless under this attack.

It was the fear in Maida's face that told Adeline what she had earlier suspected. She was as frightened of discovery as she was for her life. Adeline saw it then: Caerdoc had wed Maida, and his young sons were trueborn. He had hidden his marriage from the Normans to keep his new wife and sons safe from the threat of hostage-taking. He had hidden the marriage, even from Adeline—

She met Maida's desperate gaze and put a finger to her own lips. Maida closed her eyes in relief.

Taillebroc released Adeline's arm and broke the silence. "I owe you a chamber door," he said. "Tomorrow, I'll send a messenger to William the Marshal, to tell him you are innocent of tonight's raiding."

Caerdoc closed the door of the hut and stood before it, his sword still ready in his hand. "And what will you do to banish the insult you have given my house? Will you give your worthless oath that you'll not drag my daughter from her bed, my people from their sleep, to insult us again? This peace, Priestkiller, has become a heavy burden. Make it heavier, and I'll break it upon your body."

Taillebroc sheathed his sword. "Do not tempt me,

Caerdoc, to break it first. There is a limit to my patience.''

Caerdoc lowered his blade. 'Your limits, Taillebroc? We should ask the Hodmersham priest. He discovered them.''

CHAPTER SIX

Adeline returned to the sleeping chamber and rested upon the mattress where it lay on the chamber floor. Through the shattered doorway to the great hall, warmth and firelight reached her; the restless sounds of shepherds and huntsmen returning to their pallets, snoring beside the hearth pit, were welcome signs that the manor was once again a place of refuge for Caerdoc's people, and for his family.

His family. Adeline opened her eyes upon the darkness and began to consider what she had learned in Taillebroc's brutal night raid.

She pressed her fingers beside her eyes and willed the tears to stop. It was understandable that her father would not yet trust her with the truth about her small brothers. A half-Norman daughter returning from five years in Normandy must be a stranger to Caerdoc

and his people; they would not—should not—tell
her of Caerdoc's marriage until they were sure her
loyalties were to Caerdoc alone.

The most hurtful thing was to remember that Caerdoc had stayed in the hut with Maida and the children
until Taillebroc's threats had become too loud to
ignore. What had he imagined as he heard the sound
of splintering wood across the bailey yard? Adeline's
voice had not drawn him from the hut. How had he
planned to save the boys and his wife if the Normans
had surrounded the small house and beaten down
that narrow door? If they had brought torches to fire
the walls, what then?

Despite the night's fear and confusion, Adeline had
not believed that Taillebroc would harm the souls he
had dragged from sleep. She had somehow imagined
herself safe at Taillebroc's side as she had waited for
her father to make his move. There had been a
strange moment when she had stopped struggling
and poised herself to duck behind him should fighting erupt in the dark passageway between the huts.

Whatever he was, however ruthless he had been in
demanding a sight of Caerdoc in the manor,
Taillebroc was not a profligate killer. Adeline had felt
the truth of this before; despite the terrors of this
night, she found that she now believed that Taillebroc
wanted peace above all things.

Simon Taillebroc had ignored Caerdoc's insults
with a cold-blooded compassion that had left Adeline
breathless. He had turned his back upon Caerdoc's
naked sword and called his men to gather and leave
the stockade.

The silence following the Normans' departure had been deep and complete. Caerdoc had not noticed the silent exchange between Maida and Adeline in the moment of crisis. For all Adeline knew, he still imagined that the legitimacy of his two young sons had remained a secret known only to his Welsh household. He had said nothing of the hut, or its contents, or the presence of Maida and the children. In grim silence, Caerdoc had walked into the confusion of his hall, brought Adeline and Petronilla to the sleeping chamber, and returned to Maida and his sons.

The night might have ended in bloodshed. Only luck and Taillebroc's surprising restraint in the final moments of the raid had preserved the lives of both Normans and Welshmen in the bailey yard. Adeline closed her mind to thoughts of what might have gone wrong. There might be another time—perhaps many times—when her fiery father and the relentless Taillebroc would come even closer to bloodletting. By spring, one or both of them might die.

The throbbing behind Adeline's eyes had turned to a painful sting; she abandoned her attempt to stop the tears from flowing. All that she had discovered this night—her father's new marriage, the dangerous mistrust between Caerdoc and Taillebroc—paled beside the secret danger to both her father and Simon Taillebroc, should Longchamp decide to strike.

If Adeline went meekly to her kinsman's lands to the west, Longchamp would hear of it from his soldier Luke. Do not think to cheat Longchamp, the soldier had said. Disloyalty rouses the killer in him.

The man called Luke was too frightened of Longchamp to take a bribe and keep his master ignorant of a failure in their schemes. Somehow, Adeline must convince her father to allow her to stay and accomplish all that Longchamp had demanded.

By dawn, Adeline had decided how she would do it.

"One day," said Maida, "when the lads are grown, we will ask Father Cuthbert to marry us, and Caerdoc will tell the Norman lords that Penric must be his heir, and Govan the next in line." A cool hand covered Adeline's fingers upon the loom. "Will you mind, Adeline?"

Maida's weavers had set their hut to rights and left Caerdoc's new wife and grown daughter alone at the largest loom to speak in whispers. What they could not hear they must have surmised, for they stared down the long planked space to watch Caerdoc's kinswomen with obvious interest.

Adeline shook her head and smiled at Maida. It seemed to Adeline that Maida and Caerdoc must already be wed, and their sons trueborn. Maida was telling but a portion of the truth, but she showed courage and trust by going that far.

"Maida, I don't mind. I had never thought to bring a husband here to be lord of the valley and live here forever; to be honest, my mother had always spoken of the wonders beyond Hereford, and I had expected to see them." She looked up to see compassion in Maida's eyes.

"I saw that cold sea and the old king's Christmas

courts that my mother had described, but they were
not as she remembered. It is a strange, savage world
among the Plantagenets' vassals." She pressed Maida's hand. "You're right to hide the boys from notice
and keep them safe here. In your place, I would do
the same."

Maida frowned. "When you take a husband, he
must be told, or he might have unwelcome tidings
some years from now, when Caerdoc makes the boys
legitimate and names them his heirs. A man who
weds an heiress and loses the inheritance may turn
against his wife." She lowered her voice to a small
whisper. "If you carry through with your plan, we
cannot tell Taillebroc of your brothers. He will be
angry to wed you as it is."

"I'll be safe enough."

She shook her head. "You risk too much, Adeline,
with this plan; if it doesn't bring peace between
Taillebroc and your father, you will have lost your
freedom and squandered your life."

Adeline ignored Maida's warning. "My father must
not know why I do this." And Maida must never know
the second, darker reason for which Adeline had
determined to wed Taillebroc; her gentle soul was
troubled enough by Adeline's more obvious cause.

"And please, Maida—Caerdoc must not know that
we had this speech together. He would fret, and fear
that I would tell Simon Taillebroc."

"I have no such fear," said Maida. "But beware.
Do not give Taillebroc cause for anger. If he refuses
to wed you, do not press him."

"I promise."

Once again, Maida reached for Adeline's hand. "You may be right about the man. Taillebroc seems harsh, but his actions have shown that he desires peace. Still—remember that he killed a priest. He doesn't deny it. There may be madness within him; think again before you wed him."

Adeline rose from the weaving bench. "There is no time. If we're to do this, Maida, it must be done now."

It began easily enough. There was no need to persuade Petronilla to be silent on the matter: She was away from the manor, searching for the missing pannier bag with the hapless Howyll. Maida, as agreed, had asked Caerdoc to have private speech with them both on the question of Adeline's broken betrothal.

Adeline stood before Caerdoc with her gaze fixed upon the floor and waited for her father to complete the rush of profanity with which he had greeted her request.

"You said there was no dishonor, daughter. Tell me again, from the beginning, how the knave dared to ask for you, then spurn you. Was it your dowry? Did the young snake believe I wouldn't dower you as befits Caerdoc's daughter?"

Adeline raised her head. "It wasn't the dowry."

"Then what? What was the reason?"

Adeline drew a slow breath, and made a silent prayer for forgiveness in case any of the blameless Nevers family ever had cause to meet Caerdoc. She looked down again and found her most demure voice.

"There was a cousin, you see. She was widowed that month—she had become a rich widow."

"So? Your dowry will be nothing to despise."

"And—"

"And?"

"And he decided it would be better to have a Norman wife." Adeline glanced up and saw the predictable crimson rising to her father's brow. "Norman born," she said, and crossed her fingers.

"He spurned you? For your Welsh blood, he spurned you? I'll carve his liver from his Norman gut. I'll—"

Maida moved forward and touched Caerdoc's arm. "He's far away, and long wed by now. Your daughter is here, and wants a husband. She should wed now; those who hear of the broken negotiations will think you set young Nevers aside and found a better man for your daughter."

Caerdoc stopped in mid-rant. "I'll do that. I'll find her a husband. I thought, when she came home, that I should do that."

Adeline sighed in relief. As she had hoped, Caerdoc had forgotten he had intended to send her to Rhys's household.

Caerdoc smiled. "Well, Adeline. Who will it be?" He made a broad gesture to encompass the empty hall. "You have seen my men in this hall. Name any one of them—any unwed one of them—and you shall have him."

Adeline squared her shoulders; this was the moment she had dreaded. But it must be done. "None of them pleases me."

Caerdoc frowned. "Well, look again at nightfall, when they gather around. Take a good look. There are some good men among them."

"I want a Norman husband."

"You do not." His voice softened. "You had a fright blast night. Sleep well tonight, and think again tomorrow."

"I want a Norman husband. I have been years among the Normans. My near-betrothed was a Norman knight of good family. I want a man of equal stature, wellborn and rich."

Caerdoc stared at her for an endless moment. "You were too long in Normandy," he said at last.

Adeline met his gaze. "I was. Now I am a woman grown; what I have become cannot be undone. I want a Norman husband of good family. And rich."

Caerdoc rested his head upon his hands. "In the spring, I'll go to Hereford and find one for you."

"There's one right here. I want Simon Taillebroc."

Her father's face went pale. "You're mad."

"I want Simon Taillebroc." Adeline hesitated, then plowed on. "If you get him for me, I'll never ask you for anything again. Never again."

"The man's dangerous. He killed a priest."

"He'll not dare harm Caerdoc's daughter."

He stared at her, then, as if he knew that she had not told him everything. "If you wed him," Caerdoc said at last, "you will be a widow before you're old. Men with great sins to carry do not live long."

"I don't want to be a widow. There must be no talk of killing Taillebroc after I wed him. He may not always be in exile—"

"No." Caerdoc sat back and considered Adeline's words. He glanced at Maida, then back to Adeline. "You'll not bring him to live here in my hall."

"Of course not. I'll go to live at the fortress."

The sound of Penric's young voice drifted through the open door. Caerdoc looked out into the sunlight and saw his sons at play. "When I die," he said, "a kinsman will be chieftain here. Not Taillebroc. Do you understand?"

Adeline nodded. "I'll honor your wish."

"If you wed the man, you'd have to have a care for his temper."

If Maida had not been there to soothe, plead, and advise, Caerdoc would have balked. But she did as she had promised, and delivered to Adeline her father's vow that she should have Simon the Priest-killer to husband.

When they were done, Caerdoc waved them away and went out into the sunlight to find his sons.

CHAPTER SEVEN

The ravens had returned.

Simon Taillebroc awoke to the sound of their harsh cries and listened for their direction. They seemed close on this raw morning; they must have come back to the newly repaired fortress walls.

The great dark birds, larger than their Kentish cousins, had left the rocky heights of the fortress when Simon's men pulled down the rotting frame of the old tower and raised a new lookout post. They had kept their distance, flying far above the work as the Norman garrison hauled timber up the steep road to the fortress to build a longhouse for shelter against the coming winter. They had watched from the tall oaks below the promontory as the fortress walls rose once again to cut the north wind.

Caerdoc's people had seen an omen in the ravens'

departure from the old walls, and had come up the hill to gape when the largest of the birds attacked the first sentry to stand watch on the new tower. Simon understood little of the superstitions of Caerdoc's people, but he had known enough to forbid the archer Luke from killing the troublesome bird. After a day of harsh cries and bloodletting forays against the sentries, the large raven had departed once again.

Simon rose from his bed and broke the thin ice covering the water bucket. The hearth pit still glowed from the small fire he had built last night—only the second night he had brought fire to keep the late-autumn cold from his solitary chamber.

His midnight invasion of Caerdoc's manor had sent a chill into Simon's bones. He had learned that the old man had not been abroad in the night attacking Norman settlements; that much of the night had gone well. All else—the near disaster with Caerdoc's daughter, and the old man's choice to defend only his mistress and her by-blows, leaving his daughter and household to deal with Simon's men—was a deeper mystery.

It had begun as a discourteous but necessary confrontation. The swift confinement of Caerdoc's men by Simon's larger force had gone as expected; Simon had sworn to the close-guarded men, upon the honor of his sword, that he would do no violence to Caerdoc's people if they offered none of their own. They had understood, every man of them, that Simon had sought only to discover whether their chieftain Caerdoc was abroad in the night with the raiders, causing two distant fortresses to burn their beacon fires.

It was when the Caerdoc guards had been silenced and confined, when Simon had sent his men to search the four sides of Caerdoc's manor compound, that he had begun to fear that he lacked the skill to keep his mission bloodless.

The daughter's courage had come near to bringing her death. Simon had recognized the hoarse fear in her voice and had guessed, hearing her first words, that she lied to confuse the searchers. Still, he could not have turned away from that barred door; the wily Caerdoc and other hidden men might have emerged later to attack.

Confronted with the overturned table and mattress barricading the end of the chamber, Simon had called back his men at the last moment and brought down the barriers himself. His hands had been slick with sweat as he had done so, remembering that other night, that other dark chamber, that other blind struggle at Hodmersham. Merciful fate and Simon's risky delay to bring bright torches into the chamber had saved him from making another deadly mistake.

It had not been easy to control the second small siege at the hut. Caerdoc was a brigand of hard reputation and unquestioned bravery. Why, then, had he decided to make his stand against Simon within that single room with women and children behind him?

Simon had sent Harald and four others to search the hut before leaving, but had found no way out save the narrow door. Caerdoc had trapped himself, his mistress, the servant, and the children in that place. It was the act of a simpleton, a plan unworthy of the old bandit Caerdoc.

Worst of all, the old man had heard his daughter's voice through the door but had not answered her. Simon had seen Adeline's face in the torchlight; she, too, had been shocked by her father's indifference.

Simon raised his hands from the frigid water bucket to scrub the sleep from his face.

Bright, cold sunlight streamed through arrow slits and beneath the stout new door of his chamber. Simon reached for his tunic. Today he would ride across to the far wall of the valley and resume the task he had set himself: to find some sign of Caerdoc's method of leaving and returning unseen by Simon's patrols.

The old bandit was wily, but no wizard; he must have found a way for a mounted man to leave the valley without using the closely watched pass below the sentry tower. Once he understood Caerdoc's secret routes, Simon would know what he needed to keep the old fox confined to his lair. Once he controlled access to the valley, Simon would never again need to confront Caerdoc within the chieftain's large and baffling household.

The cries of the ravens grew louder, more raucous than before. Beyond the walls of Simon's refuge, voices rose in excitement. Had the archers disobeyed their orders to leave the huge birds in peace? Simon picked up his sword belt and swung a heavy cloak to his shoulders.

The uproar started before he reached the door. There, in the middle of the garrison yard, was Caerdoc himself, squinting into the late-morning sun. As Simon watched, three ravens descended from the sky to join a rank of glossy black predators upon the newly mortared rim of the fortress walls. The north wind had begun to blow; in its wake, small flakes of snow spiraled down upon the blackness of feathers bristling sharp as boars' hackles.

Caerdoc's head turned; beneath the grey iron of his brows, his gaze was scarce warmer than the ravens' cold regard.

"I have come to speak with you, Taillebroc."

Simon nodded. "I should have come to you first. Last night there was damage. I will restore what was broken."

"You apologize, then, for invading my household."

"No. But I regret the need for force."

To Simon's surprise, Caerdoc fell silent. Though angry, the man did not seem eager to talk of last night's invasion. Simon brushed a hand across his brow. Caerdoc had been unpredictable—perhaps mad—since his daughter's return.

The grizzled head turned once again to the ravens upon the battlements, then back to Simon. "Is it a Norman custom," Caerdoc asked, "to make a treaty, then deny an old enemy room at the hearth?"

The men of the garrison had crowded out of the longhouse, watching the exchange. There would be no privacy beside that fire. Simon pointed to the old hall. "My own hearth is scarce warmer than the yard, but you are welcome, Caerdoc."

The chieftain swung from the saddle with a lithe movement that belied his years; he tossed the reins to the nearest man without turning to look at the startled soldier. Simon managed not to show an offending smile; mad or not, old Caerdoc was still as carelessly regal as the old king Henry Plantagenet had been.

Caerdoc was puzzled to see Simon's chamber. "You live here, in this ruined hall, and give your soldiers the new longhouse?"

Simon nodded, and once again hid a smile as he remembered Caerdoc's own sleeping place, in a hut no better than a storage shed. "You will agree," he said, "that a leader of men might be happier at a distance from his followers; a small chamber far from the hall may offer more comfort."

The chieftain's eyes narrowed. "It's prudent to sleep where an enemy doesn't expect to find you."

"Of course."

Caerdoc began to pace an erratic path across the floor, stopping to inspect the few possessions Simon had brought with him in exile. Twice he began to speak but checked himself. At last, Caerdoc halted and pointed to the curved scabbard that rested upon Simon's empty saddlebag. "What weapon is that? Who made it?"

Simon drew the short sword from its sheath and offered it upon his palms. "It's a Saracen sword. Cunning shape. The blade is good—holds its edge—and hard to balance."

Caerdoc traced the shallow carving upon the hilt. "Well made."

"My father's father brought it from the Holy Land."

The chieftain sighted along the shining arc, then grunted and returned the sword to Simon's hands.

"You're a family of Moors? You have the black hair for it."

The old fox seemed eager to talk, and just as pleased to risk offense. Simon placed the sword back upon the empty bag. "We're Christians. Of course."

"Yet you killed a priest."

Simon stood up. "Yes, I killed a priest."

"Why?"

"It was a mistake." Simon turned to the ale pot and filled two wooden cups. He drew a long breath and prayed that Caerdoc had not come to provoke a fight. "Let us drink," he said, "to the end of mistakes."

"No mistakes," Caerdoc muttered. He drank deeply and set the cup down. "I have an offer to make you, Taillebroc. And I pray it will be no mistake."

Simon sat down on the pallet and motioned for Caerdoc to take the single bench beside the cold hearth. "Tell me," he said.

Caerdoc set his mouth in a short, rigid line, and growled. "I'll give you my daughter as wife, and you will swear to keep the Normans—all of them—from overruning my valley."

Last night he had dreamed of Adeline, and even in sleep had known that she was forbidden to him, that her summer gold hair would never touch his skin, or lend its warmth and fire to his bed—

"Well?"

Simon looked into Caerdoc's fierce gaze. "I cannot take her." He drained the cup.

"Are you already wed?"

He rose to stand at the arrow loop. "No. But I'll

not bring a woman into my life. You know what I am."

Caerdoc's voice darkened. "You refuse her? You refuse my daughter?"

"I refuse to burden her with my enemies. And you," he said, "should keep her clear of me. How can you offer her to an outcast?" He turned back to face Adeline's father. "I have lost my lands, and may never regain them. There is gold, most of it well hidden from the justiciars; I'll not touch it until they cease to watch me. I may never get back to it. There is nothing to gain from wedding your daughter to me."

"Do you refuse my daughter?" Caerdoc said again.

The man was mad. Had he told his daughter what he had planned? Simon met Caerdoc's angry gaze. "I would speak with her. Alone. Where is she?"

"Alone? What do you intend?"

"Why do you hesitate?" Simon pointed to his bed. "You have offered her to me, to sleep in this bed, alone with me each night as long as we both live—" He broke off.

As long as we both live. There might be a deadly reason for Caerdoc's unthinkable offer. Did he intend to make an assassin of his daughter?

Caerdoc bristled as if he had heard Simon's thoughts. "If you harm her, now or ever, I'll find you, Taillebroc, and kill you by inches. I swear it."

"If you believe I'd harm her, why are you here?"

Caerdoc stood and stalked to the door. "You may go down to her. She's at the foot of the hill."

Simon picked up his cloak once again. Beyond the open door, his men were clustered as near as they dared, straining to hear. Above them, the ravens had not ceased their calling. Simon called across to the stablemaster, then turned to Caerdoc. "Don't follow me. I'll speak with her in the open. Alone."

Caerdoc frowned. "And I'll speak to the priest."

Simon buckled on his sword. "Your priest hides from me. Do you blame him? There's not a priest in this land who would wed me to your daughter, Caerdoc."

"I'll be waiting in my hall. With the priest."

The road below the fortress was empty. Had old Caerdoc told his daughter why he had gone up to speak to the priestkiller? Had he ordered her to wait for him in the cold autumn morning while he negotiated to wed her to an exiled man?

Whatever she had been told, Adeline had decided not to wait for the outcome of her father's mad errand.

Simon turned his mount back to the fortress road. High above him, the archer Luke paced along the sentry walk, then stopped to look away over the eastern wall, toward the valley pass.

He was light-headed from lack of sleep and hunger, impatient with Caerdoc's half-truths and mad demands. Simon was in no fit state to placate the scheming Welshman; wars began under such conditions.

Simon headed instead for the valley pass. The ride would clear his head; in the delay, Caerdoc might tire of waiting and ride home to plague the unfortunate priest with his scheme.

* * *

As he neared the top of the climb to the pass, Simon looked back again to the fortress, and saw that Luke had remained on the eastern walk, staring past the ravens still perched upon the stone-topped embankment. Simon raised his hand in greeting, pleased that the archer had obeyed his orders to leave the birds in peace.

The solitary figure upon the watchtower did not return Simon's gesture; the man stood motionless, looking beyond Simon to the high ground of the pass.

A swath of green, a bright fragment of summer against the autumn land, had attracted the archer's gaze.

Adeline of Caerdoc awaited him at the crest of the deep passage between the valley walls, not far from the pitted road. There was no shifting of the vivid green mass of her cloak as it swept from her shoulders to rest upon the crupper of her palfrey, no tightening of the reins held in her small gloved hands. But as he drew near, Simon saw, from the set of her delicate jaw, that Adeline was fighting the urge to flee.

He halted a short distance from her and waited.

Her gaze had not faltered as he approached. Only when he stopped did she look beyond to the man upon the watchtower, then back to Simon's face. He glanced back over his shoulder. "My sentry will neglect all directions save this one," he said, "as long as beauty rides along this road."

His words did not please her. She frowned and looked up again at the distant figure upon the tower.

"Do I offend you?"

Adeline glanced down to the saddlebow, and to the small, shabby bundle lashed to the painted wood. "No," she said.

"Then do you mind if I ride with you?"

She raised her gaze to look directly into his eyes. "I know what my father has said to you. Have you agreed?"

Simon attempted not to smile. When she had something to say, Adeline's conduct was as direct as her sire's unflinching speech. The woman seemed to have two manners: the watchful silence he had seen in her father's hall, and a boldness that took her, perhaps too quickly, to the meat of a question. Would she have remained silent had she come to the fortress with her father? Or would she have helped to expose the madness in Caerdoc's idea?

In that moment, an odd urge possessed Simon to ignore her question, to discover how anxious she was for the answer. To discover what she wished the answer to be. He pointed to the worn leather bag at her knee. "Have you decided, in case I intend to wed you, to run away? You have packed light, Adeline. Are you going far?"

She placed a hand upon the bag as if to protect it from his sight. "It's a second cloak. Nothing more. I carry it for the rain. I do not," Adeline said, "flee my family or my duties." From the soft wool of her hood, a strand of red-gold hair curled free and floated upon the wind. Her eyes had darkened to the green of a summer sea.

Family. Duties. Adeline of Caerdoc was prepared to wed Simon the Priestkiller for the sake of her people. No doubt the old man knew that his daughter had beauty enough to tempt a king. Why did he squander her upon the warden of a half-built fortress?

Simon looked away from her gaze. A less merciful man would accept the marriage, allow this woman to bring her unearthly beauty to his bed, ask her to share in the next place of exile, and the dangers to follow.

He glanced at the sky. "You won't need the cloak today. It hasn't rained since you came to the valley. You brought the summer back."

Her fingers had tightened upon the scarred leather bag. "You have refused me," she said. "Have you?"

"Of course I have."

He caught the bridle strap of her palfrey before she could ride away. "Lady," he said, "Have you some— trouble?"

She recoiled from his question. "Leave me."

He tightened his grip upon the bridle. "Listen to me. There are only two reasons why a man would give his daughter to a man who has lost his honor and his lands. For gold, or to save an unborn child from bastardy."

Adeline dropped the reins and drew back to sit high in her saddle. "Which do you think it is, Simon Taillebroc?"

She had recovered her composure and turned his own words back against him. It took courage to use that wit against a notorious sinner. For a brief, unworthy moment, Simon imagined that this woman might come without fear to that sinner's bed.

"If it's a child you want to shelter, you must not burden it with my name. The stories are true. I killed a priest. Not a stranger, but a priest who lived on my lands. If I had not been a rich man with lands and influence, I would have died soon after. I kept my life on the condition that I work for William the Marshal in the king's service. I have enemies, madam, in the highest places; not just the church, but in the royal court—"

"Why?"

He stopped in confusion. "Why should the churchmen not despise me? I killed an unarmed priest."

"Why do you have enemies in the royal court?"

There was more than a sharp wit behind those green eyes. Adeline of Caerdoc had picked out the single item in his litany of disgrace that he dared not explain. "It's a simple thing to understand," he lied. "Those in the Plantagenet court who hadn't yet turned against me convinced the churchmen not to have me excommunicated. There was protest from the others, and accusations of bribery. In the end, those who had helped me could do no more without losing their reputations. I have my freedom, and nothing more. It could have gone worse for me."

Adeline had shown neither surprise nor disgust at his account. "The old king forgave those who killed the Archbishop of Canterbury. Their punishment was light. It is not outrageous that you have your freedom;

perhaps the priest you killed was not beloved of his superiors.''

She was calm, almost unwomanly in her discussion of his heinous sin. And she was coming too close to the truth of his troubles.

"You cannot understand," he said; he pitched his tone to be dismissive, an insult to Adeline's intelligence. "You were not there, were you? You seek to distract me from the question of your father's intentions in this matter of your marriage. Listen to me—your father has made a great mistake. Do not follow it with another."

"Speak then. I'll not distract you more."

She could not help but distract him. Where had she learned to take apart a man's words and pounce upon the lies woven within them? Simon had known a few old women—his own grandmother among them—with such skill. Never had he seen it in a maiden of marriageable age. Never had he seen in one so beautiful.

"Listen again, madam. My lands are gone. Most of the gold is gone, and my brother is exiled north. If I die in exile, my honor not restored, a child with my name would not inherit Taillebroc. My brother might try to get the land back for you, but he would fail. As I said, if there is a child you want to shelter, do not burden it with my name. You would do better to wed one of your father's shepherds; you and the child would be safer."

"And if there is no child?" Her voice was low, her demeanor was as calm as if she discussed the disposition of small household matters.

Last night, in the invasion of Caerdoc's manor, she had acted with such presence to protect her father. There had been fear, but no mistake in reason, no faltering of purpose. Only when the door of the hut had opened and Caerdoc had proved his innocence, had Adeline given way to a shocked silence. Simon frowned. If she bore a child, this woman would protect it with the same fierce intelligence.

"Is there a child?"

She looked full into his eyes, as if drawing her answer from his soul. "You have refused me," she said at last. "You need no answer to that question." Adeline looked down at the reins and began, with slow deliberation, to straighten them across her palm.

She would ride back into the valley and tell Caerdoc he had not relented. After that, there would be trouble. If there was a child, the trouble would come sooner. Simon reached for her arm. "Answer me, and swear that your words are true. Yes or no—it makes no difference. Tell me whether you are with child."

Again, she took no offense, but stared as if to read his thoughts. "I'll not swear to you. If you want an oath, then ask me for marriage vows. I offer you nothing else."

He released her arm and pointed up to the fort. "I have some gold—all I could carry in secret from Taillebroc. If it's gold you need, I'll give it to you. Tell me, in truth—what do you need from me?"

Adeline looked past him, to the archer still watching from the distant sentry walk. "Marriage vows," she said.

She had paled as she spoke. Simon's heart was heavy at the sight of her fine courage worn thin. He heard his own voice begin to give the conditions for marriage.

"Your father must promise me peace. Not a false peace, but his promise, on his honor, that he will not leave his valley without telling me. And you—"

Her eyes were darker still, and her face white as a winter field. "And I?"

"—you will understand that if I live long enough to regain my lands and honor, I will want a child. If you carry a child now, I'll give it my name. And if my honor returns before my death comes, I will want a child as well. This will be no sham of a marriage, Adeline. If you're foolish enough to want my name, these are the conditions."

CHAPTER EIGHT

He had not expected an ambush on his betrothal day. Harald saw it first, and muttered a word to Simon as they entered Caerdoc's great hall. Simon whispered back, then turned his attention to the purse-mouthed priest who waited at the end of the great chamber at Caerdoc's side. Neither the priest nor Caerdoc himself, staring with steady resolution at Simon's approach, had noticed what waited upon the largest rafter of the hall, high above the midpoint of Simon's path.

Simon kept his eyes upon Adeline's father and the pale figure of the cleric standing slightly behind, and obliged the young assassin by walking directly beneath him.

With a blood-chilling scream, the boy released his

limpet grip on the sooty beam and plummeted down upon his prey. He landed, noisy and positioned to strike, safe in the arms of his victim.

Simon held the lad long enough to recoil from a blow of his short wooden sword, then set him down. "You're a fierce one," he said. "Will you go easy on me when I'm your kinsman, wed to your sister?"

The lad thrust his sword into a soot-stained cloth scabbard. His short tunic was well sewn and had likely been, until the trip up to the rafters, a fine shade of blue.

"Sister?" the child asked.

The boy's eyes shifted beyond Simon. Running toward them was the handsome servingwoman whom Simon had last seen in Caerdoc's sleeping hut. The woman addressed a rush of Welsh invective to the child as she seized the single clean part of his clothing, at the scruff of his neck.

The boy would not be dislodged. He peered into Simon's eyes. "My sister?" he cried again.

The servingwoman was trembling. "He's confused," she said. "I beg your pardon for his foolishness. He has been angry since—"

"Since my invasion of your sleeping chamber. I beg your pardon for that as well."

"Adeline is not my sister," shouted the boy.

"Silence," bellowed Caerdoc. The lad wrenched free and ran to the chieftain and clung to his leg. A sooty patch blossomed upon the fine Norman surcoat Caerdoc had chosen for this parley; Simon wondered, as he looked down at his own blackened sleeve, whose

Norman baggage had carried Caerdoc's fine garment into range of the valley's band of raiders.

"I'm sorry I upset the lad," said Simon. "I thought him a half brother of Adeline."

"He doesn't speak your Norman tongue. And he doesn't understand who Adeline is."

Simon frowned. Did anyone in this household so much as care who Adeline was? He had noticed no great attention given to her by her father's people. The old man himself seemed cold to her.

Caerdoc growled as if he had heard Simon's thoughts. "They can't speak together, the lad and Adeline, until she learns to speak our language again. Her mother was a Norman, and spoke to her only in her own tongue."

And her years exiled as a hostage had further divided her from her father's people. Simon began to understand what he had seen. "It will be a long winter, up here in the valley. No doubt we'll all speak easily together by spring—"

"She's not my sister," repeated the boy in perfect Norman words.

"You speak well enough," said Simon. "And some of us are learning very fast."

Caerdoc had lied; this boy could speak with Adeline, if given the chance. Had he been kept from his half sister? Simon looked to Caerdoc; there was no trace of guilt in his shuttered expression.

He looked down at the lad and shrugged. "Will you agree to a treaty until spring?"

The boy nodded. His mother snatched him away

and took the lad into the kitchens. The sound of the child's displeasure continued beyond their sight.

"He's a fine boy," said Simon. "I had a half brother at Taillebroc, conceived many years after my father was widowed. Some say, with justice, that he's best of us all."

Caerdoc turned without speaking and walked back to stand beside the priest. Simon followed. It was one more mystery heaped upon many, he thought, that Caerdoc would be reluctant to discuss a child so obviously his own blood; a beloved bastard raised in his father's hall should be no disgrace to the father or to himself.

Harald had stood aside as Simon dealt with the lad's screeching descent from the roof; he drew near and walked with Simon to Caerdoc's board. "Damned private man, that Welshman."

"He'll keep the peace if we avoid speaking of his family, or of his past," said Simon.

"If you're still bound to wed the old fox's daughter and keep the peace, find a way to miss the wedding feast. When you speak, the man shows a wolf's hackles. He'll attack you over simple words, that one, even as you drink his daughter's health at his board."

There was a square of trimmed sheepskin and a pot of ink upon the trestle, and a sullen priest behind them. Caerdoc made a vague gesture. "Cuthbert here—Father Cuthbert—will hear your man's declaration that you are unwed"—Caerdoc shook his head and continued—"and not yet excommunicated from Christian folks. He knows my daughter is unwed and fit to take you to husband. He'll write all this, if your man swears your part is true, and he'll set down our agreements as well."

"Peace," said Simon, "must be the first item."

"And a dowry. I'll give her an honorable dowry."

"As I said before, any lands or gold your daughter is known to possess may be taken from her if things go worse for me."

"Do you refuse to take her dowry?"

Simon shook his head. Keeping the peace with the fiery, prickly Caerdoc would not be an easy thing. In future, Adeline might help him understand—"Where is Adeline?" he asked.

"In the chapel. Looking for altar cloths from her mother's time. I'll send for her in time to write her name here." Caerdoc nudged the priest. "My daughter can write, you know. Take care you set forth the facts in good order. She will know what you have written."

Simon raised his brows. Adeline's mother had given her more than Norman speech. He gave a warning glance to Harald; he would not mention that he himself could read.

Harald understood; he winked at Simon and turned to Caerdoc. "Simon can write his name," he said. "He learned it from his father's steward at Taillebroc. Took him weeks to get the right of it, but he can do it now."

Caerdoc shrugged. "A mark is good enough. A man's word is what matters. Now—we spoke of the dowry. There must be a dowry, for my own honor as well as my daughter's. If, as you say, the crown might take land from her, I'll give you gold instead—pure

Welsh gold, not the shabby coins the Normans drop on the road when they run from me.''

Simon managed not to smile. ''I give you my thanks. I'll need to conceal the gold—put it aside in a safe place in case we need it. You should know where it is, in case we must send to you from a distance to ask for it. Show me a good place, and we'll hide it together—you, I, and Adeline.''

Caerdoc looked up with an admirable sham of innocence in his gaze. ''I'll have to find such a place. Where do you suggest?''

''Not in the chapel,'' said Adeline. ''It's well-known to thieves, I think.''

Simon looked up to find Adeline watching them from the side of the hall. ''I didn't hear your approach,'' he said, and crossed the rough slate floor to take her hand. ''We are discussing your dowry; it's to be gold, and to be hidden away from the eyes of the crown.'' He opened his other hand to reveal the small leather pouch he had carried from the fortress. ''And this, Adeline, is my betrothal gift to you.''

She was slow to take it from his hand. ''There was no need for a gift—''

Caerdoc had advanced to watch their exchange. ''Take it, daughter.''

She had not lowered her gaze from his eyes. Simon smiled. ''They are small things, but valuable. The wife of an exiled man should have such jewels; if we have—trouble—in the future, you may use these as you wish.''

Adeline spilled the three Taillebroc rubies, each set flat within a worn gold ring, into her hands.

"Wear them always," said Simon. "They may one day buy you safe passage away from danger."

Adeline caught her breath. "Or I may wear them until I'm an old woman, safe beside the hearth."

Simon closed his hand over hers. "I pray you will."

Caerdoc sighed. "Wear them, then, and come write your name on the agreement. I'll give him forty marks of gold as dowry for you, and the priest will write that Taillebroc has given you three rubies as a betrothal gift. Cuthbert has said that he'll say the banns tomorrow, and wed you in three days' time. It's all there, on the sheepskin," Caerdoc said. "Sign it, and we'll be agreed."

Adeline did not seem displeased by the short interval between contract and wedding. *It must be a child that drives her to marry me,* Simon thought. *She wants my name as soon as possible, before the child grows in her belly.*

Adeline moved to the table with a simple grace that made Simon's blood pulse faster. If there was a child, who was the father? Had she gone willingly to that bed, or had she been forced?

However she had come to this state, Adeline had shown courage in dealing with the consequences. The mother of a bastard babe would feel something like the strangeness and constant fear of a man who had lost his honor and his lands—unable to continue a life as it had been, knowing rather than fearing that the future would bring hard times.

Her transgression, if indeed she had sinned to get that child, was a small misdeed compared to Simon's killing of a man of the church. Yet Adeline's dilemma must have been as painful as his own.

Adeline looked down at the words the priest was writing; she opened her hand and began to place the Taillebroc rings upon her fingers. To Simon, her small, precise gestures were more seductive than a Canterbury whore's promises.

She signed her name and held the quill for him to take. From the narrow, unshuttered window behind her, a ray of sunlight turned the Taillebroc rubies into unmoving, steady brilliance. Her slender fingers did not tremble.

In that moment, sensing Adeline's calm in the moment she gave her future into the hands of a landless, infamous man, Simon made a silent oath that he would give this woman no more grief than she had already known. A great tenderness came over him, and he spoke to her without care that the priest and Caerdoc and Harald would hear him. "I'll write my name, my lady, in the hope that all will go well between us."

Adeline's eyes were as bright as if she had been weeping. Did she believe his words? Would she trust him to put aside his anger at finding himself enmeshed in Caerdoc's schemes?

Harald coughed, as if to remind Simon of what he was about. Simon bent over the priest's writing and signed his name beside Adeline's letters, taking care to do so slowly, as if he found it hard to remember the way of it.

When he finished, there was a small smile on Adeline's face. She must be pleased to see the betrothal

done. Or she might have understood the small deception he had attempted, to appear unable to read.

Simon grinned back. He must discover, before
long, how to make her smile more often.

CHAPTER NINE

A bright, cold morning followed Adeline's betrothal. Tracings of frost silvered the fallen leaves beyond the stockade, and the great oaks of the valley floor rose dark bold against the sky. Beyond the old forest, the high meadows of Caerdoc's vale still bore the night mist; clouds of grey and white moved across the hills, parting to reveal the flocks of sheep upon the slopes, and long shining streams descending from rocky walls.

Caerdoc's household had roused early to hunt game for the wedding feast; they led their mounts from the stockade amid the sounds of brittle leaves beneath well-shod hooves, and raised their voices in greeting. Simon Taillebroc and half his garrison came down to join the milling confusion outside the manor walls; in the high spirits of the moment, Caerdoc's men moved heedlessly among the Norman soldiers, their differences forgotten in this moment of anticipation.

Luke the archer was mounted among them. He guided his horse to halt near Adeline's grey palfrey, and began to retie his quiver case beside the saddle. "You made a fine move in this game," he murmured. "Longchamp will be pleased."

Adeline glanced about her. Taillebroc was speaking with her father; no one had noticed the archer's presence at her side. "You will tell your master, then, that I haven't been idle?"

"I already have." He tested the knot. "See that you follow your husband, lady, when he rides far abroad each day. I cannot do that without leaving my post. You will do it."

He looked over his shoulder and gathered his reins. "Watching him inside the fortress is nothing. I do that myself. Your advantage as Taillebroc's wife will be to ride out with him, and tell me where he goes, and the names of the people you may see."

Adeline saw her father turn in her direction. Taillebroc had not yet seen her. "A husband may refuse his wife's company," she said.

"Follow him anyway. He has been riding out alone every day, even in foul weather. He could be meeting Count John's men. Rebels. Longchamp needs to know this. He wants nothing less from you."

Taillebroc had turned to look in her direction; he and Caerdoc had a clear view of the archer Luke. "Go now," Adeline said. "They see you."

"Remember your task," Luke said. "When you

hear my flute, you will know it's safe to come to the garrison walls and bring me word. Listen for the flute." He gave a last tug to the knot holding his arrow case, and spurred forward to join his fellows.

Two shaggy hounds loped behind Taillebroc as he guided his mount to her side. "You are riding out today?"

She nodded. "My father's hounds have taken a liking to you."

Taillebroc shrugged. "They're curious, nothing more." Behind him, Caerdoc bellowed a harsh order; the dogs turned and ran back to their master. "Caerdoc says he hopes to get two great harts, one on each side of the valley, for the wedding feast. It will be a long and rough day, to do that."

Adeline looked to the sky. "The weather should hold. He may manage it."

"Can you?"

"What do you mean?"

Taillebroc made a small gesture. "It will be a long, rough ride. You may wish to follow behind, at a slower pace. Or not follow at all."

She had forgotten, in the high spirits of the morning, that Taillebroc believed she might be with child; with his question, he had sought to discover the truth of her condition.

"I rode from Hantune across England to get here."

He smiled. "I have seen your father in hot pursuit of game. The road from the south coast is nothing to these hills. I'll ride with you, behind the hunt, if you wish."

He had not pursued the question. In his eyes, Adeline saw only concern. Taillebroc had meant only to keep her from harm. Adeline looked beyond him to focus her thoughts; the monster that Longchamp had sent her to watch was proving to be a compassionate man.

He waited for her answer.

He rides out each day, the archer had said. Follow him. Remember your task. Her marriage plan, the archer had said, had been a fine move in the game.

Adeline began to tremble. For the first time since Longchamp had set forth the conditions for her father's safety and her own freedom, Adeline allowed herself to consider the consequences of her task for Longchamp, and that Simon Taillebroc must not suffer the treachery the chancellor must intend. Though he had killed a priest, Taillebroc had shown her nothing but kindness in the matter of this forced marriage and his belief that he would give his name to a bastard child. He deserved better than disloyalty from the woman he must wed.

The heaviness of her shame would soon have her in tears.

She turned her palfrey around to face the stockade gates. "It's colder than I thought," she said. "I won't go. I'll stay behind until midday, then ride out again to watch the hawking."

"As you wish," Taillebroc said. He began to say something more, but checked himself and spurred his horse to follow Caerdoc's noisy departure for the hunt.

Beyond Taillebroc's path, at the edge of the naked forest, Luke the archer stared at Adeline. She lifted

her face and returned the cold gaze. The archer was
the first to flinch from the silent exchange. He shook
his head and left to follow Simon Taillebroc in the
hunt.

She left her horse in the byre and crossed the
deserted bailey yard. She could see, once she stood
in the center of the open space and looked about
her at three walls of huts and storage sheds facing
Caerdoc's long hall, that the settlement was now
much larger than it had been in her childhood. The
weaving house was longer; there was a clear change
from old timber to new halfway along the face of it.
The sleeping hut that sheltered Caerdoc's great bed
had not existed, five years ago. Her father had built
it for just the purpose she had seen: to spare Maida
and his younger children the attention they would
have attracted from outsiders.

Adeline walked across to the kitchens, but turned
aside when she saw that Maida was not among the
women working around the cooking fire.

She found Petronilla in the sleeping chamber,
brushing the nettles from her best crimson cloak.

"Did you fall?" Adeline asked.

Petronilla shook her head. "The wind blew them
into the panniers, that last day."

The saddlebags were empty; stacks of square-folded
chemises and bliauts lay upon the pallet. "Are you
packing for your trip home?"

There was a sudden silence; the brush in Petronilla's hand dropped to the floor. "I'm not leaving," she said.

"I asked my father, as I promised you, to get you back down to the coast and buy your passage home. I didn't forget."

"I'll not leave," said Petronilla. "I promised the lady Maude that I'd see you through the winter. And I will."

"My father has ten good men to see you safely to Hereford. The snows won't come for another week or two, he says."

"I'll stay with you."

Adeline sat beside Petronilla among the clothing piled on the coverlet. "You were right to want to go home, especially now that I'm to be wed. I'll be living in the fortress. There's no place for another soul, up there. You can't sleep in the garrison house, can you?"

Petronilla fell silent. "I could stay here, in the manor," she said at last.

"But you dislike this household. I promised you I'd help you get home before winter, and I'll make sure you do. If the weather is bad when you reach the coast, you'll have enough gold to stay until spring comes. But if you wait here until the new year, the snow will keep you from leaving the valley."

Petronilla lowered her head and sighed. "It's all my fault," she said. "All my fault that you had to marry that Simon Taillebroc."

"Come, Petronilla. How can you blame yourself?" Adeline reached out to stroke her maid's hair. "I made my own trouble in this matter; I want the marriage."

Petronilla began to weep. "No you don't. You wanted the young knight Nevers, and I—"

"You what?"

"Never mind. It's my fault, though. You should have stayed in Normandy and married young William Nevers. Now—"

"What are you saying, Petronilla? I left because my years as a hostage were ended. There was no true betrothal with William Nevers. How can that be your fault?"

Petronilla gulped. "They left, all of the Nevers family, before the talk of betrothal was finished. It's all my fault. And then I hadn't watched you well enough, and you have to wed as a consequence—"

"Petronilla."

"—and William Nevers's mother would never send him to you since—"

Adeline knelt before Petronilla and took her hands. "Tell me, Petronilla, from the beginning."

"It wasn't my fault."

"Of course not."

"It was his fault. He found a place in the cowshed where we could be alone. I thought we'd never be discovered." Petronilla raised a square of silk to her streaming eyes. "I was wrong," she whispered.

Adeline found, to her dismay, that she couldn't keep the laughter from her voice. "Who had you in the cowshed, Petronilla? William Nevers? That boy?"

Petronilla's tears vanished. "It was Sir Reginald Nevers, of course. Not his son." Just as quickly, the tears reappeared. "But the son must have had a way about him, too. Or so you must have thought. Oh Adeline, how terrible to be seduced by a man of good family, and to lose him and end by marrying a felon, a priestkiller, just to save the situation—"

"What situation?"

Petronilla frowned. "You might have told me. It's all the talk in your father's hall. When he's not there, of course. When he's there, they never say a word, for fear of angering him."

Adeline's heart turned over. Had Simon Taillebroc confided to his men his belief that she was with child, and had his men brought the rumor to the manor? "What talk in the hall?" she asked.

"That you returned with child from Normandy, and Caerdoc found a Norman to remedy the lack of husband. They say it's the only reason you'd take that man to husband. Though they remember your mother was a Norman lady, they don't blame her."

"Blame her?"

"For raising you a Norman and giving you the idea of marrying outside the valley. Any one of Caerdoc's men, they say, would have given you his name."

Take a shepherd, Taillebroc had said. And your child will have a chance to grow up in your father's hall. Adeline sighed. If William the Marshal sent Taillebroc on to another post, she would have to follow, and might never see this valley again.

She dragged her thoughts back to Petronilla. "How is it that you know what my father's people are saying? You cannot understand their speech."

"Some of them know our tongue."

"And tell their thoughts to you?" Adeline saw color rising to Petronilla's face. "Which of them speaks to you?"

"Howyll has been very helpful."

"The tall youth with the little beard?"

Petronilla turned away and began to smooth the coverlet. "Yes, that one. I find him eager to talk. He teaches me a few words of Welsh, as well."

Adeline smiled. Petronilla, the most worldly-wise of the lady Maude's household women, had acquired a most unworldly young companion.

"How old is Howyll?"

Petronilla's hand stilled. "A good age, I think. He's a man, full-grown."

"There are dozens of young knights in Normandy who would want you to wife," Adeline said. "I remember how you wept to see the two Sancerre brothers leave us at Hereford. They may be there still, Petronilla."

"It's too late," said Petronilla. "Not the season, but the events in my own life. The lady Maude won't let me wed any of our kinsmen. Not after the day she found me in the cowshed with the lady Nevers's husband, and there was such trouble to follow. That's why she chose me to come with you," said the tearful maid. "She said that the long trip would help me reach next summer without a babe to birth. She said that to me, in front of Lord Nevers, to shame us both." She seized Adeline's hand. "Don't send me home," Petronilla cried. "If the lady Maude doesn't forgive me, I might never get a husband there."

"I never heard about the cowshed—"

"You were thinking of nothing but your return, I think. And the lady Maude didn't want to upset you."

"—and you have spoken of nothing but returning to Normandy each day since we left."

Petronilla dropped her head once again. "This country was so wet and cold that I would have gone back as a beggar—or worse—just to be home."

Adeline remembered her own thoughts as she had left this valley so long ago. She stroked Petronilla's hair. "And now?" she asked.

"Now," said Petronilla, "it looks different to me. And I got used to the cold."

It would be comfortable, Adeline mused, to have a familiar face about the manor. There were so few Welsh faces from the past—

"Well?" said Petronilla.

Adeline squared her shoulders. "When the hunt is back, I'll ask my father to put aside the travel gold for your dowry."

"And Howyll? Will you ask him if I may have Howyll?"

"Getting Howyll to husband," said Adeline, "is your task, not my father's."

On the night before her wedding, Adeline lay wakeful in the pallet she was sharing, for the last time, with Petronilla. When the door to the chamber opened softly from the quiet hall, Adeline thought, for one wild moment, that Taillebroc had come for her. Of course he had not. Adeline sat up and whispered a greeting to Maida.

"Will you speak with me?"

Adeline pointed to Petronilla's silent form. "She's asleep."

Maida nodded, her burnished hair silvered by the moonlight streaming through the narrow, unshuttered arrow slit. "I thought, if you don't mind, that I'd take a mother's part tonight and speak to you of your marriage duties."

Adeline crept from the bed to sit beside Maida.

It would have been possible for Maida to take her aside earlier in the evening to do this. There must be something else at stake to bring Maida across the bailey yard in the cold of the night. Adeline kept her voice at a soft whisper. "I have heard a few things."

"No doubt." The woman looked into the moonlight, then back to Adeline. "First, I must tell you that I spoke but half the truth in the weaving shed. I couldn't sleep for fretting that you should know the full truth before you wed Taillebroc."

Adeline squeezed her hand. "On the night of the raid, I thought that you must be wed to my father. The boys are true sons, are they not?"

Maida nodded in the moonlight. "They are. And your father loves them to madness. As he does you."

Adeline forgave Maida that small, kind lie. "How did you meet?"

"I am the stepsister of your kinsman Rhys. Your father wed me only months after he heard of your mother's death. His obsession, Adeline, has been to keep us at his side. He will not surrender another child as hostage to the Plantagenets. And he will not, he says, have his second wife stir from his side."

Adeline sat back against the bolster, and offered Maida the foot of the coverlet to warm herself. "And when the boys are full-grown, my father must acknowledge the elder as his heir."

Maida covered Adeline's hand with her own. "I had to speak now. Caerdoc may not do so for many years. Yesterday, I asked him to tell you, before you are wed to Simon. So that you would know the extent of the risk you take. Taillebroc may be angry, one day, when he discovers that he has not wed an heiress, but a landless daughter who was passed by long before the wedding—" She hesitated. "Are you disappointed to know there is already another heir?"

Adeline shook her head. "I had expected my father to choose a nephew, a son of Rhys, to lead his people after him. He's not so much the lord of these lands as he is the chief of the people. I understood this as a child."

"The Normans see it differently; to them, he is much like a lord. Your husband will think of this valley as your inheritance. If you decide to go ahead and marry him, you must be careful not to tell him that the boys are trueborn—for your sake as much as theirs. With luck, by the time Penric inherits, there will be gold enough to give your husband something to sweeten the disappointment."

"Taillebroc is already a rich man. He won't care that the valley will go to your son."

Maida shook her head. "He was a rich man, but he's landless now, and may want the valley as an inheritance. I pray you, don't tell him the truth until the boys are grown."

Adeline remembered the warmth she had seen in Taillebroc's eyes. "He'd never harm a child."

"Please, Adeline. Swear you'll not tell him."

She sighed and pressed Maida's hand. "I swear, though I know Taillebroc would do them no harm."

The fear in Maida's voice had been painful to hear. Had this woman feared Adeline's return in the same way? Had the people of Caerdoc's household kept her at a distance, far from their gossip, because they feared she would hate her small brothers for taking her place as heir to the valley lands? Even Caerdoc himself, her own father, had intended to keep her ignorant of her brothers' true blood. Adeline opened her eyes. "Will my father suspect that you decided to speak to me?"

"No, he sleeps."

"Will he ever trust me?"

"He wouldn't trust Saint David himself with this secret, if he hadn't received his oath of secrecy on the day of our marriage. Even Father Cuthbert," said Maida, "agreed to hide the marriage from outsiders."

Outsiders. Her father had treated her as an outsider, for the sake of her young brothers.

"I'll keep your secret from Taillebroc," Adeline said. "And I'll not tell my father that I have guessed it."

Maida leaned forward and hugged her. "It is his grief," she whispered, "—seeing you taken away and your mother lost forever—that makes him hide this marriage and our sons. He loves you, Adeline, but his fear for the boys goes beyond reason."

"I'll not cause him any more grief," said Adeline.

Maida touched her hair and rose from the pallet. For the first time since she had entered the chamber, she allowed her voice to rise above the faintest whisper. "As for the other secrets," she said, "what do you know of the marriage bed?"

Adeline drew a long breath and tried to steady her own voice. Later, when Maida had left, she would allow herself to think of the past. She turned to her father's wife and smiled. " I saw a few things in the lady Maude's gardens. My window was above the darkest corner of the walls."

"My suspicion," said Maida, "is that your lord Taillebroc may be something more formidable than the knaves taking their pleasure of the maids in that garden." She paused and listened to Petronilla's steady snore. "Put on your cloak and boots," she said. "Walk with me into the bailey yard, and I'll tell you what you need to know."

CHAPTER TEN

On the morning of his wedding day, Simon Taillebroc sat against the damp chapel wall and made his confession to the terrified Cuthbert. The priest stood at a good distance to hear Simon's words, casting glances to the open door where the exasperated Caerdoc had agreed to stand watch.

"Are you not finished?" bellowed Caerdoc. "It's damned cold out here."

It was damned cold in the chapel as well. Simon renewed his efforts, and finished the long account of his sins since leaving Kent. Cuthbert did not know, and Simon did not tell him, that the Hodmersham abbot had heard Simon's confession on the night following his priest's death, and absolved him; there was no need to describe or explain that event to the trembling Cuthbert.

Simon added a brief account of his part in a brawl in the streets of Hereford. "That's the end of it," he said. "Have I your absolution?"

Cuthbert had listened with distracted indifference to Simon's account of three brigands he had killed outside Hereford, and the sins of fornication and possibly adultery he had committed in that town before leaving for Caerdoc's valley. Impatience, profanity, and neglect of the sacraments failed to rouse the slightest reaction in the priest. Simon had not mentioned his lustful thoughts of Caerdoc's daughter; it was a small sin to desire one's betrothed wife.

"That is all?" Cuthbert asked.

"All that I can remember," said Simon, "since my last confession."

The priest's dilemma was obvious: If he asked Simon whether he had received absolution for his infamous murder of the Hodmersham priest, he risked angering a dangerous man. If he granted absolution for an incomplete confession, Caerdoc's daughter would wed a man in bad grace.

Simon watched the struggle upon Cuthbert's features, and sighed. A cold rain had begun outside the chapel door, and Caerdoc would be furious at further delay.

"My last confession," said Simon, "was in Kent, the day before I left my lands."

With obvious relief, the priest began to hurry through the words of absolution. When he was done, Simon stood and approached him. "My penance?" he asked.

Cuthbert stepped back.

"I must have a penance," said Simon.

The priest made a vague gesture. "Honor your wife. Treat your wife well."

Simon smiled. "That is a penance? I thought her a sweet lady when I agreed to marry her."

"Of course. A moment, my lord." Cuthbert rushed to the door and called for Caerdoc to approach; his voice held the breathless timbre of a man delivered from assassins. "The rain has stopped for a time," he said. "I'll wed them now, if you wish."

Simon followed Cuthbert through the narrow door and looked at the lowering sky.

In Kent, at Taillebroc, the land would be green with autumn rain and the mist soft in the folds of the gentle hills. At Taillebroc, his bride would have passed well-edged fields and pastures as she came from the great walls of the keep along the abbey road. His people would have strewn the abbey steps with sweet herbs and the late, dried blooms of summer, and stood smiling as the next lady of Taillebroc drew near. At Taillebroc—

The wind gusted hard and cold at Simon's back. From the stockade gates, Adeline came walking with her father at her side, and the household's women following. Caerdoc's men, armed as ever, walked behind. Half the men of the garrison came last and stood with awkward interest behind Caerdoc's people.

Here were no children to stretch their small hands to touch the bride's fine raiment. Even Caerdoc's sons were absent from the shivering group huddled in no particular order about the chapel door.

Adeline drew near and pushed the hood back from her shining, plaited hair. She smiled a little, then raised her gaze to Simon's face.

She deserved better than this cold ceremony. The early-winter chill in the air was not itself unkind—it gave Adeline's cheeks a fine hue, and would give appetite for the wedding feast. It was the company that Simon would have changed, if he could; the fledgling good cheer that Simon had seen yesterday at the hunt had vanished. Caerdoc's people might as easily be watching a funeral, for all their dark expressions. And the men of the garrison, though smiling at the beauty of their warden's bride, were ill at ease among the silent host of Caerdoc's people.

Simon put aside the anger he felt. How could he blame the valley folk for watching this marriage with trepidation? Their chieftain's daughter was to wed a Norman outcast, the killer of a priest.

He extended his hand to Adeline and walked with her back to the chapel steps. They turned to face the huddled crowd; Caerdoc nodded to the cleric, and the ceremony began. Mercifully, old Cuthbert had chosen to speak in Latin only, and did not repeat the vows in Welsh or in French. In Latin alone, the priest intoned the promises required of Adeline and Simon, and in halting words they made their vows.

"I will honor you as my wife," Simon added. "What has begun in strife will bring peace to us all. I swear it, Adeline."

Adeline's voice shook as she replied. "I will honor you as my husband," she said. "May peace come to us both."

The wind had risen as they spoke, and cut cold into the flesh of Simon's palm when he drew the gauntlet from his fingers and took Adeline's small hand into his own. Together they bowed their heads for Cuthbert's cautious blessing and turned away from the chapel.

There would be no wedding mass this day; Caerdoc had declared that old Cuthbert would faint of fright had he done more than confess Simon the Priestkiller and wed him to Adeline. The chieftain stepped forward with a smile and passed a small flask to the shivering cleric; then he turned to his newlywed daughter and wished her well. Last of all, he turned to Simon. "Remember, Taillebroc, that we have peace now between us. I have sworn an end to raiding. Will you swear an end to your own? I would sleep peacefully now, with my daughter wed to a Norman. Will you swear to let my household sleep undisturbed?"

The old fox had picked the proper time to demand forbearance from the garrison. How could Simon deny this vow of peace, standing with his new wife outside the chapel, with the words of his wedding vows still hanging in the cold air?

Adeline's fingers stiffened within his grip.

Simon drew a long breath and drew his cloak aside to shelter Adeline from the rising wind. "I will swear never again to rouse you from your bed to show that you are not out raiding. I'll trust you that far, Caerdoc, for now we are kinsmen. But I'll not swear to leave your walls unbreached; one day, such a vow might prove impossible to keep. The future bring us things we cannot imagine; I found that to be true, months ago at Hodmersham.''

For an instant, Simon feared that his promise was too guarded to satisfy Caerdoc's mind. At his side, Adeline watched her father's face in silent concern. Behind him, he heard the priest uncork Caerdoc's flask; there followed a great, gulping swallow and the scent of strong brandywine.

At last, the old fox made a small gesture of peace. ''Come along,'' he said. ''You're making a poor beginning of this marriage, keeping my daughter out here in the cold while you trim your promise to me, and give only the half of it back.''

''We will go up to the fort when night falls.''

''There will be wine and songs past midnight,'' Adeline said.

Simon covered her hand with his own. ''Your father has been generous. My men have not tasted such wine since last summer.''

On this day of his wedding, Simon had put aside his speculations about Caerdoc's source of fine southern wine. Having a reformed brigand's daughter to wife would bring some fine rewards, until the old bandit used up the last of his stolen riches. Simon contemplated the fine crimson color of Caerdoc's wedding wine within its silver goblet and hoped, for one unworthy moment, that his new father-in-law might steal a tun or two next summer, before his reform was complete.

He drank the last of his wine and waved away the

serving girl who came to give him more. "Your father has said that the second half of the garrison may come down at nightfall to join in the feast. Harald will bring them, and be sure they do not drink too deeply and offend the women here. I must ride with the others back to the fort, and see them take the places of Harald's lot, and be sure they are sober enough for sentry duty. Will you come with me then? It would seem odd to these people if you do not."

"Of course." Her voice did not waver; the rich wedding wine had worked its spell upon Adeline.

She had eaten little of the venison, hare, and soft bread; when the maids had brought great platters of honey cakes to the board, Adeline had taken one and begun in an absent manner to pull it into small pieces. She had produced a tidy pyramid of crumbs upon her dark trencher bread and pushed it aside.

Simon began to doubt his earlier suspicion that Adeline was with child; she had neither the pallor of a woman ill in her early weeks nor the appetite of a mother in her later months. Simon resolved to ask Petronilla; the woman seemed eager to talk. Too eager.

"Your maid—" Simon began.

"Petronilla."

"Yes, Petronilla. I should have spoken of her before. There is no place for her in the fort. You said she wants to go home to Normandy. Will your father's household keep her until I put together an escort for her to Hereford?"

Adeline reached for her wine cup. "She's to stay here for the winter."

Simon attempted to keep his voice calm. Petronilla would bring serious disruption to the garrison; Simon had seen the woman's bold scrutiny of his soldiers. "It will take a little time to wall off a space for her to sleep in the old hall, near us. Until then—"

"She will stay the winter down here, in the manor. Maida has offered to lodge her in the weaving hut," Adeline said.

"And she agreed?" Simon did not manage to keep unseemly hope from his speech.

Adeline smiled. "With all her heart. She has a friend or two among my father's people."

Simon smiled back. "The lady has moved fast; she'll not be lonely, then?"

His wife began to giggle. "I think not," she said. She held her hand up to the firelight. "My father has a good eye for the wine he—finds. It comes close to the color of Taillebroc rubies."

He admired the sight. "Shall we ask him to find the same merchant next year?"

"And raid the poor fellow twice?"

He had never before heard Adeline laugh. Simon resisted the temptation to pour his wife a deeper cup of wine to sweeten her farewells to Caerdoc's hall. The lady would no doubt blame him for her aching head tomorrow morning.

At the far end of the board, Petronilla sat unaware of their attention; beside her, the young lout with the pointed beard was speaking in her ear.

"Howyll," whispered Adeline. "His name is Howyll."

"Petronilla seems to like him well enough."

Adeline began again to laugh. Simon shook his head; he had not thought his words that amusing.

Yes, his wife would have a great ache in her head the next morning.

The youth with the pointed beard and the lustful eye was more dutiful than he looked. When Simon rose and Caerdoc drank the health of his newlywed daughter and her lord, the bearded lad disappeared through the door and led forth their horses into the bailey yard. Adeline's grey palfrey was groomed to a shine, and her saddle was covered with a rich velvet cloth.

Simon was growing used to the need to ignore Caerdoc's sources of such finery; he thanked the lanky youth for his trouble and admired Caerdoc's generosity. As with the wine, he was careful not to ask its provenance.

Adeline dropped Simon's hand and walked to her palfrey; she lifted the rich cloth and touched the small saddlebag Simon had noticed earlier.

He lifted her into the saddle. "Do you want the second cloak?"

She blinked once, as if she did not understand his words. Then she looked down at the saddlebow and shook her head. "It's a short distance," she said.

As he had suspected, the bag was some sort of relic—or weapon—that Adeline wanted to keep from his eyes.

The night was cold; the north wind blew over the fortress hill and down to the manor gates. There would be time, once they had reached the small comforts of the fortress hall, to consider Adeline's small secret.

Simon mounted and turned his horse to the stockade gates. Amid the raised voices both Norman and Welsh, he rode with his wife into the early-winter night. She managed well, after drinking so deeply of the wedding wine. Only once did he have to show her where the dark road led them.

CHAPTER ELEVEN

Adeline awoke to warmth and firelight. She thrust her hand out of the heavy coverlet and snatched it back again.

"It's not a beast," said her husband. "Just the skin of a wolf, to keep you warm."

She was wearing her long chemise and nothing more. Across the room, beyond the small fire pit, her surcoat and cloak were folded upon the clothing chest she had sent ahead that morning. Beside them was her small leather bag.

Beyond the walls, there were voices and the sound of horses led past.

"It's Harald and the others," said Simon, "returning from the feast."

Her head refused to leave the bolster. "They sound like an army."

"Does that surprise you?"

"Don't make me laugh. It hurts."

"Shall I put more wood on the fire?" He was beside her in the wide pallet, his unclothed arms and shoulders dark gold against the whiteness of the linen bedding Maida had given them. Her husband pushed the coverlet from his naked body and began to sit up.

"No," said Adeline.

"No?"

"The fire is still warm. Don't get up."

He shrugged and pulled the blankets up to his chest. "How is your head?"

"How do you know it aches?"

"A guess. Nothing more."

Laughter welled up, then retreated before the drumming in Adeline's temples. Through the thin smoke curling into the roof hole, Adeline could see the winter stars. "How long did I sleep?"

"A moment or two on your horse, and then an hour here." He seemed content to lie with arms outstretched, a hand resting easy upon the soft linen of her chemise. "If you are with child, you'll have to take care not to sleep in your saddle again. You would have fallen, had I not been at your side."

Her hands slid down to her belly. He had undressed her, down to her chemise; had he discovered, as well, that there was no child?

Simon turned his head upon the bolster to look at her. "We are wed now, Adeline. Is it not time to give up your secrets?"

Her heart began to pound. "You may have taken them already."

He smiled. "Sadly, I have not. Such secrets are better given than taken."

There was silence between them. A hot, pulsing silence that robbed her of breath.

"I gave you my vow," she said at last. "I am your wife."

He reached to touch her arm, then hesitated; when she didn't shrink from him, he smiled and smoothed the linen of her bliaut. "I have taken a wife this day," he said, "and you have won both a husband and a headache from the wedding wine. This is not a time for lust, I think. I'd have something else from you."

He moved his hand back to her hair and began to toy with the end of her plait. " Give me your reasons for taking a husband. For coming to Simon the Priestkiller's bed."

She shifted to her side and lay facing him in the wide bed. The pounding behind her eyes began to subside. The firelight cast crimson light upon the darkness of her husband's hair, and illuminated his dark eyes with glittering sparks. "You have more secrets than I, Taillebroc. Enough to give me two for each of my own. Give me one first."

"Your wit hasn't deserted you." He laughed and picked up her hand, lifted it up to the firelight. "A secret, then— I'll tell you where I hid the rest of the Taillebroc rubies. They will be yours, if a miracle takes us back to my lands."

"I want a secret of my choosing," she said. "Leave

the rubies undiscovered; instead, tell me what happened at Hodmersham.''

Laughter stopped. Simon lowered her hand to rest once again upon the soft linen upon her breast. "The bishop at Hereford did his best, and Longchamp's brother, the sheriff, did more; they both failed, and you will fail as well. Hodmersham is done. It is past. I can tell you nothing of the night I killed the priest.''

She rose upon an elbow and pulled the wolf pelt to cover her shoulder. "Why the bishop at Hereford? Why—Longchamp's brother? Hodmersham is far from their lands. Was your crime so terrible that church and crown in Hereford wished to judge you again?''

His voice became cold. "I told you days ago, when your father first offered you to me, that I have enemies. Longchamp is one of them. The most powerful of them. He sent his brother to be sheriff of Hereford; no doubt there will be trouble between us.''

Her aching head began again to throb. She had learned, from speaking with the archer Luke, that his messages must go to Hereford; there was no other Norman stronghold as close. Taillebroc's enemies waited close to Caerdoc's valley.

"Hereford is only two days' march from here. You will be careful not to anger the chancellor's people?''

"I have done nothing but finish rebuilding the fortress and watch the roads. Longchamp has spies, no doubt—they may be in this fort, for all I know—but I'll give them nothing to use against me.''

"You wouldn't support a rebellion against Longchamp?''

He made a gesture of exasperation. "My lady, if I had plans to join Count John's cause and lead a rebellion in these parts, I would not have wed you. It's bad enough that you wed a felon spared through William the Marshal's mercy; that was risky enough, and your father shouldn't have forced it." He sighed. "And I should not, for my sins, have allowed it to happen. But treason is something beyond my sins; I would be damned for all time had I wed you and made you a rebel's kin."

Adeline sighed in relief. Simon Taillebroc had a dark past, but he was no treasonous fool. Longchamp had wasted a hostage in sending her to spy on this man. Unless Taillebroc had lied to disguise his loyalties, he would never give cause for trouble from Longchamp's Hereford brother.

"I didn't mean to insult you," she said.

Taillebroc shook his head. "I'm not angry. It was a fair question from one who has known me only three days. But be careful, Adeline, not to raise such questions in the hearing of others. A hint of treason can lead to death, and the punishment might reach a man's wife, and his children. Even without such a hint, there could be trouble from enemies such as Longchamp."

Simon fell silent as he watched her in the firelight; he touched her plaited hair. "It would be better if you were gone from this place if trouble comes. I have been thinking," he said, "that I should send you to William the Marshal. Of all men, I trust him best."

He sought to protect her. He would send his enemy's spy out of danger. Adeline bit the inside of her lip and willed her mind away from these thoughts. She slowed her breathing. "Once the snows come, there will no more trouble. Not until spring. The road from Hereford will be slow in the lowlands, and near the valley the snow will be so deep that a traveler would be a whole day in your sight before he reaches the pass."

Her husband shrugged. "So they told me. But the snows may not come early enough."

She sat up. "What do you mean?"

Taillebroc made a vague gesture. "There is always the possibility of trouble, while the road is clear. A foolish act, a word spoken in anger—for a man with Longchamp's enmity, an open road may always bring trouble." He touched her hair again and drew one heavy plait into his hand.

"You have done nothing foolish? Not since you came here, to the fort—"

"I spent my own gold to have this hall repaired." He smiled. "But it may not have been such a foolish move, after all. I couldn't have a wife in the garrison house."

She covered his hand to halt his slow caress. "I am serious, Taillebroc. Have you done anything to anger the chancellor?"

He became very still. "Longchamp would have seen me die for Hodmersham. He waits to see me err again."

She sank back against the bolster. "I pray he never will."

Taillebroc yawned and pulled the coverlet across them both. "There was one foolish thing—"

Adeline's eyes opened wide. "What?"

"I wed a bandit's daughter, and let her keep me from sleep with her questions." He yawned again. "Even now, your father might be riding to the pass, slipping past the sentries he made drunk on his own wine." He drew a deep breath and took her hand. "Where does he go, Adeline, when he leaves the valley unseen?"

She withdrew her hand. "If he has a secret way, he'd not tell me."

Beyond the timber walls, the sounds of the night continued. The sounds of Harald and the garrison men had died away, but the horses were restless behind the stable door. The night wind gusted from the north, strong enough to rattle the arrow loop shutters. Footsteps sounded from the watchtower as a soldier descended the high ladder and another began to climb up the cold height of the sentry post. The ravens had heard them, too, and added their hoarse cries to the night.

Simon sighed and pulled a blanket around his nakedness; he moved back to the fire pit to throw more wood on the low flames. "Is it always so windy in this place?"

"Before I left for Normandy, the wind had brought down the top of the watchtower one winter night."

"Is that why your father didn't use this lookout place?"

"It was the fear that the Normans would come and raze whatever he rebuilt. As long as I can remember, we lived in the manor stockade, and my father's men took it in turns to watch the pass from here.''

"And after you went as hostage to Normandy?"

Adeline slid from the bed and picked up her small saddlebag. She placed it upon her folded cloak. "I don't know," she said at last. "The priest Cuthbert wrote two letters for my father, then nothing. I am almost a stranger here.''

He crossed to stand beside her and began to trace the many scars upon the leather bag. "Then you really don't know how your father makes his way past my sentries, or over the valley walls, to go out raiding by night.''

"He told me he swore not to leave the valley without warning you first.''

"Still, I want to know how he did it. Where he could escape, an enemy could invade.''

"I'll ask him, but I doubt he'll tell me." She reached for the bag and took it from his touch.

"Your father is an old wizard, I think. There might be something to the tales of magic and vanishings in these mountains.''

"Your sentries must have been careless, or asleep.''

"I offered gold to the first of them to sight your father riding past by night, but none has claimed it. Caerdoc's magic must be potent, to transport a band of armed men and their mounts to and from the valley without alarming my greedy sentries.''

He yawned. "You should sleep now. Dawn will come too soon." He turned from her and dropped the blanket to pull on his tunic. She tried, and failed, to look away from his nakedness. His body seemed taller, more powerful unclothed. She looked up from her breathless scrutiny to find him watching her with amusement in his eyes.

"Will you not sleep?" she asked.

"I don't sleep the night through. I'll speak to the sentry, and be back before long. Rest now, Adeline. When your father comes to see you in the morning, I don't want you looking ill."

Adeline rubbed her eyes. "He's not coming here."

"Believe me, there will be a crowd of your father's people up here in the morning, to discover whether you survived this night."

She sat up again. "Surely they won't want the sheets?"

"Surely they will. And just as surely I won't surrender them. There's no need to cut your finger to bloody the linen." He pulled on his cloak and walked to the door. "I don't know what your father and the others will look for," he said, "but I believe the last thing they would expect is a maiden's blood."

She paled.

Simon turned from the door and gave her a quiet smile. "Don't worry about it," he said. "I have never bedded a virgin in my life, and I hope never to do so. We'll get along fine, Adeline."

CHAPTER TWELVE

Spying upon Simon Taillebroc would be a more difficult task than Adeline had expected. As his wife, she would have a great advantage in the attempt; on her first day of marriage, she saw that she would need it.

On that first morning, Adeline heard Simon rise before dawn to speak to the sentries as they changed watch at the tower. He returned to bed and fell into a deep sleep within minutes. Soon after, when she rose to warm herself at the fire, her husband bolted awake and reached for his sword beside the pallet. The small alarm had not angered him; surprise had followed fright as Adeline heard Simon mutter an apology for startling her, and put the sword back in its place. She had listened as he drifted into deep and immediate sleep.

Adeline went back to bed to lie wakeful once again; she wondered how she would manage to follow the movements of a man who woke and slept with such swift efficiency. She fretted that her own reports to the archer Luke would be difficult to arrange; Simon possessed the quick reactions of a man expecting trouble, and he would notice her absence should she attempt to leave their hall by night.

He discovered that she was awake. "Is something wrong—beyond the headache you deserve?"

"Nothing."

From the garrison yard came the clash of steel.

"It's the morning practice at arms," said Simon. "I should be out there."

The sound of iron upon iron became louder. "Shall I tell them to stop?" he asked.

"No, they would think—"

"—that we need quiet for what we might be doing here?" Simon laughed. "Believe me, wife, it wouldn't occur to them."

"Are they such single-minded soldiers?"

"They're a good troop, for a small, remote outpost like this one. But beware, Adeline. They have no pretty manners among them."

"Are they dangerous?"

"Not to my wife. But stay clear of them—they see few women; I won't permit them to come near the girls of your father's hall. Be careful. If I'm not here and you want to ride out, speak to Harald, and he will get your horse. Don't go into the stables."

"Harald is different from the others."

"He is. He's from Taillebroc."

She sat up.

Simon laughed. "You'll get no tales of dead priests from Harald. He's as careful of secrets as I am."

He placed his arm about her, and she sank into the warmth of him, and breathed his clean scent. "Last night," he said, "you slept before I could ask you if there is a child."

"Why do you ask?"

"Don't be afraid—it makes little difference."

"No," she said. "There is no child."

He sighed.

"Is something wrong?"

"If you were with child, these next few weeks would have been—uncomplicated."

Something in his voice set her heart pounding. "How?"

"We might have had some pleasure together— carefully. Within reason."

"And because there is no child, we cannot have pleasure?"

"If you're to get my own child, it must be after the springtime, when I know better what Longchamp has in mind. I'll not bring a child into the world to be hounded with his mother by that monster. A young heir to Taillebroc would be vulnerable to every greedy agent of the chancellor."

"They would have to find us first."

"You have no idea, my lady, how loathsome the chancellor would be."

"He's more an animal than a man," she said. "I have seen hungry wolves with more compassion."

His breathing stopped. "You have seen Long-champ?"

"He travels often in Normandy. I saw him in the lady Maude's household."

There came a hammering on the door, and questions about Simon's orders for the day. He rose from the bed and went out to deal with them.

When she awoke again, daylight was in the sky, and Taillebroc stood at the bedside fully clothed and ruddy from the cold morning air.

"Adeline, you must wake. Your father and his lady are riding up the hill." He placed a hand on her shoulder as she sat up. "You have a few minutes. They just left the manor."

He turned to open the shutter and look out to the stable doors as she scrambled into her tunic and surcoat from the night before.

"Did the sentry come to tell you?"

Simon turned back to her and smiled. "I was on the tower when they left the stockade."

Adeline began to smooth the coverlet and the great wolf pelt over the possible controversy of the bed linen. "Do you rise before dawn each day to spy on him?"

He laughed. "Tell him so, if you think it would please him."

Simon carried Adeline's saddlebags to the pallet and set them upon the coverlets. "That will keep the curious from burrowing for scandal," he said.

Adeline nodded her approval and returned to her question. "Do you watch the manor each day at dawn?"

"When the mist doesn't cover it. It was in your

father's honor that I built the tower so high, to over-look half the valley."

"He would be pleased to know how well he puzzles you."

A broad smile appeared on Simon's face. "The extra timber your father sold us went into the sentry walk. One day, I'll tell him."

Adeline smiled back. "Not today?"

"Not today." Simon dragged a small trestle board from the wall and lifted it onto its frame. "To be honest, I'll miss chasing your father across the hills. I was getting closer each time."

She made a small sound of disbelief.

"Don't doubt me—I was improving. The day Caer-doc found you on the Hereford road, I had been following him since first light. He rode through the pass that time, bold as his ravens. Following him through the forest was hard work. When we caught up with him, he had ten new mounts, a packhorse, a Norman lady, and his daughter in tow. The man is a wizard or worse." Simon brought wood to the fire and set the door open to await his marriage kin.

Adeline set a small veil upon her head and smoothed her surcoat. Beyond Simon's tall frame, she saw men-at-arms leading horses from the byre, the breath of men and beasts clouding the bright, cold air. She went to her husband's side; he placed a light hand upon her shoulder and murmured a word of courage.

She felt a rush of warmth in the chill of the morning. In the worries and confusion of the days since her arrival at the valley, Adeline had not had time to consider how it would be to begin a marriage with this man. She had imagined the wedding bed, and given embarrassed attention to Maida's advice, but had thought little about the small details of living as this man's wife. In Simon's gesture, there was a pleasant intimacy, a sign that they were together in a fledgling household of their own. Adeline stood close against her husband's arm and allowed herself the illusion that she belonged in this place, with this man.

Maida had brought food from the night before, and hot bread from the manor's ovens. It was her reason for accompanying Caerdoc, she had said. Adeline watched Simon's face as he greeted Maida, and saw no sign that he considered her more than Caerdoc's amiable mistress. Adeline began to hope that her marriage might be strong enough to bear the burden of secrets within her family and in Simon's past.

While the garrison's cook unburdened the pack animals, Caerdoc and Maida shared cold venison and the garrison's pottage with Simon and Adeline. The pottage was rich, Maida said, but badly seasoned. Caerdoc had muttered his doubts that the Normans would notice. Simon ignored the growled insult and offered Caerdoc a cup of ale.

Maida moved about the chamber with Adeline, discussing the gift of wall hangings she wished to bring her. When they reached the far corner, she lowered her voice to a whisper. "You are content?"

"Yes."

"Your father wants to know. He said that if you prove unhappy, or if you tire of this marriage, he'll get Cuthbert to consider an annulment somehow."

Adeline colored. Not even Maida must know that the marriage was incomplete, and an annulment still quite legal on this cold, chaste morning.

"I want to stay with him," she said.

Maida drew Adeline into her arms and hugged her. "I thought he had a look of kindness—both strength and kindness. You are fortunate, Adeline. And so is your husband."

Beyond the fire pit, Caerdoc rose and looked about the hall. "Where's the heathen sword?"

Simon smiled. "Up there, beside the arrow loop."

Adeline's father looked at the shining blade hanging from the timber planks and nodded his approval. "It's a pretty thing to look upon, and handy enough if your enemy is at the wall. That steel is thin enough to kill a man through the gap of a closed shutter."

"I would that my enemies were so easily overcome." Simon glanced at Adeline. "If there is trouble here, I want to send Adeline back to the manor, or on to William the Marshal, if the snows haven't come."

"Father, I told him I won't go."

Caerdoc sat down in heavy exasperation. "If she goes anywhere, it will be to my cousin Rhys, where I would have sent her had she not married. Keep peace with her, Taillebroc. The truce between us will endure as long as my daughter is content with her husband."

Adeline felt the gentle pressure of Maida's hand upon her arm. She moved forward. "Father, I'm content."

Caerdoc's gaze moved to her, then back to Simon. "Then all must be well between us," he said at last.

Maida's hand relaxed.

Simon's bench scraped loud in the awkward silence. He rose and pointed to the Saracen sword. "Would you like to try the blade?"

After a small hesitation, Caerdoc shook his head. "Show me the sentry tower instead, Taillebroc. I would see my valley from the height of it."

Simon turned to the women. "Will you come?"

Maida demurred. Adeline looked down at her fine wedding surcoat and thought of the rough ladder on the outer wall of the tower.

Her husband extended his hand. "Come with us. Both of you. You'll be safe enough."

He led them to a small door in the base of the timber structure and pushed it open. Within, weapons, dry stores and firewood lay stacked against the walls. In the center of the lofty space, a railed stair rose in sharp angles from the floor to a sunlit opening above.

Adeline saw her father glance about the walls and frown. "You can't defend it," he said.

"It's a lookout post, nothing more. If an enemy comes near enough to enter the tower, or burn it, we're already lost." Simon took Adeline's hand and began to climb the open stair.

Caerdoc waved Maida ahead and followed her steps. "Why did you build it so high, when you can see the pass from the fortress walls?"

Simon shrugged and helped Adeline step out onto the broad sentry walk. "Why did your ancestors build the first tower here, if they believed they needed to watch only this pass?"

A black, silent look was Caerdoc's answer.

The valley lay before them, its high meadows still green below walls of rock that rose as solid as a well-mortared castle keep. The manor and its settlement of huts were close enough that Adeline could see the fresh-hewn wood of repairs to the stockade, and each dark slab of slate upon the manor roof. Beyond Caerdoc's hall, on the far side of the valley, each croft and shed was clear to sight.

"There are so many huts up on the meadows," Adeline said.

Simon walked to Caerdoc's side. "How many people do you have living up there?"

Caerdoc shrugged. "I never counted. In the old king's time, when there was war hereabouts, some sent their young ones west, away from the fighting. Not many of them returned when peace came. I gave their huts to others who came here to settle."

"You have some old fighting men, I think, in the croft above the manor."

Caerdoc scowled into the bright sunlight. "Which one?"

"The large one, with the smoke rising below it. I rode past it some days ago, and saw them."

"I won't turn away any man who has fought the Normans." Caerdoc faced Taillebroc, his hands resting upon his wide sword belt. "They were men-at-arms who fought old Henry Plantagenet. Now they're shepherds and woodcutters. Not good ones, but they earn their bread and keep their rough ways up on the meadows, clear of the women in my hall. I'll not drive them away; not for you, not for William the Marshal. They will keep our peace as long as I wish it. Watch them, if you will, but you'll not see them fighting any but their own fellows, when the dice fall crooked."

Taillebroc nodded. "I saw your treaty with the Marshal—it says nothing of the number of fighting men in your household. If you can control them and keep the peace, they are nothing to me."

Caerdoc growled in agreement, and moved along the sentry walk to look out over the pass, to the lands beyond his valley.

"That's a fine archer down there. He bends his bow as well as a Welshman."

"It's Luke, one of my Hereford men."

Adeline looked down to the broad meadow north of the valley pass. The archer Luke had wedged a small barrel high in the fork of an oak tree where the forest bounded the meadow. He stood far from his target, surrounded by grass and deep bracken, and shot arrow after arrow into the bristling shape of the tun.

"I hope he emptied it first," said Caerdoc. "I had such a barrel among the Marshal's treaty gifts. Brandywine, it was."

"What bright arrows," Maida said. "Such bold scarlet—"

"He makes his own," said Simon, "and reddens them to claim them among others. He's a good soldier and a better archer; Luke could stop a sparrow in flight across that meadow."

They turned from the rail and began to descend the stair. Adeline looked back over her shoulder and saw the archer take a longer arrow from the quiver and send it flying high above the oak tree, far into the forest beyond his target. It was comforting to know that Longchamp's agent could make mistakes.

Simon's hand descended upon her shoulder.

"I didn't mean to fright you," he said.

Adeline shook her head. For one terrible moment, she had imagined that she had spoken aloud, that Simon had heard her thoughts. She steadied herself with an arm against the rail.

Simon inclined his head toward the distant sight of Luke plucking his crimson arrows from the brandy-wine tun. "Mark that man," he said. "Be careful of him. I believe him to be one of Longchamp's agents; if I'm right, he's dangerous to me and may be to you as well."

It was impossible to tell, from Simon's tone, whether he had noticed Adeline speaking to Luke. "He has been courteous enough," she said.

Simon frowned.

"He helped me once, at the stable here," she added.

Adeline looked back again, and saw the archer at the foot of his target tree, closing the quiver case. He stood and looked into the forest, as if straining to see where his long shot had fallen. Then he turned and began the steep walk up to the pass.

"He's careless of those arrows," said Simon. "He left the long shot behind."

Adeline looked again at the meadow, and at the

forest, and at the figure of the archer. And she knew
how Luke the archer sent his messages to Longchamp. A scarlet arrow in the stand of winter oak
would be easy to find, and Luke was skillful enough
to send it to an appointed place, even as he appeared
to overshoot.

There was no movement in the forest; later, another
agent of William Longchamp might move through
the brittle leaves, searching for the message. What
had the archer sent into that bleak forest this day?
Word that she had married Simon Taillebroc? How
many of Longchamp's men waited in that forest?

Simon was waiting at the top of the stair, his hand
extended to help her descend. "If the archer ap-
proaches you," he said, "come to me, and tell me."

Adeline nodded, and thanked her saints that Simon
Taillebroc had not asked for her to speak a promise.

Some forms of deception tainted a soul more than
others. She was Longchamp's spy, yet she hoped that
she would never need to lie to her husband.

She took her husband's hand and prayed that Luke
the archer would never have cause to send Longchamp a scarlet arrow bearing the means to bring
death to Simon Taillebroc.

And then she turned her mind to the troublesome
thing she had heard Taillebroc say about the treaty.

CHAPTER THIRTEEN

Once again, Adeline was reminded that Taillebroc would not be an easy target for any spy.

"No, you may not come with me," her husband insisted. "Go in to see your father. I'll be back soon."

"I saw my father this morning. I'm coming with you."

Simon pointed to stockade gates. "You'll stay here. Visit Maida. Weave something. Discover where your foolish maid spent last night."

"Insulting Petronilla is no remedy."

"I have no time for your stubbornness. I could ride up and back in the time you keep me quarreling here."

"That is my point. Ride on. I'll keep up with you."

"Madam, I'm visiting a camp of veteran rebels. You cannot accompany me."

"Why must you go up there? They're shepherds now. They fought in our rebellion, and now they keep sheep. My father told you this; do you not believe him?"

"I believe that he doesn't lie—"

"Then trust him, and leave the shepherds in peace."

"—and that he never tells the entire truth."

"Then ask him what you need to know. Or take me with you to the hut. They will see that I am Caerdoc's daughter, and they won't attack you."

"They know who I am. And they won't attack me. Not now, with a full garrison in place and sentries watching from the tower. I'm going alone for a reason—to question them without threat."

Adeline looked over her shoulder; even at this distance, she could feel the gaze of Luke the archer upon her back. If she let Simon go up the meadows alone, Luke would send another of his crimson arrows into the forest; Longchamp would soon know that Simon Taillebroc had spoken in privacy with Caerdoc's settlement of former rebels. Even if she managed to go with Simon to the encampment and report to Luke that Taillebroc had not spoken a single word of treason, Luke still might send the deadly message that Taillebroc was courting the old recreants.

"How will it look," she asked in desperation, "to have Simon Taillebroc, priestkiller, despised of the king's chancellor, visit a band of rebels? You said you thought that your archer Luke is a spy; if so, word of your visit will spread. Why do you provoke trouble?"

Simon looked up at the sky and began to mutter.

Adeline caught a few of the words; he was, she realized, counting in Latin.

"Madam," he said at last, "you cannot follow me wherever I go. We are wed, as you wished. You live in my hall, as you wished. All I ask is that you leave me in peace to ride about this valley. As I wish. Alone."

"You are shouting."

"Yes, madam, I am."

Adeline pointed to the stockade gate. "I am Caerdoc's daughter, and I will ride where I wish in his valley."

Simon's next words were not Latin. Nor were they numbers.

Adeline lifted her reins and urged her palfrey onto the well-worn track leading to the hut above the meadow.

Her husband followed, holding his mount to a slow pace behind her. "Do you know these men?" he asked.

His voice was low, approaching a reasonable tone. Adeline answered in her most civil manner. "No—I know none of the people who came here to settle after the rebellions."

"Then do me the favor of letting me speak to them without distraction."

Taillebroc had given up his objections to her presence. Adeline smiled. "Of course," she said.

"Then draw aside and let me pass. I should go ahead of you, for your safety."

She guided her mount to the withered bracken beside the track. Simon stopped beside her. "Since you'll be present—foolishly present—you should know my plan. I'll question your soldier-shepherds about the way they travel in and out of the valley. I don't need to know who they were before they came here, or what they did in the rebellions."

He leaned forward and placed a hand upon the neck of her palfrey. "If you want me to turn back now, and ignore your armed shepherds, then tell me how your father vanishes and reappears without using the pass. I'll not reproach him for hiding the route; he need not know that you have told me. I will use the knowledge to prepare a defense against invasion— nothing more. Will you tell me what you know?"

Adeline pointed to the end of the valley. "The slope isn't as steep at the end, where the valley widens out. A man carrying a light load could make it over the top and down the cliff."

Simon shook his head. "I'm looking for a way that armed men on horseback could come into the valley. There are caves above the meadows, but none large enough for a horse to pass into them."

"If there's a cave, men could leave horses at each end of the passage."

His dark eyes showed interest in her suggestion. "That was my first thought, but it proved wrong. The last time your father disappeared from sight, both men and horses were missing from the manor—I went through the byre and the hall in his absence. After Caerdoc's return, I saw the horses; they had been pushed hard. He might have used them in a raid, some distance from here."

His hand was still upon the shining grey neck of

her palfrey. Adeline looked away. "I don't know how he did it."

"When you were a child, when your father began his rebellion, there must have been a plan for escape. Did your parents not tell you, before the fighting started, what they would do if Henry Plantagenet took this valley?"

"No—I heard nothing of such a plan, and it never occurred to me that my father would lose."

Simon nodded his head. "I might have thought the same, when he was a little younger."

Adeline sighed. "The old king's army did take the valley. There was no talk of escape for us—for my father, my mother, and me. After the truce was made, they sent me to Normandy as surety for my father's good faith. Believe me, if there had been a secret way to leave the valley, my father would have sent us away before that happened."

Simon took his hand from her palfrey and sat back in his saddle. "Is there someone from the early days—among the women, the weavers—who trusts you enough to tell you what has happened here since you left?"

It was a difficult thing to admit. Adeline shook her head and looked down at her saddlebow. "Most of the people I remember are gone—missing after the rebellion or gone west to live far from the borders. In my father's hall, there are many new folk who came to the valley to escape the Normans; I haven't yet learned their names. And the old ones"—she stopped to draw a shallow breath, then rushed on—"the old ones don't trust me. If they have secrets, they wouldn't give them to me. I had little Welsh when I was a child, for my mother was Norman and raised me to remember that. I can't understand my own father's people unless they slow their words. They do not."

There—she had said it without faltering, and her eyes were still dry. Simon was silent for a time, then shook his head. "A sad homecoming, then marriage to me. Which was worse?"

Adeline saw a small smile twitch the corners of Simon's mouth; the sight of it brought her a giddy, unreasonable levity of her own. The dull ache in her throat was eased and she found that she could smile back. "The homecoming was difficult, but the marriage may prove still worse."

"Has it yet?"

"Not yet."

His eyes were darkened gold in the sunlight, and his mouth, now curved in a deep smile, was temptation itself. "I am your wife," she heard herself say, "yet you have not kissed me."

His smile broadened. "Would you like me to?"

"Yes."

"Would you stay behind and wait for me if I did?"

"Of course not."

He dropped the reins and slowly drew the gauntlets from his hands. With a touch so gentle it could have been the brush of a leaf in the wind, he brought his hand to her cheek. The warmth of his palm moved down to her neck, and hesitated above the curve of her breast. "By all the saints," he whispered, "you are so beautiful—" He slid his hands behind her head and his lips were upon her mouth.

There was a moment's teasing as he whispered her name upon her lips; there was a great rush of warmth through her blood as the teasing ended and he began to kiss the corner of her mouth.

She had been kissed before—by a Breton who had caught her to him in the midsummer dancing, and by the nervous young Nevers in the corridor outside the lady Maude's solar. It had not been like this. Nothing like this.

She turned to take his kiss full upon her mouth; the beating of her heart grew loud in her ears, and she heard with distant surprise her own soft cry of wonderment .

He took his lips from hers and moved his palms to her shoulders. "You are right," he said. "This is not the time for more than a kiss."

"I—I don't mind." She reached to his hands and brought them down to the place where he had hesitated above the small swell of her breasts. "Again," she said. "Please—again."

Her palfrey tossed his head and backed away from Taillebroc's steady mount. Simon braced her in the saddle and caught the reins. "Careful," he said.

The world was still around them, bitter cold and vivid in color. Adeline looked at the country before them and wondered at the sight. Something had shifted within her mind; she had seen the winter green of the meadow as if for the first time.

"Your mount has more sense than I do," said Simon. "The camp is just beyond here. Forgive me."

Adeline nodded once.

They rode in silence across the meadow. She knew

that had she spoken, she would have heard the voice of a stranger. She had changed; everything had changed.

Everything—

Simon drew his horse to a halt and reached for her arm. "What on God's earth is that?"

A distance from the track, in the middle of a stand of rowans, bright colors hung from the bare branches of an ancient tree.

"Is it—"

"No," she said. "It's not a hanged man. I remember this place, and the tree. Those are gifts to the saints on its branches."

"The clothing?"

"They're offerings—for luck, or health, or a babe safely born. My mother left her best mantle there before my birth. She told me when I was a child."

"Though she was Norman, she believed all this?"

"She may have. That tree is very old, and has a strong reputation."

He started toward the eerie confusion of tangled wool and drifting silk.

She reached to stop him. "Don't approach, unless you have a great favor to ask the saints, and a good length of cloth to leave there."

He shrugged. "It's too cold to leave my cloak, and my wishes might be too great—even for your pagan tree."

"Come away then. It's not good to stay here without purpose."

It took only minutes to reach the far side of the meadow. The brightness of the day, the clarity of each bird's song, the white rush of excitement—it had all subsided during that short ride across the grassland. As they neared the shepherds' hut, low clouds had gathered to block the sun; in the sudden darkness, Adeline sensed the hillside returning to what it had been before—

Simon turned in his saddle and made a small gesture of warning. "Stay close beside me," he said. "There will be no trouble, but stay where I can see you."

The slow smile that followed his words sent another message to Adeline—one that had nothing to do with the shepherds' camp.

At first sight, she thought that the hut must be aflame, and burning to the ground. Thick, resinous smoke surrounded the camp, obscuring the large hut that Caerdoc had built for the failed rebels. Beyond the large campfire, the hut rose straight against the base of the cliff, and a line of sheepfolds extended along that same rocky wall above the meadows. From the high smell and the sound of milling sheep, it seemed that Caerdoc's former rebels had managed to keep a large flock together through the summer grazing.

They didn't look like shepherds, nor had they changed their short swords and hauberks for shepherds' boots and crooks. The largest of them, a burly man with only one ear, rose to his feet at the sight of Taillebroc and Adeline.

"Caerdoc's daughter and the Norman warden. Wed now, are you?"

Taillebroc halted and signaled for Adeline to stop as well. The well-armed shepherd stood with his back to the smoking fire; the fumes billowed around him.

Simon seemed not to share Adeline's superstitious wish to ride away from this image of the devil. He leaned forward to address the man. "Yes, we were wed yesterday. I am Simon Taillebroc. How are you called?"

The man glanced about him, as if looking for a trap. "Gruffud," he said at last.

"You and your fellows are shepherds?"

"We are."

A fresh gust of wind drew a billow of dense smoke from the campfire. "You're burning green wood," said Taillebroc. "It will be a hard winter up here, if you don't find better fuel."

Gruffud inclined his head to the hut. "We have dry wood for the winter."

"May I bring my wife into the hut?"

"There's men sleeping there." Gruffud shrugged. "And a woman or two."

Adeline looked past Gruffud to the nine men who sat before the wide, listing door of the hut. Unconcerned with the heavy smoke, they sat upon blocks of wood in a semicircle, throwing dice. One of them was watching Taillebroc; the others ignored him.

Though their clothing was patched and their swords scarred from strife, the edges of their weapons gleamed lethal in the setting sun.

Taillebroc pointed to the folds. "You own the sheep?"

"It's Caerdoc's flock. We watch them, day and night, and get half the fleeces."

"There's better work to be had, up at the garrison."

The men around the dice game looked up.

Gruffud frowned. "We're through with wars. That's what Caerdoc promised the Normans. The fortress is none of our concern."

Taillebroc drew a small leather bag from his hauberk and weighed it in his hand. "There's gold here for the men who can tell me how an armed horseman gets out of this valley without using the pass."

There was silence beyond the smoke. Adeline saw Taillebroc's free hand move with slow precision to rest upon the hilt of his sword.

Gruffud pointed to the sky. "He rides into a Norman garrison, draws his sword, and damns the soul of Henry Plantagenet to all in his hearing. He's in paradise within the hour, so the priests say."

"Your priest suggested this?"

The one-eared shepherd grinned. "He's a fair nuisance, that one—discouraging the women from showing us a little kindness. If I say the priest is promising salvation to rebels, will you rid us of the old man, as you did the other churchman?"

"No!" Adeline rose in the saddle and grabbed Simon's arm. Her horse shied from the sudden movement; Adeline fought to keep her precarious balance. Simon's gold coins fell to the ground as he turned to steady her.

"Say nothing," he growled. Simon set Adeline back

in her saddle and turned once again to Gruffud. "Better men than you have tried to provoke me in that way. I'll not draw my sword to stop any man's talk of the dead priest; this I have sworn, and I'll keep that oath. But I make another oath to you, Gruffud One-Ear: You and your soldiers may live here and play at shepherds as long as you threaten no one— not the men of my garrison, not my wife and her kin, and not even the sour-faced priest. The day you do so, you'll die by my hand. Any of you. All of you. Caerdoc cannot protect you from me."

The men stood in their semicircle, swords at the ready. Gruffud shook his head. "Let the churchman live, then. Up here, we harm no one. Not even that pest of a priest."

Simon looked beyond Gruffud to the hut. "Then you will live here in peace."

Gruffud's eyes narrowed. "Your gold is there on the ground."

"Keep it," said Simon. "And pay some lads to cut you some decent firewood."

Laughter broke from the door of the hut, then spread to the men standing about the forgotten dice. The great fists of Gruffud One-Ear uncurled and left the scarred sword belt.

Before them all, the scattering of Taillebroc's bright gold shone upon the cold earth.

With a curt word, Simon sent Adeline back down the meadow track. Within moments, she heard him behind her.

They rode in silence all the way back to the fort.

CHAPTER FOURTEEN

At the end of his first day of wedded life, Simon Taillebroc rode back to the fortress with his new wife at his side and the setting sun behind him. They rode in silence, heavy with thoughts of their encounter with Gruffud at the former rebels' campfire.

Simon used that long silence to consider other mysteries unresolved by the day's events. He was no closer to discovering why Caerdoc had given his daughter to an exiled Norman, nor why the daughter herself had consented to the marriage. Nor could Simon understand why she wished to follow him about his errands in the manner of an infatuated bride.

The most likely answer was obvious: that Caerdoc was using his only daughter to watch the Norman garrison's workings and discover Simon's intentions toward the people of Caerdoc's valley. That was reason enough; and if the daughter were to be widowed and her father able to claim part of the confiscated Taillebroc lands and riches, so much the better. The old fox Caerdoc would not ignore a source of gold, even if he had to come down from the mountains, travel across the breadth of England, and pluck it from the civilized lands of Kent.

Simon smiled as he imagined Adeline and her ill-tempered father descending upon Taillebroc to wrest it from the Longchamp partisans who must, by now, be collecting the rents. His own brother Savare would get the lands, of course, if Savare outlived Longchamp's days of influence; Simon must write to his younger brother to tell him of Adeline, and the need to give her an income should she become Simon's widow and need refuge at Taillebroc.

As in all things, the future of the Taillebroc lands might not follow the most obvious path. Though he had already told Adeline that they should not dare conceive a child this winter, he was tempted to change his mind. One day, now or in the springtime, she might conceive a Taillebroc child, an heir to those lost lands.

Simon's veins ran hot at the thought of bedding his wife. This night, there would be no prolonged feasting at Caerdoc's board, no flagons of rare wine in which Adeline might attempt to drown her nervousness and make herself ill. They would be alone in the old hall, undisturbed by his garrison across the fortress yard.

But like all the other questions that plagued Simon's

mind, the matter of Adeline and the possibility of a child would have no simple resolution. Though she had the wit and courage to defend a child, or hide it for years if necessary, Simon's bride was already watched by at least one possible agent of Longchamp. The archer Luke might have fellow spies in the garrison, working for the corrupt chancellor.

Once the winter snows came, Adeline would be safe from Simon's enemies for many months. Trouble would come next spring; a pregnant, widowed Adeline would be unable to risk herself as a fugitive in these mountains.

A prudent man would leave his wife free of a child until spring.

A prudent man would not have wed Caerdoc's daughter and brought temptation into his bed.

Simon looked to his wife and saw that her thoughtful gaze was upon him. Was she thinking of the same dangers, feeling the same temptations that sent his blood pounding hot in his veins?

In that moment, the remedy to Simon's dilemma became clear. He would ask his wife to tell him what she wanted from the long, intimate winter they would pass together in the ancient hall. He would let Caerdoc's daughter decide the question.

Simon drew breath to speak to her, but thought better of it. They had reached the foot of the fortress hill and would soon be among his men. This night, when the fire blazed upon the great hearthstone of the old hall and the door was barred against the rising wind, he would ask his question of Adeline.

The fortress looked better than it should in this

light, with the valley in new darkness and the last light of the red sun striking the heights above the pass. The hurried repairs to the stone curtain walls and the uneven colors of old timber and new repairs to the hall were not visible in the dying light. Even the stark new planks facing the sentry tower were darkened to amber as the sun began to leave the sky.

Torches bloomed at the fortress gate, and a great curl of woodsmoke and drifting sparks rose from the garrison's cooking fire. Simon dismounted and pulled the heavy gauntlets from his hands. He caught Adeline about her small waist and set her upon the mounting block, above the frozen mud of the bailey ground. She lifted the hem of her cloak to step down and picked her way past the ice-covered puddles to the old hall.

Harald stood beside the hearthstone, prodding the fire to life beneath a great web of kindling. "There's cold venison and stew on your table," he said. "And the last of Caerdoc's feasting wine." He cast a shy glance at Adeline, then addressed Simon. "The cook has a big kettle of water over the kitchen fire. If you want to have it for bathing, I'll tell the men to wait their turn."

Adeline blushed brighter than the young flames around Harald's kindling.

"Tell the men to wait," Simon said. "We won't be long."

She was silent until Harald had left the hall. "I can't bathe in the kitchen," she said.

Simon shrugged. "There's no one there after the day's food is ready. Our cook doesn't fret much over the place; he's a man-at-arms who gets a little extra silver to keep us all from starving."

Adeline did not seem reassured.

"If I live past spring, and if the well stays full, I'll build us a proper bath shed, like the one at Taillebroc. Come," he said, "the kitchen will be warm, and I'll bar the door for us."

"I think not."

Simon frowned. After her years in Normandy and the liaison with her foolish betrothed, his wife seemed as shy as a nun. He felt his intentions slipping, unsure that he should leave the important question of consummating this marriage to his wife's discretion. One should not expect a woman with the soul of a nun to make a clear decision.

"I don't need to bathe," she said. She was shivering from the cold, and there was an edge of ice upon the hem of her tunic.

"Stay here, then." He grabbed the water bucket and walked outside to the kitchen shed to fill it with steaming hot water from the cauldron over the fire.

When he returned and pushed open the hall door, he found Adeline sitting at the table. The food was untouched. "Here." He pointed to the small bucket of water. "Bathe here in the hall. I'll go to the kitchen fire and be back soon." He watched relief transform her face. "Bar the door until you're done."

She looked happier still at those words. "I will," she said. "I thank you, Simon."

He picked up a clean tunic and managed to get back to the kitchen shed before the others came and muddied the water with their washing cloths. Back at Taillebroc, there was a cistern on the roof of the large keep, and plenty of servants to carry the buckets down to heat beside the fine wall-hearth in the lord's sleeping chamber. When the widowed lady Aelis had come to Taillebroc, she had bathed in Simon's warm chamber and forgotten to find her own bed that long summer night—

Simon turned his mind from thoughts of the lady Aelis's delicate skills and rinsed his washing cloth in the bucket of cold water set apart from the fire. He hesitated, then passed the chilly cloth over his body and willed away the memories of days when a woman would look at Simon Taillebroc and see him as he had been—before that night at Hodmersham.

The night air was colder still when he came out of the kitchen shed. He stood looking at the early-winter stars and began to compose the words he would use for Adeline. Nothing forceful, but warm enough that she would know he wanted her. She would know. By St. Peter's great toe, she would know that he wanted her.

To have a woman in his hall—to have a wife—had been beyond Simon's imagining even a fortnight ago. Even had he married Mathilde Bouteville a year ago, when her brothers had first approached him, she wouldn't have followed him to this desolate place. Simon sighed at the memory of that timid white face peering out from her brothers' hall when Simon had broken the betrothal. Had she been his wife before that night at Hodmersham, Mathilde's brothers might have killed him in order to free her from sharing his disgrace.

And now he had an unlooked-for wife of more beauty than a Plantagenet's mistress and the courage to live in Simon the Priestkiller's hall. He looked again to the stars and thanked his saints for this good fortune—

He blinked and saw that his second glance confirmed the first. The torches at the fortress gate were burning high, casting their light upon the south wall, and up the side of the sentry tower. There, at the edges of the torches' loom, was the figure of Luke the archer; there was no mistake about it—no other man in the garrison who stood watch with a longbow at his side. The other figure was a woman.

It was Adeline.

He would have gone up, but stopped himself because of Adeline. It was a small, precarious place, too dangerous for a woman if a struggle began.

He made no sense of it all in that first cruel moment of recognition; he forced himself to stand immobile in the cold of the night and consider the consequences of action and inaction. At Hodmersham, he had moved too fast and come to grief for it. Hodmersham had taught him more than he cared to remember.

Simon stood watching his wife and Longchamp's spy, too far away to hear their words, but close enough to see that they were speaking fast, with swift gestures of disagreement. It seemed no accident that they had found each other on the sentry walk; they had much to say to each other. For they were, both of them, Longchamp's creatures.

Both of them.

Both of them.

It was not necessary to deal with both of them together.

It was not necessary to do anything at all.

They had only to look down into the bailey yard to see him. He pushed away from the kitchen wall, walked to the hall that he now knew would be empty, and shoved open the door that he knew would not be barred.

The bucket of hot water that he had fetched for her stood cooling upon the planked floor. A square of green linen hung drying upon the end of a bench, its delicate, straight web drifting in the draft of the fire. Her tunic was beside it; the ice had melted from the hem and fallen in a broken line of water drops along the floor.

She had bathed and dressed and seen to the tunic. Adeline had not been very long in the sentry walk. She had spoken very little, by now—

Simon slammed his fist into the wall and wondered, somewhere in the back of his mind, why he felt no pain. He was a fool to count the minutes Adeline had been speaking with Longchamp's spy. Longchamp's other spy.

He was a fool to imagine ways to diminish the proof of her disloyalty.

He was a fool to have allowed the marriage.

He was a fool to have imagined, having wed Caerdoc's daughter, that there would be an end to his lonely nights without the comfort of a willing woman.

He had learned many bitter lessons since Hodmersham. But he had not learned enough.

He had managed to leave no hint of his anger in the hall. The edge of his fist was throbbing and would soon begin to pain him, but aside from a mark on the soft wood face of the wall, Simon had avoided doing damage.

Harald had left the last of Caerdoc's wedding wine on the short board beside the fire. Simon sat down and began to drink.

A moment later, he sensed rather than heard Adeline's approach. Simon set down the wine cup and stood to watch his wife's return.

She seemed to realize, as soon as she came through the door, that he knew—that he had seen her on the tower. He watched her hesitate at the threshold.

"Why?" he asked. "Why did you not wait until tomorrow to meet the archer? Did you want to be discovered?"

Her stony courage as she stood silent before him was gall to his soul.

"Do you imagine yourself a lamb to the slaughter, in Longchamp's cause—to be beaten or killed by your angry husband the priestkiller, to give the crown yet another reason to put Simon Taillebroc to death?"

She stepped backward into the frame of the door. In that moment, he knew that if she ran for the gates, he would let her go.

She hesitated.

He gestured for her to approach.

She shook her head.

"Come," he said. "Do you believe I will oblige your wish to sacrifice yourself for Longchamp's cause? I could do it quickly, Adeline. With no pain for you."

She spoke a soft, strangled word.

"Speak up," said Simon. "A martyr must learn to make her cause known. If you mutter, you will lose the effect."

Adeline stood straight and took her hand from the doorframe. "I did it for you," she said.

Even now, in this hour of deadly accusation, his wife had not lost her power to astonish. She reached behind her for the door. Let her go. Let her go back to Caerdoc's hall, far from her notorious husband. Only God knew how far she might push him and his credulity if she stayed. Only God knew—

The door closed. She was still there, beside the portal. Between them, the heat of the hearthstone rose in shimmering undulations, confusing the eye.

"You should go," he said. "Take a horse from the stable and go back to your father."

"Listen to me."

He sat down on the bench and put his head in his hands. "Is your father part of this—effort of yours? Is he allied with Longchamp as well?"

"He knows nothing of this."

"And you? Is your loyalty to Longchamp, or is it to the archer?"

"My loyalty is to my father. He's all I have."

Simon took his hands from his face. "God only knows your father's loyalties. Or his daughter's."

She glanced at the heap of saddlebags; for an instant, Simon thought that she would reach for the small, ugly bundle she earlier tied to her saddlebows. It might be a weapon. Or poison. The woman had so damned many mysteries about her that only a fool should have considered wedding her.

Only a fool would have given her, by marriage, a kinswoman's link to the disputed lands of Taillebroc.

"Your master Longchamp is my enemy, and he will try to strike me down in any way he can. But know this: I have kin waiting to return to Taillebroc, and even if I am lost, they will regain the lands one day. No one—not a harlot in maiden's clothing, not Caerdoc, nor the devil himself—will push me far enough to endanger my kinsmen's right to take back Taillebroc. If that is your plan, madam, abandon it now."

"I don't want your land."

"Longchamp has already sent his creatures to occupy it." Simon pointed to the chests pushed against the eastern wall. "There is gold here, as I have told you. Take it, and trouble me no more."

"No."

"I can't have Longchamp's spy in my bed, Adeline. In the garrison, or among your father's people, I expected one or two. But not in this place, not in my bed."

She had not moved from the door. He had seen her expression before, on that first night in her father's hall. Impassive, watchful, and brittle with unease. "If I leave," she said, "the archer will know that we are discovered. He will disappear, and report this to Longchamp. There may be more danger in that than in tolerating a spy."

There were courtiers in the Plantagenet court who had never learned, as this woman had done, to think with such clarity under attack.

"And you? What would happen to you?"

"Disaster. For me, and many others."

"I don't trust you, Adeline."

"You don't need to trust me. The archer was with you before I came. I have discovered nothing Longchamp wants to hear."

"Treason? An alliance with Count John's supporters? Is that what Longchamp hopes to find?"

She put her hand upon the wall. "Yes. All of that."

He stood and threw a small piece of wood on the fire. Adeline took her hand from the wall, but did not retreat as he approached her.

"What did you tell him tonight, then?"

She looked full into his eyes. "That you were not hiring my father's old rebels, or bribing them to support Count John's insurrections. He saw us ride up to the shepherds' hut; one day soon, he might have discovered that you had scattered gold among the rebels. I told the archer that I heard all you said to them, and that there was nothing of treason in it."

"And you climbed up the sentry tower to tell him, in full view of the bailey yard, and the kitchen door."

Her eyes darkened in anger. "It is night, is it not? I needed only a moment, and that moment proved to be the wrong one." She pushed away from the wall and pointed to the unlaced neck of his tunic.

"If you had taken more than that tunic to cover you, and taken the time to dress as the warden of this fortress should do after bathing, I would have been back in this hall before you reached the yard."

Simon caught her wrist; the small tremor in her hand belied the boldness of her words. "Now you'd have me beg your forgiveness for my haste?" He released her arm and pointed to the hearth. "Sit. And listen to me."

She sank onto the bench as if exhausted. Simon looked away, disturbed by that small flaw in her brittle show of courage. Though she was Longchamp's creature, he had no wish to see her near the limits of her spirit.

He took the other bench and drew it near her. "Do you have no care for yourself? Only hours ago, I warned you that I believed the archer a spy; why did you risk meeting him tonight, when you knew I might see you on the tower?"

She made a dismissive gesture. "I might have been too late, if I had waited."

"When does he send his next message?"

Adeline's eyes widened. "Don't think of stopping him. Not this time. Please, for your own sake."

"Who takes word to Longchamp?"

"I don't know." She hesitated, as if weighing the wisdom of her next words. "I saw—I saw him shoot one of his long arrows into the forest, past the target, and leave it there. I believe he can write, and sends messages with the stray arrows into the forest."

Twice in the fortnight past, Simon had seen Luke's carelessness with those precious scarlet arrows, and resolved to watch his targets. "That's why the archer doesn't practice inside the valley," he said. "Luke rides out, beyond the pass, because someone waits there for his messages." Simon sighed. "We have our differences, Adeline, but our suspicions are the same."

He placed his hands at the sides of her face and looked into the darkened green of her eyes. "With your wit, you might survive the Plantagenet court in its most hazardous times. With your beauty," he said, "you may be a danger to the peace, wherever Longchamp sends you next. What am I to do with you, Adeline? How can I send you back to your father? How could I keep you here?"

Her breathing was shallow now. "Don't send me away," she said. "We'll both suffer if the messages to Longchamp cease."

If she drew him into promises this night, he would end by spying for Longchamp himself. He rose to his feet and gestured to the table. "The food is cold. But you should eat."

She sat back in obvious confusion. "I'm not hungry."

"I'm weary of speaking of Longchamp. We'll eat now, and sleep."

"What will you do?"

"To the archer? Nothing yet." He glanced at the bed, and back to her pale face. "Did Longchamp demand that you fascinate as well as wed his enemy?"

Adeline met his gaze without flinching.

He had been right to think her brave—capable of

protecting the child of a dishonored Taillebroc. But there must be no child of his own. Not now.

Simon managed to look away from her. "It will be a long winter," he said. "One day, when I drink enough to forget that my wife is the chancellor's spy, you must show me what you do to keep your victims content."

She did not answer.

He pushed the platter of venison across the table. "Eat, now. The chancellor's spy must keep her strength."

CHAPTER FIFTEEN

Her husband had reacted to the ruin of their short marriage with indifference.

Simon had been distant—kind in small matters, but cold when his wife attempted to discuss the future. Adeline, who prided herself on her own silence and discretion in times of strife, could bear her husband's remote courtesy no longer.

The mornings were the worst of it. Determined to search every part of the valley walls for the passage or cave that Caerdoc must have used to avoid the pass, Simon rode out each day at dawn. He never missed a morning; too soon, her husband had told her, the snows would put an end to his quest.

Adeline rode with him each day. He had tried to avoid her company by rising early and leaving soon after; he set an exhausting pace, and would speak no more than a rare word of caution. He had not, in all those chilly mornings, humiliated her by showing his displeasure before the stableboys or the men of his garrison.

At last, he had ceased to resist her company. She was welcome, he said, to send William Longchamp any news she cared to report from Simon's futile survey of the valley.

At the end of the fortnight, Adeline found herself longing for Petronilla's chirping gossip and sly vision of the world around her. Given the shape of the problem but not the true cause, Petronilla might have some advice to offer Adeline from her store of worldly experience.

The morning rides had become a torture for her. She had never before known the intensity of longing that she now felt for her aloof and dangerous husband. For years in Normandy, Adeline had longed for home, for her mother's impossible return, and for the faces she had left behind in Wales. Strong as they had been, those desires had not given Adeline half the pain she now felt when watching her own husband in the firelight, knowing that though he would sleep beside her, he would disdain to turn to her in the night. And each morning as they rode forth, the silence between them grew more painful.

The strain of the fortnight had sent Adeline in search of a friend's comfortable speech. Simon was free, on this cold morning, to invite an army of rebels through the pass and burn the fortress, for all Adeline cared. Longchamp would hear about it soon enough from the archer Luke. There was nothing, Adeline thought, that she could tell anyone about Simon Taillebroc's activities in this wide valley; she knew less about the man than did his lowliest stableboy.

So she had stayed abed after dawn; Simon had left for the stables, then returned to ask, in a voice colder than the morning frost, if she was ill. She had answered him in a single syllable and pulled the coverlet over her head.

Adeline had remained in her warm refuge until Simon left the fortress. Only then did she ride down to Caerdoc's hall.

In the distance, at the far edge of the frozen fields surrounding the manor stockade, Adeline saw Petronilla's bay palfrey and another mount standing motionless before the forest. She turned her horse into the small western track that led through the cultivated ground to the trees.

Petronilla had been abed on the day after the wedding feast, nursing a wine-sick head; Howyll had brought her message and a chest of fresh linen to the fortress, and promised that Petronilla would soon recover. She would work with Maida within the manor hall and the weaving sheds, Howyll had said. On that evening, and on the following days at twilight, Adeline had watched from the fortress gates as Howyll and Petronilla had crossed the frozen, stubbled fields together; she had smiled to see Petronilla's richly clad presence beside Howyll's tall, untidy figure. Even at a distance, there was something in their gestures that told Adeline the incongruous pair had already become lovers.

Adeline slowed her horse to a walk and looked

about the frost-silvered valley. High above her, Caerdoc's sheep huddled on the bare meadows; the rising wind brought their distant bleating to her hearing. Soon, they would be shut into their folds for the winter.

She shivered. Those gentle beasts could be more certain of warmth and shelter in the coming months than she.

During a fortnight of Simon Taillebroc's cold companionship, Adeline had lain awake, thinking of leaving the valley; if she left soon, she would reach William the Marshal's camp before the snows came. Caerdoc's hall should have been her first choice of refuge, but her presence would lead to strife between her father and Taillebroc.

Simon would not object to her going; he had suggested that she seek the Marshal's protection before they had wed. He might be glad to see her leave; he would be free to bring another woman to pass the winter nights in his bed.

Each time she had thought that far, Adeline had decided to stay.

She reached the edge of the fields and saw that Petronilla's horse and the large roan beside it were tied to a sapling oak. There was no sign of Petronilla and her companion.

She shivered. It was a cold day for dalliance, if that was what Petronilla and Howyll sought in this place. Adeline had heard gossip of lovers taking their pleasure in byre lofts; on this cold day, Petronilla and her Welshman should find such a place. Still—it was possible to feel the heat of summer in any season, beneath a lover's touch. On the day after her wedding—an eternity ago—on the track to the shepherds' hut, there had been a moment when Simon Taillebroc's kiss had filled her body with exquisite heat.

A raven's cry brought Adeline's thoughts back to the frigid, solitary present. She looked about her; beyond the horses, there was no still no sign of Petronilla. Adeline lifted her reins and rode past the tethered mounts to the winter grey waters of the valley's single lake.

A tracery of ice had formed at the edge of the still water. Adeline watched the wind ripples move beneath the frost, breaking the delicate pattern, sending the silver shards back to the water's edge. High above the valley walls, the wind was rising.

Adeline smiled. If the north wind held, the first snows of winter would fall within days. Only then, when the pass filled with deep drifts to stop all but the most determined travelers, would the archer cease to send his messages. Only then would Taillebroc and the people of Caerdoc's valley be safe from a sudden attack by Longchamp's followers.

Only then would it be too late for Simon to send her away.

Behind her, she heard the two horses stirring. In the distance came Petronilla's high laughter and Howyll's amused croak. Adeline turned her horse back toward the manor and trotted away from the sound of lovers' mirth.

* * *

Maida seemed content to have her company for the short distance up to the rebel-shepherds' hut. Adeline offered to take the halter rope of the pack-horse, and rode behind her father's new wife. Maida sat her horse with a grace and ease that the lady Maude would have approved. Caerdoc's unacknowledged wife must be a woman of noble family; she had used much skill to present herself before strangers as a servingwoman aspiring to do well in the weaving hut.

Had the keen-eyed Petronilla discovered Maida's background? Adeline smiled to herself; Petronilla's natural curiosity must have been occupied with the gangly Howyll of late. She looked down the long hill to the manor and the forest beyond the fields. In the distance, she could see Petronilla's horse still tied among the saplings.

Maida laughed as if she had heard that last thought. "Your girl Petronilla has been gathering herbs in the forest these past two days."

"In this cold, is there anything still green?"

"Not much, but she brings a basket back each day." Maida's smile deepened. "When the snows come, I'll ask her again to help the weavers."

Adeline could see the hut before them. "Is it food in these panniers?" asked Adeline.

"Bread, and woolen coverlets. The snow will come soon."

"Who are they, living in the hut?"

Maida's smile faltered. "You have met them?"

"With Simon, two weeks ago. We stayed only a short time; they weren't eager to talk."

"They lived rough for years, in the days of the old king Henry, and now they have settled here to keep the sheep. Your father knows that there may come a day when he'll be grateful to have fighting men close at hand."

"What does he expect to happen?"

Maida made a vague gesture. "He has nothing in mind, but he's a cautious man. He likes to know that the old rebels are here for him, and they are grateful to have a little land." She pointed back beyond the packhorse. "Adeline, your husband has followed us."

She turned in dismay. After all the days he had attempted to leave her behind as he rode out, Taillebroc had decided to follow her—to spy upon her. She watched his tall, black-cloaked form come up the slope of the frost-covered meadow. If their marriage had remained cordial, if some small hope of passion had endured, she might have imagined a trace of concern in her husband's features. She looked away as he slowed his bay stallion to a walk.

"I'll ride with you," he said.

Maida smiled. "I'll take the packhorse and go ahead, if you wish."

"Please stay to ride with us, if you would—"

The warmth of his open smile was more cruel than a blow. His gallantry was for Maida; for Adeline, there would be no such greetings. Ever again.

He moved his horse close and took the halter rope from Adeline's hand. "I'll lead the packhorse," he said.

Linda Cook

"When we return from the hut," said Maida, "will you come with me to the hall? Caerdoc wanted to ride up to the fort, but I shamed him into leaving you in peace, these first weeks of your marriage."

"Adeline?"

To others, his question would seem a courtesy. For Adeline, who saw that Simon's gaze was focused just beyond her shoulder, it was a reproach—yet another sign that Taillebroc would never forgive her. "Of course," she said.

They reached the shepherds' camp soon after. Once again, there was green wood on the smoking campfire and a circle of men playing at dice outside the door of the hut. Beyond the ragged cowhide that hung in the darkened doorway, there seemed to be no movement.

Once again, Gruffud stepped out of the smoke to speak for the others. Adeline saw, in that moment, that something had changed.

The faces of the failed rebels held nothing of the displeasure Simon and Adeline had seen two weeks earlier. Gruffud nodded his head in respect and held Maida's reins as she dismounted. "Lady Maida," he said, "we'll drink your health, and that of Caerdoc, and of the boys."

Simon's gaze turned upon the one-eared rebel. "I'd gladly drink with you."

There was a small hesitation, then Maida's voice again. "Will you save the ale for next time? I must ride back now; there are more coverlets to hem, and little sunlight left this day."

Gruffud bowed his head again, and gestured for

his fellows to take the panniers from the packhorse.
"We thank you, and send greetings to Caerdoc."

Adeline turned to Simon; he, too, had noticed the
change in Gruffud's manner, in the behavior of the
men about the open fire. He made a small gesture
of silence, then turned back to watch the men unload
the packhorse.

Within moments, the small party was leading the
unburdened pack animal back down the meadow.

Maida broke the silence. "Caerdoc will ask you to
spend the days of Christmas with us in the hall. With
half of your men at a time from the fortress, of
course—just as we did for your wedding feast."

Christmas. A longing for the happy, crowded days
of Christmas came over Adeline. In all the years in
Normandy, there had been no festival to compare
with the Yuletide nights in Caerdoc's hall.

She looked up to find Simon watching her.

"May we go there, Simon, for all the twelve nights?"

He shrugged. "If you wish," he said.

"Caerdoc will offer you the lord's sleeping chamber, where you slept with Petronilla, Adeline. He
hasn't used it since your mother left."

Simon's gaze moved to Maida, then back to Adeline. In the short distance back to the stockade gates,
he did not speak again.

The north wind returned that night, carrying sleet
to cover the walls of the fortress in glittering ice,
driving the ravens to shelter in the lee of the watchtower. The sentries took shorter watches, and used

the inner stair to climb the tower and descend from it; after an hour on the sentry walk, each man hurried to seek the warmth of the garrison fire.

Each hour, at the changing of the huddled sentries, Adeline heard the muffled curses of those who wrested open the door at the base of the tower, and a vast, hollow boom as the wind blew it shut.

At her side, Simon grew restless as the gusts increased. He was gone from their bed when Adeline dozed into her own troubled sleep, and returned soon after the sentries' midnight report had awakened her once again.

.It was in the darker hours before dawn that Adeline sat up, shivering and wakeful in the certainty that she had heard the archer's call. A high-pitched whistling rode above the rushing of the wind, faltering, then forming into an eerie pattern. Listen for the whistle, the archer had said.

Even now, the archer must be in the frozen darkness without the hall, breathing summons into the polished bone whistle he had brought with his longbow and scarlet arrows from Hereford—from that adders' nest that Longchamp had created at Hereford.

The ill-pitched notes sounded again, louder this time, near the barred and shuttered arrow loop.

To open the door of the hall would be foolish. The sound and the cold wind would awaken Simon before Adeline could manage to signal the archer, let alone speak with him. She slipped from the warmth of Taillebroc's bed and moved across the frigid floor to the arrow loop.

She drew back for a moment, and stood trembling in the chill of the chamber. She must have been dreaming. The archer Luke would not have expected her to hear his whistle above the storm. Had she been sleeping well, the sound of that small flute would never have wakened her.

Though she had not touched it, the oaken bar rattled in the darkness. Adeline stepped closer; by the faint light of the hearth's embers, she saw that the single tall shutter was still in place. She reached to make sure that it would remain so.

A large hand closed upon her shoulder.

"Hush," growled Taillebroc. "You'll have the whole garrison at the door." There was a second swift movement in the darkness, and she was pinned to the wall, Simon's hand upon her mouth. "Listen to me," he said. "Do you listen? Don't scream again."

He lifted his hand. "Say you understand," he said. "Yes—"

"You're foolish from the cold." He picked her up and tossed her upon the bed. From the hearth pit came a string of obscenities as Simon poked the embers with new wood and scraped the draft-blown coals about the great stone.

The bone flute had stopped its call. Adeline strained to listen for its return.

Simon turned from the hearth and pulled the wolf pelts across her shoulders. "If you take sick from wandering about in your tunic in this cold, your father will have my liver for it." He adjusted the coverlet over her, and sank back upon his bolster. His arm remained across her body, as if he feared she would rise again.

"Did you dream?" he asked.

"I might have."

He lifted himself to peer at her by the light of the sputtering flames. "Or did you hear the archer's flute?"

Once again, his hand pushed her back into the warmth of the bed. "I heard it, too," he said, "but thought it was the wind at the corner of the tower. Was it the archer? Had you promised to meet him, despite the foul night?"

"No, I hadn't promised."

He had not moved his hand. The warmth of it was upon her shoulder; Adeline imagined, in a moment of disjointed madness, how it would feel if she moved beneath him, and brought the heat of his touch upon her heart.

He shifted away as if he had heard her thoughts and despised them.

"Will you stay here when I speak with the sentries, or must I stay to keep you from straying?"

"Why do you go up to the sentry walk so often?"

He sighed. "These are the last days before the snows come. If Longchamp wants to strike before spring, he must do it now."

"You didn't lock the archer away, or question him."

"I didn't want Longchamp to be alarmed if the messages ceased." He frowned into the struggling firelight. "You have kept your word, and not told him I understand what he's about?"

"I did. I swear it."

"Well. Then I don't have to worry, do I? My good wife has given her oath upon it."

In his voice there had been the trace of a smile. "Will you never tire," she said, "of mocking my mistakes? You smile at me, or ignore me—as if I had done but a small disservice to you; then you turn on me as if I were a felon."

"How do you want me to treat you? As the woman who did me—what was your word for it—a small disservice? Or as a felon—dangerous—shut away from decent folk? It's hard to know, Adeline. Choose for me."

She refused to be drawn into his trap. "I'll think on it," she said. And arranged herself at the very edge of the bed.

Simon heaved a long sigh. "Madam, you bring to mind the dilemma of a traitor spared the hangman's noose but unhappy with his quarters in the king's dungeons. With the threat of death behind him, the traitor begins to complain of his life among his fellow prisoners; should he hope to find a remedy for his discomfort? Or should he be silent, knowing that the only remedy must be death?"

"You considered putting me to death? For speaking to an agent of your own king's chancellor?"

He sat up and piled the wolf skins upon her once again. "Must you wave your arms when you speak? Be calm, madam. I spoke of an example, nothing more. I don't kill liars; I cease to listen to them." He sighed again. "In your case, it's often difficult to do so."

"I do not lie."

He moved his bolster to the far side of the bed and lay down in silence.

"I didn't lie to you," she said again. "I never will."

Simon turned back to look upon her in the faint light of the fire. "Then tell me," he said, "what you would have done if I had not seen you with the archer, and had returned to this chamber believing that we would complete the marriage? What then?"

"There is no question in that. I would have done so."

"Because of Longchamp." He was close enough that she could feel the heat of his body.

"No. To keep my father safe, and to stay in the valley. He wanted to send me away, you see. He would have hidden me from the Normans."

With delicate skill, he began to toy with her plaits where they lay between her breasts. "He might have hidden you nearby, or among his serving people, as he did with your young brothers."

She sat up and pushed him away. "What do you mean? He doesn't hide the boys. They are Maida's sons—"

"Have you not guessed that Maida is a wife, and that the boys are trueborn?"

It was impossible to read Simon's expression. "How long have you thought this?" she said. "The boys are no threat to anyone—they are so young—" She attempted to slow the rush words. "You are Caerdoc's heir, now. Everyone knows it. Because you are my husband, you will have the land—"

His hand closed over her arm. "Stop it. Stop it now and listen. I didn't wed you for land. God knows I had land enough at Taillebroc; I lost it for my crimes. Do you imagine that Longchamp would allow me to inherit your father's lands? No— Let your brothers have it, when the time comes. If I get my honor and my lands back, Taillebroc will be enough."

"Swear it."

"Stop thrashing about and I'll swear it." He released her and drew back. "Like you," he said, "my life is entangled with the devil Longchamp. And like you, I do not lie." His hand reached once again to her plaits and smoothed them upon her breast. "I swear it. On the beauty of my wife."

There was no levity, no mockery in his gaze. Only desire.

Her own eyes burned on the edge of tears. "I have made a miserable start of this."

"Of what?"

"Being a wife—your wife."

He took his hand from her braid and touched her cheek. "If I live—"

"You must live—"

"Shhh. If I outwit Longchamp, and live through the spring, will you take me as your true husband?"

She blinked through a haze of tears. "You are my true husband. Now and forever."

"I hope to be," he said, "in the spring and forever."

She managed a shallow breath, and found her voice. "I am here," she said, "and I am yours."

He raised her hand to his lips, then set it down upon the coverlet. "After the winter," he said, "Longchamp may send more than a ferret-faced archer to watch us. If trouble comes, we may need to travel fast. If you are with child, the danger for you will be greater." He closed his eyes. "If Longchamp discovered you were with child, carrying an heir to Taillebroc, he would destroy you both."

"Simon—"

"If I had known that Longchamp had demanded your loyalty, I would never have wed you. He knows who you are, and by now he knows you're my wife. He will turn against you, Adeline, because we are wed."

"He hates you that much?

"He hates and fears me. My brother is at risk as well. The threat is real."

"Why does he fear you?"

"I—I killed a priest. That is enough."

The quiet chill in Simon's voice hinted at a darker reason for Longchamp's enmity. Adeline hesitated. "Is there nothing you can do to make peace with him?"

"I would rather give my soul to the devil himself."

The wind gusted again, sending red sparks up to the smoke hole. Adeline closed her eyes and prayed that the lord of evil would not hear her husband's words.

CHAPTER SIXTEEN

The north wind died before Christmas night, leaving a crust of ice to silver the last of the fallen leaves. In the waning afternoon, Simon and Adeline led their horses down the frost-slick fortress hill and joined the small party of manor folk who were dragging a middling log of oak out of the valley forest.

Caerdoc was there, directing the efforts of his men as they lifted and shoved the great log between the standing trees to emerge at the edge of clear land beside the frozen lake. Adeline's small brothers were there, scampering among the white clouds of laboring breath, shrieking in mock alarm as their father warned them clear of the heavy slide of the Yule log.

The children retreated to gather stones to fling upon the thin ice of the lake, whooping in tune to the weird song they struck from the broad drumhead of ice.

"You'll wake the dragon," bellowed Caerdoc. "Don't look to me for help when the great worm wakes and comes down to your beds to get you."

"You'll frighten them," said Adeline.

"I hope so," her father growled.

Adeline picked her way across the swath of frozen mud in the wake of the log; at the border of the lake, she found her half brothers digging stones out of the hard turf.

"You're not my sister," said the older one in fault-less English.

"You think not?"

"Mother told it to me. It's important not to be your brother, if the bad people come."

Adeline ruffled the younger boy's hair. "And you, Govan? Am I your sister?"

The smaller child shrugged. "Penric is right. Penric is always right."

Adeline smiled. "So he is. If I'm not to be your sister, then, may I be your friend?"

Penric frowned. "I think so." He looked beyond Adeline. "Don't tell the big man, or the people in the tower."

"All right." Adeline followed the child's gaze and saw Taillebroc stripping off his cloak to take a place among Caerdoc's men. His massive shoulders strained as he hefted the fresh-cut end of the Yule log past a willow stump; a moment later, Caerdoc himself joined the party to slide the great log along the ice-slicked track between the fields.

Young Govan removed his thumb from his mouth and pointed to Taillebroc's tall figure. "You must be brave to live with the big man. Petronilla says so."

Adeline stood up and looked about her. "Where is Petronilla?"

Penric shrugged and put down his digging stick. "Howyll took her on his horse." He lifted a small stone and glanced at the lake.

"That will be a loud one," said Adeline. "That will surely wake the dragon."

"Not with the big man here." Govan grinned as Penric dropped his rock upon the ice and set the lake's surface ringing in eerie pulses. "The dragon won't come out now, while the big man's here."

"He's going now," warned Adeline.

The children turned and ran after Taillebroc.

The fine linen cloth upon Caerdoc's trestle board was covered with platters and trenchers enough to feed every soul in the valley. A broad silver cup rimmed in ancient design held mead, then brandy-wine for Caerdoc as he sat in the great chair beyond the table benches. In the talk and jesting and confusion of the great hall, Maida and her sons took their places at Caerdoc's side.

Petronilla, resplendent in her Norman tunic and a surcoat embellished by Maida's skill, darted between her place at Adeline's side and the noisy crowd of young men at the end of the table. Among those young men were faces Adeline had seen at the shepherds' hut; their leader Gruffud had not yet come down to the hall. Ten of the Norman garrison's men sat together a short distance away from the shepherds, with the priest Cuthbert close beside them; so far, there had been peace at Caerdoc's board.

Adeline made room for Petronilla's latest return to her side. "Do you see," said the maid, "how fine Howyll looks with his hair trimmed?"

She looked down the board to see the young Welshman's strong jaw grown even more prominent below his well-cropped hair. The wispy red beard had survived the trimming. "He does look fine," Adeline said. "I missed you both when they brought in the Yule log."

"Howyll was taking his turn to guard the shepherds' hut. I went with him."

Adeline raised her brows. The Petronilla who had embarked at Calais would not have considered spending Christmas day beside a smoking campfire with a mere youth, no matter how well he had trimmed his hair. Even odder was the good chance that Petronilla herself had done the trimming as they sat upon rough blocks of wood in that cold and smoky place.

"What were you guarding," Adeline wondered aloud. "The sheep?"

Petronilla made a vague gesture. "The wolves will come down when the snow falls." Her manner was still that of a Norman woman in a great household. The scratches on her hands and her two broken fingernails were not.

"Were you not nervous of the men who live up there?"

Petronilla shrugged. "They went away—left us

alone for hours. Howyll must have asked them; he knows them well." The maid looked down the board and waved her imperfect hand in the direction of her rough-edged suitor. Howyll's face turned crimson red.

"He seems infatuated," Adeline said.

"Yes, he is. He wants to wed before Lent. But I don't know whether I will have the weaving done by then. I think we should wait until midsummer."

"Wedding? Weaving? Petronilla, I thought you wanted to return to Normandy next year, in your young cousin's household."

"It would be no better than my years with the lady Maude." Petronilla extended her arms in a broad gesture that would have sent the lady Maude into tirades of correction. "Why should I leave this place? There's no one to frown at me if I'm late to rise in the morning, and no one to forbid my riding out with Howyll. And no one to point out that my dowry is small, and my hopes of a husband younger than my father even smaller." Petronilla looked up at the fresh holly branches upon the dark walls of Caerdoc's hall. "And with a little direction, the weavers may begin to make some splendid hangings. Better than the lady Maude's."

Petronilla's voice had risen to a happy shriek. At the head of the board, Caerdoc frowned in puzzlement. Maida smiled, indulgent of Petronilla's newfound happiness. Father Cuthbert heaved a visible sigh.

Adeline looked back to young Howyll's fresh-shorn head. The lad wouldn't have a hope of influencing

Petronilla's plans; nor did the lovestruck youth look as if he wanted to change a single word of them.

Taillebroc covered her hand with his own. "We'll give her the gold I had for her journey—tell her it's a part of her dowry," he whispered. "But don't tell her now; she might bring the rafters down."

By midnight, Caerdoc's people had begun to claim their places beside the hearth pit to sleep through the long night. The garrison men were gone, the shepherds had slipped away an hour before, and the priest Cuthbert had made his way back to his hut beside the chapel.

"Poor man," Maida said. "The bishop at Saint David's had promised him a relic of Saint Govan this yuletide, but if the monks haven't come by now, they'll wait for spring." She lowered her voice. "Cuthbert suffers from aching bones; he had hoped for the saint's help this winter."

Caerdoc snorted. "If anyone will need a cure for the bone ache, it will be the man foolish enough to travel in this ice."

Taillebroc rose to his feet. "My grandfather brought home a splinter of the True Cross from Palestine. The priest may have that for the winter."

Maida's eyes widened. "You have it now?"

"I brought little with me, when I left Taillebroc. But Harald had his wits about him, and brought a pack mule with us. It held everything of worth that he judged small enough, or useful." He smiled at Caerdoc's sudden interest. "Some may be of use as gifts to my bride's family."

He crossed to the doorway of the great sleeping

chamber that Caerdoc had given them for the twelve days of feasting and returned with the Saracen sword upon his palms. In the blaze of firelight from the long hearth, the small jewels upon the scabbard shone as if alive.

"I can't take your grandfather's booty," said Caerdoc.

"Why not? It was honestly won—as much as anything was—and now, honestly given."

Caerdoc grinned, and shed all appearance of indifference. He drew the deeply curved blade from its scabbard and held its perfect silver crescent to the firelight. "How do the infidels use it?"

"I don't know. It rested upon the wall at Taillebroc as long as I can remember."

Caerdoc began to ply the blade through the firelight. "I'll learn it," he said.

"I thought you would." Taillebroc handed the scabbard to Caerdoc.

"My thanks."

Taillebroc bowed his head in a brief gesture of respect. "I thank you for your daughter."

"Her wit is sharper than this sword. Have you learned that?"

"Oh yes," said Taillebroc. He smiled across the board. "I have learned at least that much." He rose again and extended his hand to Adeline. "Will you walk to the fortress and back, to bring the relic for Cuthbert?"

The bright Christmas moon lit their way up the icy slope to the fortress. Twice, Adeline's thick sheepskin boots slipped on the worn stones and sent her giggling into a swift descent of the hill. And twice, Taillebroc caught her and demanded a kiss for her rescue. They reached the gates in some disorder, and returned the gatekeeper's greetings with some chagrin.

"Caerdoc promises a great feast tomorrow," said Taillebroc. "You and the others who stayed behind will have a better turn for yourselves, so the old man says. I'm going back now; we will look for you at noon."

The gatekeeper nodded. "There's a traveler here— came through the pass at sunset too weary to go on to the manor. Harald went down and brought him up the hill, and took him into the garrison house. Says he has something for Caerdoc's priest."

Adeline stamped her feet and kept herself warm by walking back and forth outside the garrison door while Taillebroc dealt with the half-frozen priest. At first, she avoided the sight of the sentry tower; then she looked up and saw the archer Luke staring down at her in the moonlight.

She made no gesture, no signal of greeting. The archer stood as still as the ice-covered timber around him, meeting Adeline's gaze with silent intensity. When the garrison door opened again, the archer had retreated from sight.

Taillebroc cast a quick glance at the tower and took Adeline's hand. "It's good luck for Cuthbert, and for us. It's a Norman priest they sent with the relic. He's too cold to follow us down the hill, but he's happy to sleep in the longhouse tonight. He's already hearing

confession from the garrison men. This may mean
the end of Cuthbert's complaints about ministering
to a swarm of Normans.''

They crossed to Taillebroc's hall and brought in a
torch from the gatekeeper. As Taillebroc searched his
strongboxes for his gift to Cuthbert, Adeline waited
beside the cooling hearth. "It was generous of you
to give the Saracen blade to my father. Maida said
he had spoken of it many times in these few days
past."

"He'll learn to use it. He knows it will frighten
the liver out of his enemies." Taillebroc smiled and
opened his hand to show a small ivory box banded
in silver wire. "Cuthbert's gift," he said. "This should
buy some goodwill from the old badger."

"He's our priest. Don't speak of him that way in
my father's hall."

"There are worse things to call a man. I happen
to respect badgers." He picked up the torch and took
her hand. "Let's get back to Caerdoc's hall before
someone decides to bed down in our chamber."

She drew back and pointed to the strongbox. "May
I look?"

He hesitated. "You may have anything you wish.
What would you like?"

Adeline stood. "You don't want me to go through
the strongbox?"

Simon shrugged. "I'll fetch whatever you want."

"Then bring me the copy of my father's treaty with
William the Marshal."

He drew a long, ragged sigh.

"Or, if you prefer, keep it to yourself, and read it to me."

"I—"

"You lied, Simon Taillebroc. You can read. Your strongbox is filled with documents, and a book of hours."

"You read them all, I suppose."

"Yes. I opened it yesterday and looked. There was nothing to hide. Nothing but your ability to read them. Why did you lie to me, on the day of our betrothal? You and Harald spoke as if you might write your name more easily with the quill between your toes than in your hand."

"I didn't trust you."

"What other skills have you hidden from me?"

He heaved another sigh. "Skills? Lady, if you will cease to burrow about these strongboxes, and trust me again, I'll show you."

"What? Heathen languages? Potion-making?"

He caught her to him and stopped her words with a long, thorough kiss. "I'll show you one day. I swear, lady wife, that one day I'll show you all you want to know."

On the way down the hill, they passed the garrison men who had eaten at Caerdoc's board and watched them make their way up the icy slope. They reached the hall as the last of Caerdoc's own men slid from the benches to stretch out near the fire. On a low stool not far from the chieftain's great chair, one-eared Gruffud sat with a small harp upon his knee,

telling a tale of blood and a dying hero. The priest
Cuthbert had returned to the hall, and sat bright-
eyed with the children as Gruffud concluded the
ancient story.

As the final dissonance of the harp strings died
away, Caerdoc raised his silver cup. "Well told,
Gruffud. Well told."

Young Penric rose and pointed to Simon. "You
should have heard it. A very big man killed the dragon
worm, and then he died from the poison."

Simon brushed aside the trencher crumbs from
a corner of Caerdoc's long board and gestured to
Adeline. She stepped forward and set down the small
reliquary that Simon had pressed into her hand at
the fortress.

Her husband cleared this throat and looked at the
priest. "A gift for your chapel. A piece of the Cross,
brought home by my grandfather from Palestine."

Caerdoc reached out and touched the carved ivory
panels. Cuthbert's face paled in awe.

"Come. Take it," said Simon. "It's better in your
chapel than in my strongbox."

Penric crept forward to look at it. "It's not very
big."

Cuthbert moved close enough to touch it. "That's
only the casket you see. The relic will be smaller still."
He took the relic in his hands and turned to Simon.
"I thank you."

Simon nodded. "There is more. The priest from
Saint David's church came through the pass late this
night; he's up at the fort. My men will bring him
down in the morning."

Cuthbert clasped his hands together, cradling the delicate ivory panels. "He brings a gift from the bishop, I think. A piece of Saint Govan's cloak."

Adeline smiled. "Before long, you'll have pilgrims gathering at the valley to worship, and be cured of their pains."

There was a muffled sound from Caerdoc. He sat down and reached for his drinking cup. "Better to keep these things quiet. We don't want a crowd of strangers coming here—brigands among them. They'll steal the relics, and we'll have nothing but trouble in the end."

Maida beckoned to her sons. "Pilgrims will want lodging," she said over her shoulder. "Soon, there would be more huts outside the village." She led the small boys out of the hall.

Adeline saw Gruffud set down his harp and moved to Caerdoc's side. She placed a hand upon Simon's sleeve.

He covered her hand with his own and turned to face Cuthbert. "Hide the relic well, and keep it secret, as you wish. My men know nothing, so won't speak of it." Cuthbert muttered his thanks once again, clasped the carved ivory box to his breast, and followed the women of the household as they carried half-eaten platters out to the storage huts.

Caerdoc heaved a great sigh. Gruffud moved back to hang his harp upon a peg in the timber wall; he picked up his cloak and walked into the night. Behind him, the men of the household lay sprawled along the edge of the hearth pit. Only Caerdoc remained at the board.

Simon looked down at Adeline. "It's time we slept," he said. Together, they walked to the door of the old sleeping chamber.

Caerdoc raised the drinking cup. "No. Come. Drink your health. Drink my health." He lowered the cup and braced his hands upon the table. At his side, the Saracen sword winked and glittered in the crimson light of the Yule fire.

CHAPTER
SEVENTEEN

Simon felt his wife's hand tremble where it rested upon his sleeve. Her father looked more like an angry bull than a fond parent eager to draw out the festivities of Christmas night.

He should have sent her alone to speak with her sire; she had been absent for years, and there should be talk of the past. He had no place in that past.

Her fingers tightened upon the velvet of his tunic, and he understood that she wished him to stay.

"I'll drink your health," he said. "And my gratitude for the gift of your daughter."

Caerdoc reached for the flask beside his drinking cup and cast an irritated glance about the hall. "The women have taken the others away."

Adeline disappeared into the shadows of the far

wall and returned with a wooden beaker. "We'll drink together, Simon and I, from this."

Caerdoc poured a rich stream of brandywine into the beaker. "So you will," he said. The dark, narrowed gaze moved from Adeline to Simon. "For a hasty wedding of strangers, you have done well. So far."

He took the beaker and offered it to Adeline. Old Caerdoc was of a strange mind, this night. In the weeks since the wedding, Adeline's father had not sought his daughter's company, nor had he encouraged his lady Maida to befriend her. Now, in the dark hours after the moon had set, with his men sleeping beside the Yule fire and the women of the household gone out to the manor's longhouses, Caerdoc had decided it was past time to drink with his daughter and her husband.

Simon put his arm about Adeline's shoulders and met Caerdoc's intense gaze. "We have done well enough," he said.

"Her mother was a lot of trouble, at first."

Adeline set the beaker down. "How so?"

"She came to me as part of the first treaty I made with the Normans. Old Roland de Gras had her fostered in his household, and wed her to me on the day we marked the treaty." Caerdoc drank again from the silver rim. "She was a good wife to me, but never thought much of the people here. Kept you apart from the others, wanted to send you to be fostered when you were but a babe." He set down his cup. "I wouldn't allow it."

There was regret in Adeline's expression, and something more. "I wasn't lonely," she said. "I was happy here."

Caerdoc nodded and looked up to the rafters. "She was angry when I went up against the old king Henry. Said I'd end by putting us all in danger and losing the valley. She might have been right, but back then we fought so well that old Henry's men were the first to sue for peace with us." The scarred hands became fists upon the table. "And that was when you went to Normandy. As surety for the peace."

"I remember the day."

"I remember the week. You wouldn't go, and cried at the stables. Old Henry's man was ready to sling you over his shoulder in a bag, he said. So your mother went, too."

Adeline was silently weeping.

Caerdoc looked away and drank again. "How did she die?" he said. "I asked you on the day you came home, and you never answered. How did she die?"

Simon pushed the beaker away and rose to his feet. Beneath his hand, Adeline's shoulder seemed frail. "This is not the time for this tale," he said. "Adeline is weary, and the moon is down. It's Christmas night, Caerdoc."

"No," said Adeline. "I should have spoken of her on the first day."

The cropped hair on Simon's neck bristled at the steadiness of her voice. Here, once again, was the unnatural calm that he had seen on that first day; she must have been frightened then.

And she seemed to be now.

Simon looked away from Caerdoc's intensity.

Beyond the louvers of the smoke hole, the embers of the Yule fire snaked into the blackness of winter sky. He shuddered, and imagined he could feel the cold of it descending into the hall.

"She died on the boat. The seas were high, and we were in the shelter. She stood up, and the wave came—"

"Your mother drowned?"

Adeline shook her head. "She fell against the shelter post. Her head hit it. They—the king's men—tried to help her, but she was dead."

There was a long silence. Though Adeline had managed a calm demeanor, he felt the faint trembling of her body where it touched his thigh. This ordeal had gone on long enough. Simon took Adeline's hand and stood up. "We'll sleep now, and talk again—"

"Where is she buried?" Caerdoc continued as if he had not heard Simon's words.

The subtle trembling was becoming visible. "Not—in the sea," said Adeline. "At Caen. In the abbey. I watched as they laid her to rest. And then they took me to the lady Maude." She hesitated. "Did they not write to you, to tell you all this?"

"There was a letter. Cuthbert read it. But I didn't know whether they wrote the truth in it."

"About her death?"

"Whether she had died, in truth."

Adeline did not seem surprised by the answer. "She meant to come back to you. Many times, as the seas grew worse, she fretted about the trip back to Hantune. She was to stay with me until I was settled. Until I wasn't afraid."

Caerdoc pushed his cup away. "In the end, it didn't matter. She was gone." He rose and walked to the door. "Good night," he said. And walked into the blackness beyond.

With effort, Simon managed not to follow Caerdoc and force him back to say whatever words of forgiveness Adeline would have believed. "Come," he said. "We have a chamber and a bed to claim." He picked up the untouched beaker of brandywine and led his silent, benumbed wife into the bedchamber.

Simon left her there in the darkness and returned to Caerdoc's board to seize a handful of costly tapers from the bracket on the wall. He lit the first of them from the great Yule log and returned to his wife.

"If you're going to think about it," he said, "drink first."

She looked at the beaker and shook her head.

"Your father is an idiot. His wife was unhappy here, she took her first chance to see Normandy again, and died of bad luck on the voyage." Simon raised the beaker and drank a swift draught. He pressed the cup into her hand and folded her fingers about it.

"It's my fault."

He spilled hot tallow upon the clothing chest and set a candle into the pool as it hardened. "That's nonsense. You were a child. And she wanted to go anyway."

"She went because I cried when they came to take me to Normandy."

Simon heaved a sigh. "Of course you cried. All children cry. All the time. Drink the brandywine and think of the future. Will you drag your guilt with you in this life?''

She looked at him and shrugged. ''My husband carries such a burden. I have his example.''

''It's not the same. I killed a priest.'' He lit a second taper from the first and began to melt a bed of tallow for it.

''I killed my mother.''

He set the second taper upright and returned to Adeline's side. ''In our short marriage, you have insulted me, spied upon me, betrayed me, and tempted me beyond belief. But never, until now, have you said something witless. Your mother died by chance, Adeline. Had she stayed here, she might have died on the road to Hereford, or slipped on the ice as you did this night.''

''And your priest? Did you kill him by daylight, knowing who he was?'' She looked up, mercifully distracted from her own sorrow. ''You do not seem a heretic, or a bloodthirsty man.''

''I thank you.'' He reached for a third taper and held it to the flame.

''How did the priest die?''

With effort, he kept the taper steady. ''I do not speak of Hodmersham.''

She made a small gesture of impatience. ''I do. It is my right as your wife to know it.''

''As my wife, you will do well to think of what you will do if I continue this fall from grace. I was mad to wed you, but believed that you might survive my future troubles through secrecy and your good wit.''

He shook his head. "It was fool's delusion in a moment of weakness. I thought—"

"What did you think?"

It would do no good to speak of his dreams of a child, and the certainty that Adeline would know how to protect the babe, no matter what fate Simon would face from Longchamp's enmity. He set the last of the tapers upon the chest.

The chamber blazed in light, and turned her hair to the color of mead.

"I didn't think," he said at last. "That was the problem. That, and your father's offer of peace if I wed you, and deep trouble if I did not."

"Yet you made your decision, and should tell me now why Longchamp hates you so." She hesitated. "I won't take your words to the archer spy."

He shook his head. "Be grateful you know no more than you do. That ignorance may help you, if Longchamp questions you and your father." The thought of Longchamp near Adeline sent a sudden coursing of anger through Simon's veins. "Had I known that Longchamp had sent you here, and would watch you henceforth, I would have risked a war with your father to avoid this marriage. If there is more trouble, you will fall with me."

"Foolish or not, you wed me, and you must tell me why Longchamp still wishes you dead. What happened with the priest? Was it more than just the killing?"

She was standing mere inches away, her eyes green and dark as holly in the light of the tapers. A scent

of summer roses and broken rosemary came to him.
"Will you not cease to ask me?"

"No. I will—"

He stopped her question as he covered her exquisite mouth with his own. It was impossible to draw
away from the delicate warmth of her mouth, from
the fragrance of her hair. Impossible—

Beneath his lips, she murmured a soft word, then
another.

He took his lips from hers to kiss the softness at
the base of her throat.

She cried out softly. "Come," she said.

He raised his head and smiled into her half-closed
eyes.

"Come. I cannot stand." She stepped back toward
the pallet and drew his hand to her breast.
"Simon—"

It would not be a sin to follow his wife to that taper-
lit softness and put her surcoat aside. To touch the
curve of her breast beneath the fine linen of her
tunic. To have her, for one blessed moment, against
his straining body, to feel her skin against his—

His hands shook with the beauty of her. "Your
hair," he whispered.

She understood, and loosed the silken cord from
the braided glory at her shoulder. In two swift movements she freed that golden fire of it, and lay back
against the bolster. "Again," she said. "Kiss me
again."

He cast away his tunic and drew the soft linen down
from her breasts. She cried softly as he lowered his

mouth to the trembling sweetness of her body. "Beautiful," he muttered. "Too lovely—"

She touched his hair, then held him to her bosom with shaking hands. The light of the tapers shimmered as if trembling with her. She was breathing with the frantic pulse of a hart facing the hunt. She was—

He caught her hands and kissed them, and caught them again as she returned to the neck of his tunic. "No," he said. "This time is for you. Only for you."

He took her mouth again, and found the hem of her chemise. Beneath it, her body still trembled, racked with the pace of her racing heart.

Once again, her hands went to his body, and he felt the trembling of lust begin for him as well. He raised himself away from his wife and whispered a sweet oath of desire as he found the warmth of her thigh beneath the chemise. "This is for you," he said again.

"No," she said. "For you as well."

In the silence between them, he could no longer hear her breathing. "I cannot," he said.

"Do you not want me?"

"My lady, I want you as the earth wants the sun."

She sat up beside him and pulled her chemise to cover her breasts. Upon her shoulder, her unbound hair still held the convolutions of her ruined plait. "Then how can this be for me alone?"

He allowed himself to touch her cheek. "I will not get you with child, Adeline. Not until we are free of the danger that I have brought you."

She took his hand to her breast. "Simon, give me a child. I want it. I want you—"

Beneath his palm, he felt her heart begin again to race. "Do you think it is easy to deny you?" He drew away from her and tried to think of the valley's ice-brimmed lake, and the rivers of cold that flowed into it. The image vanished before the golden splendor of her firelit hair.

Her eyes had lightened to the green of summer, of richness and of promise. "If there is a child," she said, "I'll hide it well. No one will know. No one will tell—"

He drew a ragged breath. It would be a lecher's delusion to believe her. It would be splendor to believe her. He thought again of the frozen lake. "Too late. Longchamp knows you, and knows we are wed. The danger to you is grave. The danger to your child would be greater."

"You have survived despite his hatred of you."

Simon moved aside and drew the coverlet over Adeline's disordered chemise. "He plays with us, Adeline. We cannot bring a child to join us in this trap."

She rose from the bed and found her surcoat on the bare planked floor. He followed her and took her arm. "Adeline, stay and take the bed. I'll not trouble you—"

His wife straightened her garments and smoothed the coverlet over the tangled linen. "I'm not running away, Simon. I'm thinking."

He threw back the coverlet and attempted to pull the linen straight. "Then think in bed. It's a cold night, and the tapers will soon burn down."

With a brisk, annoyed gesture, Adeline once again smoothed the pallet and sat upon it. "A trap," she said. "You called this a trap. It's not yet closed, is it?"

"It's all around us."

She turned to him and placed a hand upon his shoulder. "We must run away. There's nothing here for us. My father has his secret wife and sons, and try as I might, I cannot bring him to trust me with that secret. If we go, no one will be disturbed, least of all my father. He may realize, at last, that we don't want to take an inheritance from the boys."

Simon spread his hands in frustration. "Don't let him drive you away. Without him, you have no protection from Longchamp."

"I have you."

He sighed. "You have me until Longchamp makes his move."

"Why do you wait here, inside the trap?" She pointed to the saddlebags they had brought down with them from the fortress. "You have your sword, and your hauberk and I have—everything I need. You wouldn't even have to go back to the fort before riding away. You and I, Simon, could saddle our horses and ride through the pass at dawn. Your sentries would see it—the archer would hear of it—but Longchamp would not know for days. By then, we would be far away; no one would find us. Ever."

Simon sat on the bed and ran his fingers through his hair. "I considered that." He looked up and smiled at her agitated beauty. "God knows, I have considered such a plan every hour since we wed. But it won't work. Longchamp has too many spies in too many places. We know about the archer Luke." He raised his brows. "And we know about you."

"We are not talking—"

He put up a conciliatory hand. "I know—we're not discussing your brief mission as a spy. But there will be others reporting to Longchamp near this valley. Maybe within it. The man has hundreds of followers, each more greedy than the next. Within two days, they will know to look for us." He reached out and touched her hand. "I cannot live with the possibility that you would die with me."

She took his hand in her own. "Then go without me."

"And leave you for Longchamp's vengeance? You have cheated him, Adeline, by giving me your loyalty. If I disappear, you and your father and Maida will be blamed. And Harald, if they remember that he once lived at Taillebroc."

It was an argument he had repeated many times, in the darkness of his hall. Running from Longchamp would do more harm than good.

Her hand held steady to his own. " Yet you have a plan. I can hear it in your voice—you have a plan."

"Only the beacon fires. One for raiders. Two for a military attack. The distant forts, like this one, are in the hands of the Marshal's men. If I have warning that Longchamp is coming, I'll light them both, and hope that the double beacon will be lit all the way up to the Marshal's camp. If we can hold them off long enough, the Marshal may arrive to find Longchamp's men attacking a Norman fortress. That, in itself, will be our salvation."

"Yet you gave the archer Luke a watch at the sentry tower."

Simon smiled and kissed her hand. "My lady, the Marshal would steal you from me, if he knew you have a swifter wit than half his advisors."

"It takes no special wit to know that you don't put an enemy in your watchtower. You had others watching him?"

"Only Harald. He spelled the gatekeepers when Luke was doing sentry duty. He could see a little beyond the pass, and watch Luke as well."

"I begin to hope that you will live beyond the spring thaw, Simon Taillebroc."

He drew her down beside him on the pallet. "And I begin to hope I'll catch Longchamp's creatures in their own trap, and live to see Taillebroc again. With you, my lady wife."

Simon left her to pinch the candles out, and returned to find his wife naked in the darkness.

"Show me," she said, "Show me how to pleasure you without getting a child. Petronilla said there are ways."

"Bless her."

"Simon?"

He turned to her with such passion that she thought—and rejoiced—that he had abandoned his care not to get her with child. The heat and weight of his passion was hot against her belly as his hands sought the curve of her hip; the sweet assault of his mouth upon her breast sent all reason from the tumult of her thoughts.

The whispered litany of pleasure that sounded in

the darkness about their bed was strange to her ears, and brought her staggering pulse to beat louder than the hushed voice that must have been her own.

Then all voices ceased as his lips moved to hers and took the rush of pleasure-words into his mouth, and returned them as a silent, skilled tribute of his own making.

His hand caressed her thigh, then hesitated in sweet anticipation before seeking her most secret pulse; his touch brought shimmer after shimmer of pleasure, then sharp joy that hungered for completion.

She made way for him, and with trembling fingers sought the solid heat of his sex. He caught his breath, and she came to the place where pleasure took wing and held her aloft for a moment of the divine.

He caught her hand within his own and stilled her striving to bring him within her. He held her to him then, and stifled a hoarse groan as the heat of him flowed between them, and onto her flesh.

She lay beneath him, her eyes still closed, watching the stars diminish in her secret sight. He kissed her again, then moved from her and returned to draw a cloth across her belly.

"I would have done more," she said.

"We cannot risk a child."

"I would have done more—for you."

He sighed. "My lady, I have looked upon you and wanted you these many days past. My desire was so great that a single touch would have been my undoing"—he shrugged against her, and brought her head to his shoulder—"as you have seen."

She murmured a question into the hot salt taste of his skin.

He turned his head, and she sensed the deepening curve of his mouth against her cheek.

"It was no jest," she said.

"We have tempted fate already," he answered.

"If there is no danger of a child, then tomorrow night you must show me—"

A thorough kiss stopped her next words. "Hush," he said. "No more talk of it—that danger has already begun to rise again."

CHAPTER EIGHTEEN

The archer Luke had missed the first two days of feasting. He had chosen to do so, and pointed out to the others that it was folly for half the garrison to leave the fortress each day. Even worse, Luke had said, the absent men would be within a Welsh stockade, surrounded by former rebels and young warriors eager to test their blades against Norman flesh.

The wedding feast had been bloodless, or nearly so, the others had reminded him. They had returned from Caerdoc's hall with decent food in their bellies and no great harm done to the peace. The same would be true of these days of Christmas feasts. And if Simon Taillebroc, a hard man with a sinful past, believed he could sleep in Caerdoc's hall each night of the twelve feast days without waking to find his throat slit, then his men should not fear a few hours in that same hall.

Luke had scowled at those words, and pointed out that the old Caerdoc was mad and his daughter crazed to take the likes of Taillebroc as marriage kin. To that, the men of the garrison had no reply. But still they went down the hill, half of them at a time, to eat at mad Caerdoc's board.

On the fourth day, the archer Luke relented and went down to Caerdoc's manor. The men who walked beside him were careful not to speak of his change of mind. He was not a man that many would care to taunt.

Harald, armorer to the last lord of Taillebroc, kept the archer in sight as he joined the company of men walking down to Caerdoc's manor.

"I think we'll wed soon after the Twelfth Night," said Petronilla. "Howyll frets that he should go and fetch his mother from over the mountains to be here, but I told him she'd know soon enough in the spring-time." She turned from the empty loom and straightened the long woolen tunic she had slipped over her fine linen kirtle. "It's easier for Maida, we think, to add a day of feasting to the twelve."

Adeline set down a final stitch in the hem of the great hall's new wall hanging. "Is this not sudden, Petronilla? Last month you were hot to get back to a Norman town for the winter, then last week you were speaking of a summer wedding with a Welshman, and never returning to Normandy. Now, you think of an

early-winter wedding—" Adeline raised her brows
and smiled up at Petronilla. "Is there a particular
reason for this recent haste?"

"Not the one you think," said lady Maude's former
mistress of tapestries. "It's the visiting priest who
changed my mind."

Adeline had noticed the smiling, rotund cleric moving among the Norman guests, giving them the attention that old Cuthbert begrudged all foreigners. "He
wants you to wed sooner?"

"I don't want to have that sour-faced Cuthbert wed
us. He'd speak the banns for months, hoping to hear
some opposition to Howyll taking a good Norman
wife."

"He made short work of the banns for me," said
Adeline. "So short a time that I wonder whether it
was done right."

Petronilla sniffed. "It's too late to think of that."
Her face softened into familiar curiosity. "How is it
with your husband? Is he as lusty as he looks? Black
hair and dark eyes are the look of the devil or a skilled
lover, they say."

Adeline felt the color of heat flood her face. She
pushed aside the heavy cloth and brushed the skirt
of her own tunic. "Don't repeat that to your Howyll.
He'll think you mislike his red beard."

A secret, satisfied smile came to Petronilla's face.
"He knows I like it fine." She looked beyond Adeline
and assumed a more innocent demeanor. "There
he is—the Norman priest. Will you vouch for me,
Adeline, and tell him I'm an unwed maiden of good
character?"

"I'll tell him you are of fine character, and unwed as well." The question of Petronilla's maidenhood was one that Adeline thought she would prefer to ignore.

"He said he would hear confessions this afternoon before the feast. You could see him then—" She broke off and smoothed her kitchen tunic. "Here he comes. You could tell him now."

Adeline stood and smiled at the burly priest. His round, ruddy face creased in a toothy grin as he neared the weaving shed. "Hard at work, my children?"

Petronilla bowed her head, all meekness and nervous confusion, and pointed to Adeline. "This is the lady Taillebroc, Father Ambrose. I spoke of her yesterday."

The priest's grin widened to cover his broad face. "I heard of your fine gesture, and your father's generosity in wedding you to the lord Taillebroc. A move toward redemption for Taillebroc, and peace for all. If you wish, I'll bless your marriage this day."

Adeline managed to keep her smile steady. Taillebroc was out riding the valley's high perimeter, still searching for Caerdoc's hidden passage. He would not take kindly to an interruption, however well-meant; and he would not care to revisit a ceremony he considered a hazard to Adeline and her kin. "I'll tell him of your kindness," she said.

"I'll go up to the garrison later today, to visit those who haven't taken the sacraments. Will I find him there?"

"No, he's at the far end of the valley."

Ambrose frowned. "Will he return tonight? Cuthbert has agreed to offer a mass of thanksgiving for the peace."

"He doesn't go far—just past the lake and a mile over the meadows. He'll be back long before sunset; I'll send him to you."

Petronilla coughed. Her gaze moved with heavy significance between Adeline and the priest. "Oh yes," said Adeline. "I would like to offer to vouch for Petronilla in the matter of her betrothal to young Howyll. I can tell you that I knew her for the past five years in Normandy; she had a place in the household of the widowed lady Maude des Roches. Petronilla has no husband, and is free to wed."

Ambrose nodded as he listened. "Bring the young man to me," he said. "I'll hear his confession—and yours, Petronilla—and speak to you of marriage."

"He's there," announced Petronilla with all the breathless pride of a green maiden. "Right there, before the stables. I'll fetch him, if you wish."

The priest glanced out at the bailey yard. "I'll come with you," he said. Ambrose turned back at the doorway. "Come to speak with me, my lady Taillebroc. It may be some months before you see any priest but Cuthbert; I fear he's not as zealous as he might be with his Norman charges."

Adeline laughed. "He tries to do his duty by us all, though he finds some of the garrison men a challenge. Tell your bishop that Cuthbert strives to save us all, Welsh and foreigners alike."

Ambrose hesitated. "I do not come from Hereford," he said.

"I meant the bishop at Saint David's church."

He smiled again. "Of course."

She watched the priest make his way to the middle of the bailey yard. Howyll's face was pale above the fiery beard; he stood with all the grace of a poleaxed ox as Petronilla spoke to the priest. Adeline smiled and looked back to her work. There was a small sound, and a pebble on the broad plank at her feet. Adeline looked up and gasped.

The archer Luke stood in the doorway. "You have been silent of late," he whispered. "And absent. We agreed that you would come when you heard my call."

"I didn't see you there."

"I'm never very far. You should have come out to me."

"I could not, without alarming Taillebroc. He sleeps light." Beyond the archer's shoulders, Adeline saw a stream of men from the garrison passing on the way to Caerdoc's hall.

"You might have spoken in passing, the next day. The fortress is small, and it was not easy for you to avoid me." His voice became lower. "You did avoid me."

To show fear would make her seem guilty. And this man could set disaster in motion if he believed Taillebroc had won her over. "Avoid you? When there was nothing to report, of course I avoided you. If I had not, I would have risked angering my husband for nothing. He's jealous, you know. Jealous and foul-tempered."

"I heard you speaking with the priest. Your lord is
out riding, and you aren't watching him."

"There was much to do here. He would have been
suspicious had I left it all to ride with him."

The archer shrugged. "Where does he go, when
he rides out?"

"You heard me tell the priest. He rides past the
lake, and then toward the end of the valley."

"You must ride with him, and tell me who meets
him."

Adeline pitched her voice low, and attempted a
shrug. "I did. For days, I followed him about. There
was never anyone waiting for him. I tired of the
effort."

"I'll tell you again—follow him. Every day, you must
ride with him or follow him. If there is ever a meeting,
Longchamp must know it. And then—"

"What?"

The archer looked over his shoulder, and back
to Adeline. "After the Twelfth Night, send him to
Hereford. Or better, ride with him."

Adeline drew a long breath and managed to keep
the tremor from her voice. "Hereford? Why must he
ride to Hereford?"

Luke shrugged. "You and I may never know. It is
not our place to know."

Adeline managed to sigh. "I can't make him go
anywhere. He's impossible to influence." She looked
down at her hands and wove her fingers together.
"To be honest, he frightens me."

The archer seemed to believe her. He stepped forward and lowered his voice to a whisper. "Whatever

he might do to you is less than you will suffer with Longchamp, should you fail him. You have already failed in your duty; pray that I will forget to send word of this to Longchamp."

He seized her arm and pitched his voice still lower. "Do what you must to get Taillebroc out of the valley on the day after the Twelfth Night. Tell him a lie. Tell him many lies. Get your maid to tell him you have gone before, to meet a lover. Do what you must, but get him onto the road as Longchamp demands. My lord chancellor is not of a mind to wait for William the Marshal to discover his presence and interfere. The timing must be right."

Adeline's heart stilled. "Longchamp will take him prisoner?"

The archer released his grip upon her arm and flexed his fingers. "He may."

"There is a garrison of men up there—"

"All of them Normans, and loyal to the crown. And too few to stand up to my lord chancellor's men." Luke's gaze went from his gloved hand to Adeline's throat. "Get Taillebroc on the road to Hereford and there will be no bloodshed."

Adeline managed to nod. "I understand. But why now? Longchamp was content to have him watched—"

"Ask Longchamp yourself, when he comes." He glanced again at the bailey yard and spoke faster. "If he has to come into the valley to find Taillebroc, my master will be angry. You and your kin will regret it."

Beyond them in the manor yard, Adeline could see Petronilla and her lover out in the thin sunlight, deep in speech with Father Ambrose. Here, inside the weaving shed, the shadows seemed to deepen across the hanks of dyed wool pegged upon the wall. "Go now," she said. "You will be noticed here."

The archer Luke stepped back to the door. "In a few days, my lady, that won't matter. Pray your father still has a roof over his head when Longchamp leaves this place. Pray, and do as my lord chancellor demands." He looked over his shoulder, then walked in the direction of Caerdoc's hall.

Adeline moved away from the door and slumped against the near wall. She had thought they would have the winter. At least the winter—a winter of long, undisturbed nights in which she might persuade Simon to vanish, to take another name. To lure Simon from his fortress to live as a common man-at-arms, far from this place, safe in anonymity. Now there would be only eight days, maybe fewer, before Simon's enemy would appear with his small army to destroy Simon Taillebroc.

The double beacon would summon William the Marshal. Timing was all, as the archer had said. If summoned too soon, the Marshal's troops would find no trace of an attack under way, and might ride on. Longchamp's scouts would see the Marshal's men and arrange Taillebroc's slaughter beyond their protection. If summoned too late, the Marshal would find the valley decimated. In either case, William the Marshal would not believe, unless he saw it happening, that the king's chancellor would strike a Norman warden, or attack a Welsh chieftain who had pledged a truce with the crown.

When the way was clear and the Marshal gone, Longchamp would return to kill Simon, and go on to slaughter Caerdoc's men. Only the snows of winter blocking the pass would halt this inevitable evil.

Adeline sank to the cold, lint-strewn floor and huddled into the corner. From the bailey yard came winter sunlight and the voices of Caerdoc's shepherds outside the ale shed. Petronilla and her Howyll had moved to the stable door, deep in speech and happy in their ignorance that disaster might visit before they could be wed.

Adeline did not attempt to stop the tears that came to her then. The archer had hinted that the valley might be saved if Taillebroc were taken far beyond the pass, on the road to Hereford. He was a fool to suggest it; Longchamp was too wily to leave behind those who knew of his enmity. Caerdoc, who had wed his daughter to Longchamp's prey, would not survive this strike.

Petronilla had crooked a finger into Howyll's sword belt and was drawing him into the shadows of the byre. Adeline looked away. There would be no wedding for Petronilla and her lover; the sweet young lust that the pair had shared this fortnight past might be their last.

She put her hands over her ears to block the happy din of the manor yard. Days from now, there would be fighting at the stockade gates, then greater bloodshed as Longchamp's men broke through.

He would take Simon Taillebroc first. Adeline sobbed in silence, then bit her lip to dispel the image of Simon under Longchamp's cold gaze, dying beneath the swords of the chancellor's army. Simon dead, taken across a packhorse to Hereford. A broken trophy, sacrificed to Longchamp's schemes.

Through the blur of tears, she saw the empty shuttles and pegs upon the timber walls and despised her womanhood. Men learned young to heft a sword, and to strike hard. They would not be left with only wits to help them save a lover from disaster. The rush of blood in her ears grew louder; this must be what men felt when they fought an invader—pure, killing rage.

In that moment, Adeline knew that she would kill William Longchamp before he could strike her husband.

She wiped the tears from her face and drew a deep breath. She would need little more than a kitchen knife to strike down Longchamp . . . if she could get near him.

Her last night in the lady Maude's solar came to mind. Longchamp had been alone with her, a mere arm's length away, unprotected by his guards. That night, an eternity ago, she had feared the king's chancellor and wished herself far from his black regard; now, she would give her life to have that moment back again. To take her fine silver eating knife and ram it into Longchamp's evil heart.

There would be an unprotected rider on the road to Hereford, easy prey for Longchamp.

It would not be Simon Taillebroc.

A cry of alarm rose from the bailey yard, sending Adeline to her feet. Had Longchamp come already?

Maida ran past the door in the direction of the stockade gates, heedless of the mud that dragged at

the low hem of her crimson surcoat. Adeline moved
to the door; Maida was pushing her way through
the small crowd surrounding Simon Taillebroc's bay
stallion and his half-naked, tousled rider. Through
the crowd, two cloth-wrapped bundles floated from
shoulder to willing shoulder, to end in Maida's arms.

"Help her," shouted Taillebroc over the excited
voices. "They're heavy."

Maida staggered, then sank to her knees, still
clutching her untidy burdens. Adeline ran forward,
then halted to gasp her dismay. From the nearest
bundle, she saw a small head plastered with tangles
of wet, red-gold hair.

From the other bundle, a formless bulge came to
life, then surfaced as a small foot thrust through the
sodden cloth.

An enraged bellow came from the hall. Caerdoc
staggered from the stoop, his gaze fixed in horror
upon Maida's hunched form and the small, shroud-
like forms upon the skirts of her tunic.

Adeline saw it before the distracted crowd, and
moved to block her father's mad rush at Taillebroc.
He pushed her aside and hurtled toward the bare-
chested horseman.

Simon ducked Caerdoc's first blow, then rose to
trap Caerdoc's wrist in his hand. Adeline saw the
sinews of her husband's massive arm strain to pin her
father's wrist to the saddle bow. With his other hand,
Taillebroc struck at Caerdoc's fist and wrenched the
jeweled hilt of the Saracen sword from his grasp. The
bright, curved tip of the blade slipped to the neck of
Taillebroc's mount. The enormous horse plunged

and screamed; Caerdoc fell back and rolled clear of the deadly hooves.

Howyll launched himself from the byre door and dragged Caerdoc aside. "Look," he shouted. "Look at them. They're alive."

Maida had not raised her head to watch the deadly clash at the gates. Shucked of their wet covers and wrapped again in cloaks drawn from those nearest them, the children had begun to whimper. Maida struggled to rise with her blue-lipped, shivering sons in her arms. She wouldn't give them to others to carry, but stumbled, with many willing hands around to steady her, into the hall.

There were cries and small shrieks from the crowd still watching Taillebroc's struggle with his wounded mount. Caerdoc staggered to his feet and bellowed an order. Howyll darted forward and seized the bridle, then dropped it and ducked clear of the stallion's bared yellow teeth.

"Stay back," called Taillebroc, and allowed the maddened horse to back against the stockade wall. He spoke again in lower voice to the trembling beast, then dropped down from the saddle, the reins still in his hand. "A cloth," he said in steady tones. "Get a cloth, and bring it slowly."

"Here." Petronilla ducked out of her woolen work tunic and handed it to Adeline. Taillebroc glanced over his shoulder. "Come up behind me. Slowly." He was holding the side of the bridle in one hand, and with the other, he stanched the stream of blood down the shivering, sweat-slick neck.

Adeline snatched the woolen tunic from Petronilla's shaking hands and advanced. Taillebroc reached back to snatch the cloth without looking. "Go back," he said. "Get back now."

"Open the byre door," she told Howyll. "The second one—open it wide and move the other beasts back."

The horse was still skittish as Taillebroc walked it into the shadowed shelter of the byre. "Stay back," said Simon. "He's not a warhorse—hasn't been taught to stand after a blow." He moved the cloth aside and saw that the flow of blood had diminished. "As I thought," he said, "it's a deep scratch—nothing more."

"I'll treat it," said Howyll.

"He'll kill you," said Taillebroc.

"Tie him to the post and I'll unsaddle him and salve the wound." Howyll pointed to Taillebroc's chausses. "You're near naked, sir. You need dry clothes."

"Bring a halter." Taillebroc removed the bridle with unhurried, gentle movements, and slipped a stout halter over the bay's head. His hands were shaking with the cold. Adeline brushed past him and tied the halter leads to two posts.

"Come," she said, "you're in greater danger than the horse. Howyll will unsaddle him, and treat the wound."

Taillebroc muttered something.

"What did you say?"

"Cover him. Blanket." His teeth were chattering.

Adeline had no cloak to give him. He walked slowly toward the stockade gates.

"To the hall," she said, and took his hard, cold arm in her hands.

"Not yet," he said. He waved away the gaping shepherds at the stockade gate and leaned down to pick up the Saracen sword where it lay in the mud. His hands moved slowly and could not grasp the hilt.

Adeline caught it up and carried the curved blade beside her as she led her husband into the warmth of Caerdoc's hall.

CHAPTER NINETEEN

The children were squirming in their mother's arms, their faces once again colored with young life, their arms gesticulating above the thick coverlets wrapped again and again about their bodies. A stream of disjointed explanations and contradictions rose from the children. Maida held them upon her skirts and kissed their small faces, again and again. "My babies, my sweet—"

Cuthbert and the Norman priest had knelt in prayer beside Maida and her sons; within Cuthbert's blunt hands, Simon saw the small ivory reliquary held high above the small tousled heads.

The heat from the hearth was painful, almost cold upon Simon's skin. Icy water still dripped from his chausses, staining the fresh-bound rushes at his feet.

Adeline loosed her grip upon his arm and stepped before him.

"Don't come near us," she said.

Her father halted a small distance from Adeline's fury. "I was mad with grief," he said.

Maida looked up. "He understands now that you saved the boys. But for a moment, he thought they were dead."

"At my hand?" Simon began to shiver. He brushed away Adeline's attempt to draw him closer to the fire. "Did you believe I had killed your sons, Caerdoc?"

"I was mad."

The old chieftain would come no closer than that to an apology. Simon nodded. "So you were."

Caerdoc opened his surcoat and thumped the fine velvet that covered his chest. "Strike here, if you wish. Strike with the blade you gave me, the blade I turned against you."

"It was a mistake. I was at fault as well."

Adeline stepped aside. "Is there no cloak to cover my husband?" She pulled a length of soft wool from Petronilla's hands and cast it about his shoulders. Simon shuddered. His benumbed skin hardly felt the contact.

His wife turned back to her father. "Simon is right. It was his fault as well. In this mad place, he should have known that as he brought your sons back from death at the frozen lake, he should have thought to shout ahead, and tell you that he was half-naked and freezing because he had gone in to save them. And you, sitting beside the hearth and brooding about your treaty with the old king, had no idea that your own sons were missing."

Simon let his hand fall upon her shoulder and pulled her back. "No. I share the blame for it. They followed me."

The Norman priest rose from his prayers and went to Simon's side. "My lord Taillebroc, you are ill from the cold. Caerdoc understands—we all understand—this was not your fault."

Simon shook his head. Soon, he would crawl into his pallet and collapse. They should know how the boys had come to grief. They should know—

"Simon?" Adeline had her arm about him. In her other hand, the Saracen sword still dragged along the rushes.

"Let me speak." He drew a long breath. "I pass the lake each day, on the track to the valley's end. Yesterday, they waited in a tree."

David stirred in his mother's arms and pointed at Taillebroc. "We got him."

Simon shook his head. "I should have told you they were out there. I didn't think they would do it again. Today, they ran onto the lake—"

"And you swam to get them?" Ambrose's voice was suffused with emotion. "God will bless you for this, and forgive your many sins."

"I waded to get them. The ice broke near the shore. I got them out and hauled them home." He placed his arm about Adeline's shoulders. "Give your father his sword back, and help me find dry clothes and bed."

Maida looked up from her children. "Why has

someone not given this man brandywine? Petronilla, get the lads to carry the bathing tub into the sleeping chamber, and set water to heating.'' She smiled at Simon. ''After you have recovered, you will hear our thanks once again. Bless you, Taillebroc. You will always be in my prayers.''

Simon bowed his head. ''Come, Adeline.''

Caerdoc stepped back. ''You would give me back the blade that might have killed you?''

Simon shuddered beneath the warmth of Petronilla's cloak. If he didn't shuck his wet chausses before long, his manhood would shrink into nothingness. ''I'll be safe enough until you learn how to use the thing. I thank God you weren't wearing an honest straight sword when you came at me.'' He squeezed Adeline's shoulder. ''Give your father the blade, before I freeze waiting.''

Caerdoc cleared his throat. ''I owe you my life.''

Simon shook his head. ''You owe me a bath. A hot one.''

The sleeping chamber was soon more crowded than the hall. Simon sat on the side of the pallet with the bed's linen to cover his nakedness and watched Caerdoc's servants drag a wide, sturdy bathing tub into the room. Adeline emptied his saddlebags, found his second-best tunic and chausses, pronounced them too shabby for Caerdoc's hero, and sent Petronilla in search of better.

''I wore those the day after we were wed,'' said Simon.

"And you tore the tunic since."

"You didn't notice before."

"Well, I see it now."

He caught her hand and kissed it. "Sit beside me," he said. "Tonight we—"

Two grinning servant lads came through the door and began to pour buckets of steaming water into the tub. "Close the door," Taillebroc said.

Adeline leaned to one side to get a view through the doorway. "They're not done, Simon. I see a great cauldron set in the hearth, and more lads with buckets."

"Tell them to use it on the boys."

"They have. Maida has them back in the sleeping hut, soaking in warm water and rosemary."

He lowered her hand, still covered by his own, onto her lap, then down to her knee. "Adeline, I have been thinking about our dilemma."

"I thought of little else, this morning."

"There are ways—" Simon broke off as the servant lads returned with three more buckets of hot water. "Thanks, lads. That will be enough—"

They were gone before he finished. Simon shook his head. "I must learn your odd language, wife."

"I hardly remember it."

"Do you remember enough to warn the next troop of servants away, and shut the door?" He slid his hand beneath her knee. "As I was saying, wife—"

Petronilla darted through the doorway and set down a neat stack of clothing and linen toweling. "There. Nearly all we need for your bath."

We. The woman didn't intend to leave. Simon cast

an imploring glance at his wife; she was picking
through the pile of clothing, speaking with Petronilla
and setting aside the best of the heap.

He stalked over to the bathing tub and dropped
the bed linen from his body. The water was hot, deli-
cious, and almost bearable. He was scarce settled into
the tub when he looked up to see Petronilla draw
closer, her face colored by curiosity. "Here," said the
sultry-voiced woman. "You should have herbs in the
water." She produced a great bundle of dried stems
and peered down into the tub.

Simon hunched forward in the water. "Adeline—"

His wife came forward. "Rosemary? Good idea.
Scrub his back, Petronilla."

Beneath the surface of the water, there was a stirring
near his manhood. Simon raised his elbows and saw
a thick bunch of herbs floating near his belly. He
brushed it away. "My back, Petronilla."

Howyll came through the door and approached
the tub. "Your mount is fine, Taillebroc. The blood
stopped soon after you left, and the beast is quiet."

"Did you—"

Howyll grinned. "Yes, I remembered the blanket
for the beast. He'll be as snug as any soul here this
night." He reached beyond Taillebroc's ear to
Petronilla; there was a small, pleased squeak close
behind him.

"Fine," said Simon. "I thank you."

Howyll seemed in no hurry to leave.

Simon reached for Adeline's arm. "Will you bathe
me, now? We should manage well enough alone."

"Ah—" said Howyll. "I almost forgot. There's rain coming down, and the byre roof is leaking."

"On my horse?"

"No, he's under the good part. We had to move the stock around, and the shepherds who slept in the straw last night must bed down elsewhere—"

Simon closed his eyes. This was a matter for Adeline.

"—so Maida's bringing them into the hall and sending the women in here to sleep. On the floor."

Simon opened his eyes. "In here?"

Maida and Caerdoc had materialized in the doorway. Caerdoc's color had returned; the scent of strong brandywine permeated the chamber. Adeline's father strode to the tub and struck a friendly blow to Taillebroc's shoulder. "Do you mind the company? It will take a few days to thaw out your treasures, I think. By then, the rain will stop, and you'll have this chamber to yourselves again."

To have a bedchamber alone with his wife in the Yuletide season with the whole population of the valley crowded into the manor had been a sign of Simon's uncertain reputation. Now that he had become the savior of Caerdoc's children, that same population had accepted him, and would crowd into the chamber for the rest of the feasting days. Simon put aside a foolish wish to insult Adeline's father in order to regain that privacy.

A stream of scented oil began to flow upon his head. "Relax," Petronilla said. "When the lads bring the next bucket of water, I'll rinse your hair."

Across the chamber, Adeline glanced up and saw

his distress. Her mouth twitched, and he heard a soft sound very like a giggle.

It was a thing he hadn't expected to hear in these circumstances, with Adeline's mad kinfolk gathered around. He sighed. It had been worth it—the plunge into ice water, the near disaster with Caerdoc's sword, and the prospect of sleeping cheek by jowl with half the household. It had been worth the trouble to see Adeline happy with her folk.

Simon lay back and watched his wife's kin move about the sleeping chamber and dreamed of taking Adeline back to the drafty, solitary hall in the timber fortress. And prayed for an early end to the rain.

CHAPTER TWENTY

He rose after dawn to find Caerdoc's household still asleep. Simon pushed back the coverlet and kissed Adeline's brow as she lay in the crook of his arm, her golden hair a pool of light in the dimness of the sleeping chamber. With gentle stealth, he eased her head onto the bolster and slipped from the bed.

There were six servants wrapped in their bedrolls on the wooden floor beside the bed. Simon made his way past them and took his clothing and sword from the great chest in the corner. Beyond, in Caerdoc's long hall, the trestle boards were set against the walls, and the rushes scarce visible beneath the sleeping forms of those who had chosen not to return to their huts during last night's downpour.

The long hearth pit glowed warm despite the night's deluge. The great flat stones where the Yule log had burned were still hot to the touch, making plumes of steam from the blackened drops that still fell from the edges of the louvers high above the rafters.

Caerdoc's people lay warm and snoring beside that hearth, sleep-heavy from the night's feasting and brandywine. Simon stepped past a row of sleeping forms and recognized the heavy jaw of Howyll protruding from a bedroll at the door. Petronilla lay nearby; in sleep, she looked as innocent as she must have been a decade before.

Above the bailey yard, the sky was clear again; rain had stopped, and winter's cold had returned to the valley.

Simon hesitated at the byre door, half-tempted to return and awaken Adeline to ride with him. To be with her alone—just to speak in privacy—would be a great boon in these crowded feasting days in Caerdoc's hall. After yesterday's rescue of Caerdoc's sons, Simon had found it impossible to avoid the attentions of the entire household. He and Adeline would be lucky to have a moment's peace.

They had slept with the covers drawn up over their heads, not for warmth but for privacy. Despite this attempt, their smallest whispers had seemed loud to their ears; early in the night, they had given up words and slept.

Simon turned from the hall and opened the byre door. For a moment, he considered returning to the bedchamber to wake Adeline and bring her with him, but dismissed the thought; he would let his wife rest while she could.

In the byre, his bay stallion was tied to a single post, dozing three-footed beneath a soft woolen blanket. He placed a gentle hand on the beast's withers and gave the beast a solid pat and saw that his wound was clean, so far, and not as large as Simon had feared.

He hesitated, then drew the blanket from the stallion and hefted the saddle to his back. Caerdoc's sword had scratched high on that glossy brown neck, near to the roots of the thick, cropped mane; bridle and reins would run clear of the small wound. A slow-paced ride would give Simon a chance to gentle the great horse once again.

There were women in the kitchen house when he led the stallion across the bailey yard; one of them picked her way across the frozen mud to give him a slab of bread. He nodded at her rapid greetings and smiled his thanks.

He turned his mount to the garrison hill, then thought better of it and nudged him west, to the manor's fields and the lake beyond. There would be time enough, in the busy feasting this night, to speak with Harald of the small tasks the garrison must complete before the snows came. For now, another solitary ride in search of a flaw in the valley's steep walls would do more good for the garrison, and for his own concerns.

There were two small hawks flying above the fields, soaring and plummeting in search of prey. A flock of sparrows rose from the naked forest beyond and flew west, drawing the hawks in their wake.

Simon began to eat the bread as he rode and watched the hawks among the now distant birds. In

his life of privilege and comfort, he had kept hawks
and flown them at many kinds of prey; only now, in
these months of uncertainty and hard living, could
he look at a hawk and see the predator not as an ally,
but as the fearsome creature it was to its quarry.

Longchamp and his spies were watching him, with
mind and sight as clear as any bird of prey, waiting
for the moment to plummet from the blue and end
his exiled life. Each day he had lived after the blood-
bath at Hodmersham had been a gift of fate, and
brought him closer to the day when he would face
an enemy even stronger than any the old lords of
Taillebroc had seen.

William the Marshal, in saving the life of his old
comrade's son, had merely prolonged a life already
marked for early death, and provided Longchamp
with an occasion to fly his hawks—his spies—across
Taillebroc's new life in exile.

The image of Adeline's green eyes came to mind.
What would Longchamp do with a hawk who would
not come back to the lure, or a spy who turned that
green gaze upon the prey in friendship, then love?

A cold wind was blowing across the lake, filling the
jagged hole where the boys had fallen and Simon
had broken his way through the thin ice to find them.
Already, the water was thickened with new tendrils of
frost floating upon the still surface. Simon shuddered.
Had he not heard the lads go in, they might even
now rest on the muddy floor of the lake, with a silver
web of ice closing above their bodies, concealing
them until spring—or forever.

This season had brought peril to each of Caerdoc's

children: Longchamp's lethal notice of Adeline; and the deadly thin ice that had tempted Penric and Govan to folly. Simon looked back over his shoulder at Caerdoc's manor, now far in the distance behind him. Would Adeline's ill-natured father be willing to risk Longchamp's displeasure long enough to ensure that his daughter might escape the troubles to come?

Simon narrowed his gaze. This night, he would ask a reward of the old chieftain in return for saving his sons: He would ask that Caerdoc conceal his daughter, by force if necessary, at the first hint that Longchamp might be near. And he would compel the old man to swear that he would take Adeline out of the valley in secret, south to the Marshal's new stronghold at Striguil.

The wind gusted harder across the lake, turning the open water to beaten silver, and the ice to the smooth, polished blue of the sky. Simon frowned. Caerdoc had said that the snows came to his valley each year before Yuletide. In this season of Simon's desperation, the winter had not brought a barrier to keep Longchamp from the valley pass.

Bad fortune had followed him since the night he had entered the abbey at Hodmersham to find thieves at work. From that hour, only the Marshal's mercy had saved Taillebroc from obliteration; it remained to be seen whether that delay in misfortune would prove to be more cruel than merciful.

Simon shook his head. If he continued to brood about the past, and the uncertain future, he would earn himself a visage as morose as old Caerdoc's face. He threw the remaining crust of his bread into the forest and watched the sparrows gather at a distance to consider the temptation. High above him, the hawks' circling narrowed to watch the sparrows' next move.

He laughed and raised his fist to the keen-eyed predators. Even these birds of prey could mock a small gesture of mercy and turn the act to their advantage.

One could not change the workings of the world and hope to control the outcome. But if he was careful, and lucky, Simon would extract his wife from the trap closing about them and send her free into the world. More than that, he could not hope to do.

He spurred past the silver lake and followed the track to its fork. High on the south wall of the valley, above the meadows, a stand of rowans clustered about the source of the valley's third stream. In their branches, the dark, dried berries still held a touch of crimson. The hawks must have been busy at that place; the smaller birds had not yet stripped the rowans of their burden.

Simon turned south and slowed his mount's pace up the winding track. The unleaved, open forest lay behind him; the track wove its way through moss-covered boulders and stands of aspen as he neared the broad slope of the bare grazing lands. The air was colder now, and the wind cut sharp into Simon's face.

The bay whickered and shook his neck. Simon reached forward to place a calming hand well behind the small, puckering wound.

The track turned sharply to traverse the slope, then back along the last of the rocks that pierced the turf.

Ahead, the land was desolate of life; only the dark crimson of the withered rowan berries interrupted this wall of grey rocks and winter-burnt grass. Far to the east, Simon heard the bawling of sheep penned for the coming weather.

He rode higher still and found a view of the shepherds' hut. From here, it seemed a crude thing, built rough against the wall of rock, its doorway a large, ungainly panel of black against the mud and timber walls. The builders, likely the rebels themselves, had left the entrance gaping large through laziness, or lack of timber to finish the hut. They would suffer, in the deep of winter, from the north wind blowing through the cracks of the door.

The hawks had flown east up the slope, following him, no doubt, in the hope that he would tempt more sparrows to a mortal feast of bread crumbs below the predators' narrowing circles. Simon raised his fist again and checked himself before he shouted an obscenity at the graceful killers. He lowered his hand; if he didn't keep control of himself, he would become as testy and bitter as old Caerdoc and lose himself in anger.

He had a task, and should look to it. The caves he had found earlier on the lower slopes had been too small or too shallow to allow a horseman to walk his mount into the passage. In the days remaining before the snows came, he would continue his search for a large cavern. The stand of rowans seemed as good a place as any to begin this day's attempt.

A whistling of flight came to his ears, and he ducked as if under a barrage of archers. The offending hawk rose again and began to circle the boulders far down the slope below Simon. The second bird was higher still, above the same place.

It was as good a place as any to let his mount rest. Simon guided the stallion to a scrub hazel and dropped from the saddle. He twisted the reins about the small, leafless trunk and began to walk down the slope. Though the sheep had been moved down to shelter, there might be a stray among the boulders.

Simon smiled to himself. Only in fierce Caerdoc's valley would he suspect the hawks of preying on sheep. The old man would laugh at his new Kentish kinsman if he could see him now, spying on the hawks' hunting scheme—

He dropped to the earth and raised his head slowly to look again at the sight. A dark-clad man was a stone's throw below him, stretched upon the upper side of a boulder, watching the track. A mud brown cloak covered the burly form of the watcher, and beside him—

Beside him was the impossible—six crimson arrows. Long ones, made fine and straight by a master. Made by the hands of the archer Luke. Yet it was not Luke clinging to the moss-shrouded boulder; Luke was slighter than this cloaked archer, and a taller man.

The longbow beside the arrows was strung tight, ready to use.

He shifted onto his elbows and drew his sword from the scabbard to lie flat before him on the cold turf. The man below him had watched him ride past, and had not struck. Simon glanced behind him and saw that his mount was not visible this far down the hill.

If the beast stayed tethered behind the hazel stand, and didn't whicker again, the archer below would not suspect that Simon had stopped. The dark archer was awaiting better prey, or had taken a defensive position while waiting to meet someone in this desolate place.

Simon pushed his sword ahead and crept closer. The arrows were Luke's, and the only man in a position to receive them must be the elusive messenger who had carried Luke's news to Longchamp.

This, then, was a Longchamp spy, now moving about within Caerdoc's valley. To capture this man, and to force him to reveal his task, might make the difference between life and death for Adeline and her kin.

Simon tensed and reached for the hilt of his sword. A swift, silent rush upon the watcher, if done with skill, would silence the man without killing him. Once the dark archer was disarmed and bound, Simon could wait in that place and see who would come to meet the spy.

He counted backwards in Latin, as he had been taught to do before acting upon an important decision.

There was another course to follow: He might hold back and watch the archer. Though he was well armed as an assassin, the archer might be waiting to meet Luke, or another Longchamp spy. If he remained motionless, and the wind continued to blow up the hill, Simon might hear their speech before making his own move.

Simon released his sword and flexed his fingers. If

the archer was poised to kill, there would be time to distract him before he could draw the bow.

High above him, the knife-sharp rush of sinew and feathers continued to circle. The archer moved once, to look up at the hawks. He reached for the bow.

Simon lay flat upon the cold earth and snaked his hand once again to his sword. If the archer stood to shoot the telltale hawks, Simon would have little time to rise and rush the man; the archer would be surprised, and take some time to change his aim and shoot a moving, uphill target.

The archer turned back to resume watching the track.

Simon breathed his thanks into the withered grass and rose to a crouch. He would rush the archer now, before his luck failed.

There was a jingle of bridle bit, then a slow, steady beat of a horseman walking his mount up the hill. The archer crouched in readiness and placed a hand upon the crimson arrows. Without turning his face from the track, the burly man fumbled for a shaft and dragged it with the bow to his side. He must have seen the rider, and recognized his appointed quarry.

The long, ugly head of Adeline's grey palfrey came into sight. The archer rose with swift precision and drew his bow.

"No." Simon's bellow sent the archer reeling from his balanced stance. The hooded face looked to Simon's naked sword. Simon hurtled on. The distance was greater than he had imagined. The first arrow would be for him. Adeline might escape the second. He bellowed again. "Go back," he called. "Turn back."

The dark eyes of the archer turned away from Simon's furious charge; in an act of deliberate suicide and determined murder, he raised the bow again in Adeline's direction, leaving his broad back exposed to Simon's sword.

CHAPTER
TWENTY-ONE

Maida touched Adeline's arm. "Please, come with me," she said. "Your father needs to speak with you."

The kitchen maids had seen Simon ride out only moments earlier. With Howyll's help, Adeline could saddle her palfrey and follow her husband soon enough to join him. To do less would anger the archer Luke and prompt a bad report to Longchamp. She glanced up at the fortress hill and imagined that she saw the archer on the sentry walk.

Adeline turned back to Maida. "This afternoon, when we return—"

"Would you come now? He hasn't slept. Caerdoc isn't a young man, and has taken yesterday's mistake too much to heart."

The bailey yard was filling with activity as the sun rose higher in the sky. Howyll was nowhere to be seen. By the time she found her saddle and gear, Simon might be too far ahead to find him.

"Will he fret if I delay?" said Adeline.

"He already does. Will you go alone? I believe he wants that." Maida glanced at the stockade gates. "Your good husband won't get far ahead. I'll ask Howyll to saddle your palfrey and have her ready outside the byre." She smiled. "Caerdoc will not keep you long, you know. He never does, when there's an apology to be uttered."

Adeline hugged her stepmother. "I'll go to him, Maida."

She went to the door of the sleeping hut and once again marveled at the difference between the unremarkable exterior and the riches within. Adeline stepped through that doorway and felt the past around her with all the poignancy and shock of the night of Simon's raid of the manor.

Her father was sitting back against the rich, velvet bolsters that kept the draft from his bed. He had dressed for the day in his feasting clothes, but had returned to bed and pulled layers of deep-woven coverlets about his shoulders. Despite the opulence of the tapestried walls and rich carving upon the bed frame, the hut was colder than a shepherd's hovel.

Caerdoc beckoned her to sit beside the great high bed and handed her a coverlet for her shoulders. "Here. It's cold this morning."

"Why do you sleep in this drafty place?"

He made a vague gesture. "Maida has her women bring a brazier in here to warm the place before we come here to sleep. The cold comes slowly after they carry it away."

Adeline shuddered. "You might perish of the cold one night."

Caerdoc shrugged. "We manage." He cleared his throat and turned his intense gaze upon her. "You didn't guess, did you, until the night your good husband invaded this place, that Maida is my wife, and the boys my true sons?"

"No," Adeline said. "I thought you were sleeping in the weaving shed with Maida. In sin." She looked around the room. "All these things—Mother's tapestries, the chests, this very bed—I thought destroyed, or given away."

Caerdoc's face had brightened. "The weaving shed? That's good. Yes, a sinful reputation is a good disguise. Your husband—is it possible he does this, too?"

Adeline shook her head. "His reputation is no sham. There was a priest on his lands, and Simon killed him. I'm afraid the tales are true."

"Still, he's a fine, strong man—for a Norman. And he saved my sons. Did he know he gave up your inheritance by preserving their lives?"

This was dangerous ground. Had Caerdoc decided to reveal his marriage, or was he trying to discover whether his daughter and Taillebroc already know of it? She looked into her father's eyes and decided upon the truth.

"Simon had guessed that the boys are trueborn; many days ago, he had spoken of it." She looked about the frigid chamber. "You have no need to hide your marriage bed and deceive our people. You should return these things to the lord's chamber in the hall, and live in the comfort you had with my mother. In your rightful place."

Caerdoc shivered. "I may. My people know that I wed Maida, but on pain of banishment they keep outsiders from the knowledge. They kept it from the men of the garrison, when they snooped about, and—"

"And me? You feared to tell me? The manor folk wouldn't speak to me, Father, when I first came here."

"We couldn't know where your loyalties would rest, and whether the Normans had turned you greedy."

Adeline sought to calm her voice. "I am your daughter. Five years isn't a lifetime. You must have remembered how we were before—"

"Before Normans took you and finished the job your mother began. You were never even half-Welsh, not to my mind." He extended a blunt, veined hand from the coverlet. "But you are my beloved daughter, and I am pleased that you have a man near worthy of you—"

She took his hand and pressed it to her cheek.

Caerdoc cleared his throat. "For all he's a great sinner, I owe him my sons' lives. I'll not forget, little Adeline, that your man has proved himself as good as a son to me."

"One day soon," she said, "you may have a chance to prove that you are good as a father to him. He has enemies, and few allies. We may both need your help if the snows don't close the valley soon." She raised her gaze to his dark, hooded eyes. "Will you tell him, Father, how to leave the valley unseen?"

Caerdoc withdrew his hand from her cheek. "There is no secret way."

"Father, can you not trust me—trust my husband and me—with the knowledge?"

He shook his head. "Come to me, if you have trouble. I'll see what can be done."

"Is that all you will say? And if you're hunting, or absent from the valley through your secret way, when trouble comes—we'll ask Longchamp to wait at the pass until you return. Is that how you will repay Simon's deed? He's my husband, Father. I'll not see him perish while you look on."

He looked away. "I'll not deceive you, Adeline. I will do what I can for you and your good husband. No more. No less. I saw the Normans take my child, and then my wife; I'll die before I allow such a thing to happen to Maida and my sons."

Adeline stood and looked about the room. The tears of sentiment that had filled her eyes vanished in the face of her father's obduracy. "I suggest that you trust us to keep your marriage a secret from the men of the garrison, and from Longchamp." She took the coverlet from her shoulders and folded it with slow deliberation. "Move back to your proper chamber, and sleep in comfort with Maida and the boys. It would be a sad thing if you fell ill from this coldness, Father. Simon and I will move back to the garrison this night, and hope that you will take the warm chamber back.''

She placed the coverlet at his feet.

"Tell me how it was for you, in Normandy.''

Adeline turned at the door. "Another time, Father. Now, I'll follow my husband as he rides out. There are precious few in this place who care whether he will live or die. I'll stand by him, unlike my kinfolk.''

Adeline did not allow herself to weep as she rode from the stockade, for she needed clear vision to find Simon's path up to the high ground of the valley. She set her palfrey to a steady trot past the frozen fields; beyond, at the lake, she saw the bay's huge hoofprints in the morning frost at the water's edge.

She kept her gaze upon the track as she rode past the lake. If she had looked upon the surface of that deep, ice-crusted water and imagined the moment in which her small brothers had fallen within—if she had imagined Simon breaking past the sharp ice, stumbling as he ran into the chill and darkness of the pool—she might have turned back at the sight. She did not know, and wished never to know, how far into the blackness the children had descended before Simon reached them.

The track went on through the aspen trees, then curved right, then back through the boulders that marked the edge of the forest and the beginning of the open land above. This much of the track was familiar to her, for her mother had loved to ride this far and sit upon the great stones and look at the sky. The manor was out of sight here, and the sky, her mother had said, was the same she had left behind in Normandy.

Adeline drew her cloak back from her face and braved the bite of the northern gusts as she looked up at the dark front of clouds advancing before the wind.

She smiled, and prayed for those clouds to deliver their burden of snow into the valley pass. A pair of hawks flew past above her head, and into the wind-blown limbs of the aspen stand.

An eruption of sound brought her palfrey's heavy head up in alarm. Simon called to her from some-where above, then bellowed an order; the clash of steel upon stone and a terrible, inhuman scream oblit-erated his words.

Adeline turned her horse to gain control of the backing beast; she dared not slip from the saddle, for she knew not what she would find ahead. If Simon was under attack, she could not help him afoot. She hauled the grey mare's head back to face the rocks and forced the animal up the track.

Again, Adeline's horse shied away from the boul-ders. She looked up and saw her husband's blood-spattered face above the largest rock. He wiped his brow with a gore-stained hand, leaving a swath of crimson across his face. "Go back," he said. "Stay clear." Simon looked down and considered his scarlet-bladed weapon as if he did not recognize it.

With a sound of horror, he dropped the sword upon the moss.

His attacker must have been defeated at his hand.

Adeline looked about her and saw no sign of a living creature to harm or help. She slipped from her saddle and led her reluctant palfrey up the slope, between the ancient stones.

She saw the arrows first, then the crimson blood spilled brighter still across the back of the boulder. And beside them, fallen into the mossy space between the rocks, lay a man near death.

"Come no closer," Simon snarled.

"Are you hurt?"

"I am damned," he said.

She stepped forward, and he moved to stop her. For a terrible moment, she feared that the blood upon his hands was his own. He heard her gasp, and looked down at his hand. "I won't touch you," he said. "Go back. You must not see this."

The bloodied cloak heaved once, then stilled.

"He must be dead," she said. "Come away from him."

"Turn away. You cannot be part of this."

"Simon—"

"Hush." His gaze went to the sky, then up the slope of the broad hill behind them, and then to the scarlet arrows. He uttered a low oath, and moved past her and caught the reins of her palfrey in his crimson-stained fist.

Adeline stepped forward and looked into the face of the dead man.

It was Ambrose.

Ambrose, the priest.

The small, unseeing eyes in the broad face looked back at her as if surprised by what he had found in death. The small mouth, open as if to speak, had curled back from his teeth. The wind ruffled lank, yellow hair across the gory brow.

Adeline stepped back and steadied herself against the rocks. The spots of blood upon the moss began to move in a spiraled dance.

"You weren't to look."

She spoke to him, but the words would not sound.

"It's the priest. The Norman priest," he said.

"It cannot be."

"It is, and I am damned."

Simon shook his head as if to clear his thoughts and led the palfrey to her. He knelt on one knee beside the stirrup. "Use my shoulder," he said. "Mount up now. There might be others. Not here, but nearby."

"I won't leave—"

"Up the hill. Quickly." He raised his bloody hands to lift her and set her in the saddle, then struck the mare's hindquarters with his open palm to send Adeline bolting up the hill.

She took control and brought the mare to a nervous, sidling halt. Simon was running up the hill behind her, his reddened sword in hand, the crimson arrows and bow in the other. Below them, nestled among the rocks, the dead priest lay beside the last of the crimson shafts.

"He's not a priest," Adeline called out.

"Keep riding. Up to the thicket." He turned from her repeated words and ran ahead.

The sky had darkened, as if to obscure the scene of death at the bottom of the hill. Simon ran past the thicket, and led his horse from concealment. "Up there," he said. "Ride straight up. Stop at the trees."

He led his horse after her and stopped often to look behind them, to the line of trees below. He had thrust the crimson arrows into his saddlebag and still carried his sword in hand.

Adeline reached the rowan stand and turned her mount to face the valley below. The body of the priest was no longer visible among the distant rocks.

Simon reached her then, and pointed to the rill that flowed beyond the rowans. "Drink first," he said.

They led their horses to the brook. Adeline knelt beside the stream and drank the icy water from her hands. Simon waited until she had done, then moved downstream to wipe his sword upon the turf and plunge his bloodied hands into the water. He bathed his face and rose, still dripping from the brook, to look uphill. "There," he said. "We'll shelter there, and watch."

She touched his arm. "Simon, he couldn't have been a priest."

He shook his head. "This is the end for me. Can you not see what will happen? Priest or not—" Simon broke off and caught the reins of his bay. "Quickly. Up to the cave. We need to be out of sight, until we know who follows."

Adeline looked above the rowan stand and saw what Simon intended. "A cave? Is it—"

"No." He sheathed his sword and picked up the reins of both mounts. "I saw it two days ago. There's no passage from it." He looked at her with angry regret. "There's shelter from sight, and a view of the hill. But there is no escape."

CHAPTER
TWENTY-TWO

There was a bad moment when the bay stallion refused to move into the broad, shallow cave behind the stand of rowans. Adeline took her palfrey's reins from Simon and persuaded the ugly, gentle horse into the rocky shelter. Soon after, the bay ceased its nervous protest and moved forward to stand beside the smaller beast. Simon dropped the saddlebag from his bay and tied the reins to it.

"If no one comes by sunset, I'll try to get you to your father. If we wait for the moon to rise, we should manage it. He must send you south, to Striguil. To the Marshal."

He was speaking as if he intended to vanish from the valley, and from her life. *I am damned*, he had said. Adeline looked at his hands, washed clean of blood, steady as he smoothed the stallion's neck below the small imperfection of the wound.

"Simon, that man was no priest. How could he have been?"

He turned his head and looked beyond her to watch the hill. "Does it matter?"

She recognized the chill in his voice, and the care with which he avoided meeting her gaze. Those were barriers—weapons she herself had used, when alone among strangers and hiding her fears. Did he think himself alone in this trouble?

He muttered a word to the restive stallion and checked the girth of the saddle. "Stay here," he said. "Keep the horses quiet."

Would he leave her here, without farewell, and send her father to get her? There was a desperation in his eyes; would this be her last sight of Simon Taillebroc?

He flexed the bow and picked up the scarlet arrows.

Adeline looked past him, down the hill. "Where will you be?"

"Near the rocks, watching the track."

"I'll come with you."

"No. Stay here."

"Simon—"

He dropped the bow and caught her to him in a crushing embrace. "I'll come back, and get you to your father. But if—" Simon drew a ragged breath and whispered against her cheek. "But if you hear fighting, wait until the sun is down, then loose the bay—strike him to make him bolt. Then ride down another way. Keep off the track—you won't be seen—"

"If I come with you, I'll be halfway down the hill already. Closer to home. Please, Simon—"

He muttered an oath and took her face between his hands. "If someone comes to meet the priest, they must not see you. We can't risk it. Listen, Adeline—the priest was a scarce five feet from the track. I passed him there. It was an easy shot—an easy kill. He must have seen me, yet he let me ride by. When I was far uphill and spotted him, I saw him watching the track below us, with his weapon ready."

Simon's hands moved down to grip her shoulders as if he feared she would fall. "When you appeared, he began to draw the bow. It was you, Adeline. It was you he wanted to kill."

He put his arms about her and drew her to the far wall, where the sunlight fell in a narrow slant upon the stone floor of the cave. "You nearly died because you are my wife. They strike at me through you. You must leave me, Adeline. At my side, you are a target."

She blinked back the hot tears that had come to her eyes, and drew a deep breath. "Why do you put this upon yourself? The priest let you pass unharmed, but aimed at me. If Longchamp hates you so, why were you not the target? He could have—"

"Adeline, don't think of it—

She steadied her voice and continued. "—he could have killed you first. Then shot me, when I came."

Simon began to speak, then hesitated. In his brief moment of indecision, Adeline saw that there was more at the root of Longchamp's enmity than her husband was willing to tell. Even now, he would not speak the words.

A forced smile crossed Simon's face. "Have you given Longchamp a reason to want to kill you? Did you deceive him, for my sake? Or refuse a task?"

Adeline shook her head

Simon threw his cloak onto the floor and sank with her onto its small warmth. "Soon, your people will miss us and come to look. I'll keep them from riding far enough to see the body. You will go to your father and leave under his protection, to hide among your kin."

"I'll not—"

"I'll stay long enough to discover who wanted you dead, and I'll kill them before I leave this place. Your father must hide you well. No one, not even Petronilla, must know where you will go."

She began to weep. "If I had known we'd have so little time—"

He tightened his arms around her. "No, Adeline. Don't think that. We'll be together again."

"Swear it."

"There will come a time—"

"In this life?"

"My lady—" His voice was hoarse with passion.

She clung to him with trembling, desperate force. "Stay with me," she said. "This place. This hour. It is all we will have."

"No. Stay here. Live for me, Adeline."

She turned her face to rest upon his chest, and looked out across the winter meadow and the trees beyond. "There is no one near," she said. "Even the hawks have gone. Give me this hour, Simon. Give me your child."

He shuddered as if she had struck him. "Would you have me forget all caution? You know what you would suffer, bearing the child of a man damned by his deeds."

"Do you know what I would suffer, if I never saw you more, and had no child of yours to comfort me? If we must part, give me this hour. Just this hour—"

He stopped her words with his kiss, and the world ceased to matter. There was only his mouth upon hers, and his arms enfolding her, and the desire that ran swift and hot in her body. She raised her arms to pull the cloak from her shoulders; he moved to stop her, then tore his outer tunic away and wrapped it about them both.

They sank onto the warmth of his cloak upon the stone, his arm beneath her head, his hand beneath the skirts of her tunic and surcoat. His kiss was slow and deep; he stirred her desire with leisurely care, as if he had a lifetime to inflame and delight her.

He would not allow her to draw the tunic from her breasts, but suckled them through the soft wool, sending a blaze of sensation to her woman's flesh beneath his hand. She pressed against the magic of his touch and thrashed free of her skirts to draw him closer.

"A crime," he muttered. "This is a crime, to take you here, in this way."

"If you leave me now, I'll lose my wits," she whispered. "Please, Simon—"

He moved from her, and covered her protest with a plundering kiss that left her breathless with need of him.

Then he was with her once again, his skin hot to her touch, his manhood pulsing at the center of her desire. He muttered soft words that passed unheeded somewhere beyond the glorious vertigo that had overtaken her. A swift, sharp pain flew into the maelstrom that was her mind and vanished, sublimated by the glory that followed.

He shuddered over her, silent in completion, then wrapped his arms beneath her and rolled her onto his chest. She lay content upon his chest, still filled with the warmth and temptation of his sex. Simon reached for the empty cloak and drew it over her body.

She looked out to the daylight beyond the cave. "The world is still there."

"Did you doubt it?"

"I was sure it would be gone." She raised her head and looked into his passion-darkened eyes. "And you?"

He drew her plaits across his shoulder and brought them to his lips. "Your hair is the color of summer wheat and honey," he said, "and your body holds the warmth of the sun. For me, the world stayed about me, but the winter was gone—turned to summertime."

He began to speak again, but hesitated.

"Tell me," she said.

"When I first saw you riding in your green cloak with your hair unveiled, you didn't seem of this world. You were summer itself, lost in the cold."

"You are a poet."

He pulled the cloak over her shoulders and held

her close. "And you, madam, are a liar. You were a virgin, with no idea what you were asking for—to lose your maidenhood in a cave. This was no crime, my lady. It was a sin."

"I loved it," she said.

Within her woman's flesh, she felt his sex begin to pulse and grow rigid. "Shall we do it again?" she whispered.

"Don't move."

"Shall we?"

"I am a great fool," he said. "You should have had a bed strewn with roses, and a fire in the hearth."

"There will come a time," she said, "when we will have such a night."

He drew a long breath and smoothed her plaits back upon his cloak. "I pray we will trick fate and have many such nights," he said.

His voice betrayed the hope in those words.

CHAPTER
TWENTY-THREE

She awoke in the early twilight, wrapped in Simon's cloak and tunic, alone upon the cold stone floor that had been her wedding bed. The scent of woodsmoke still lingered from her dream of warmth, and firelight, and Simon at her side.

Adeline sat up in alarm. Simon was nowhere in sight, and she dared not call to him. Had his faceless enemy appeared at last, and had Simon already gone down to distract danger from her hiding place? In her deep passion-swoon, had she lost her chance to follow her husband to that danger and bring her kinspeople up the hill to bring him clear?

Without Simon's warmth beside her, the cold of the coming night had entered her very bones. Across the cavern, the horses whickered and sidled from the open front of the rocky shelter.

Simon appeared in the gloaming light, naked above his chausses, his breath and the heat of his body sending a mist of white into the grey luminescence behind him. He knelt beside her and drew a cloth from beneath his arm. "Here," he said. "I tried to warm it for you." He gave a small, rueful laugh. "I'm afraid it did little good; my skin is as cold as that stream."

He began to bathe her with the cloth. In the dying light of that day's sun, his body was heat and strength and the world to her.

"We are one," she said.

Simon smiled in the pale grey light. "We are that," he said. "If two can become one, we have done so."

"It shouldn't matter, should it?—how little time we have."

He placed a warm hand upon her belly. "I go with you, wherever life must take you. Whether or not there is a child, I will go with you."

She sat up and pulled her kirtle over her shoulders.

He found her surcoat and wrapped it about her, then drew on his own tunic. He shook his hair free of the cloth and reached again to touch her cheek. "You will take great care with yourself, Adeline? There may be a child. If not, I will still be with you. You'll never be alone, now."

She caught his hand and rested her head against that broad palm. "You thought I'd manage not to live, if I lost you. Before this hour, is that what you feared?"

"The thought had come to me. One fear among many. Was that one true?"

"It might have been. It seems so long ago. Only an hour has passed—everything has changed."

He frowned. "We took a risk for that hour. There will be no more risks for you. If you love me, my lady, you will keep yourself safe."

She looked up and smiled. "I promise. But don't regret the hour, or any danger that comes because of it. I wanted you, Simon. If the worst happens now, never regret that we had each other for this time."

Simon drew a quick breath, then pulled her with him to stand looking out over the valley. He pointed to the distant glow of torches at the fortress gates. "This time," he said, "has been damned uncomfortable, compared to the nights we spent in that drafty ruin of a hall. I swear to you, my lady, that if we both live beyond this day, you will discover this hour is nothing to the times we will have before us."

He spread his hand across the back of her kirtle and gave her bottom a gentle tweak. "I'm flattered, my lady, that you say you'll die happy now. But oblige me and make very sure that the day won't come too early."

She caught his hand and turned to face him. "Then tell me what happened at Hodmersham. I am your true wife now. I should know."

He nodded. "I meant to tell you as we rode back."

"Tell me here, where the hawks can't listen."

Simon moved to the horses and began to untie the reins. "It's not a long tale, but one that only few may know. If you take shelter with William the Marshal, speak freely to him, for he knows it. So does Harald, and my brother Savare. They will help you, if ever it's safe to return to Taillebroc.''

"When will that be?''

He handed her the reins of her palfrey and lifted her to the saddle. "When Longchamp no longer hoards a third of the royal treasury in the abbey at Hodmersham.''

"The treasury? A part of the Plantagenets' treasury?''

He swung up to his saddle and looked again at the darkening hill. "It's in the abbey crypt. My brother and I had brought gold for the monks, to pay our father's burial price and buy prayers for his soul. There were torches in the crypt that night, and sounds of digging. We thought they were thieves, and went down to chase them out. Before the torches went out, we saw armed men and strongboxes. Then there was darkness, and they were upon us with weapons drawn. It was the darkness that saved us, and the darkness that put a priest in the way of my sword.''

"Would they not trust you with the secret? The abbey is on your lands, is it not?''

"Longchamp had chosen the abbey because it was close to the Dover road—waiting beside his escape route should he have to flee the country. He had not told me he would use the abbey, because he didn't intend to give the treasure back.

"It was our bad luck that we found him with his men and recognized him. It was our great luck that William the Marshal arrived the next day and made a pact with Longchamp. Savare and I would give up our Taillebroc lands while Longchamp is chancellor and we would remain silent about the gold; in return, Longchamp would not use his position as justiciar to bring us low."

"The Marshal has already fallen low if that good man is trading promises with the likes of Longchamp."

Simon shook his head. "Savare and I were hot to kill Longchamp for his treason, but the Marshal thought it dangerous. He hates Longchamp as much as any man does, but knows that while the king is abroad, his chancellor must remain in power. There will be war if the king's brother sees weakness and tries to take the throne."

"So you left the gold in the crypt, Longchamp's people on your lands, and sent the chancellor back to rule the kingdom?"

He held up his hand in mock surrender. "Peace, Adeline. I knew you wouldn't like the tale. Believe me, the Marshal thought hard about it before he proposed the oaths."

"But Longchamp has not kept his word."

"My lady, we never imagined he would. The oath stopped him from making an open move against my family; he fears William the Marshal and will not cross him in obvious ways. The Marshal found us places in the king's service, far from the center of power; Longchamp waits and watches and sends assassins, but he takes care to hide his links to them. I fear that this attack was to be a new reason for Longchamp to condemn me—the death of my bride at the hands of a soldier from my garrison."

Adeline pulled her cloak about her. "I see why you didn't want to take a wife."

Simon shook his head. "Longchamp had a strong reason to send you here from Normandy. His first plan might have been to stage the death of Caerdoc's maiden daughter at my hands during the Yuletide feasts."

The last light of sun was gone. As they rode downhill in the full moon's light, it was impossible to see, among the boulders, which of them sheltered Ambrose's cloaked corpse.

"We can't leave him there."

"We won't." Simon pointed to the distant torches at the high gates of the fortress. "Ambrose will be Luke's problem. I suspect he has been just that for months now. We need the body hidden for a few days, until you are safely gone."

"Why must his death be hidden? The man—priest or not—tried to kill me. I was there. I will tell my father exactly what I saw. He was armed, ready to shoot—"

"There is no way to prove it. Longchamp is the king's justiciar. He will pay judges to consider that the priest borrowed the bow to shoot rabbits and died an innocent man—at the hands of Simon Taillebroc, the priestkiller."

He turned to her then. "This is no ordinary enemy we face. To think the worst is to imagine only half the evil that will come."

A dull pain began to grow in Adeline's chest. She had found love with her husband, but would lose him in this trap of Longchamp's. She would lose him to

a perfidious spy who had chosen and died in the
one disguise that could reduce Simon Taillebroc to
a hunted fugitive.

"Simon, he was no priest. He had the shoulders of
a soldier—an archer. And he must have been Longchamp's courier—the one who would find Luke's
arrows in the forest, and take the messages to Hereford. That's how he had the arrows."

"Of course. He may have been all that. And he
may have been a priest as well. Longchamp himself
is a bishop, for all his crimes."

He reined his mount to a halt and waited for her
to stop beside him. "Don't make this harder than it
needs to be. We have—we have had our hour. I must
be a fugitive for the winter, maybe longer, and you
can't share that life."

"No—"

"The Marshal himself can't save me from the consequences of this second killing."

"Then leave it undiscovered for the winter. Or forever. No one knows he came up here; no one need
know what happened. Don't tell Luke—I'll help you,
Simon. We'll bury him together."

"I'll not have my wife digging graves for my kill.
He will be missed tonight, and the search will go on
for days. No one, not even an old bandit like your
father, would allow that priest to go missing without
a search of the valley twice over." He made a gesture
of futility. "It's too late."

"Simon, promise me you'll not decide before I
speak with my father. Stay here, and I'll bring Harald
to you, and then go back to Caerdoc. He owes you

so much, Simon. Take the help he must give you, if you must go into hiding. He has a cousin west of here—"

He shook his head. "I must leave this place, and you must go to your father's kin. I'll find the priest's fellows, and make sure they can't harm you more. You must disappear; your father will know how to arrange it. Adeline—don't make this harder for me."

"I hate them. Longchamp, Luke, all the others— I hate them."

Ahead in the moonlight, Simon laughed softly. "Is this my cold-minded, sharp-witted wife speaking? Is this the woman who would hold her tongue and think while others shrilled their thoughts to all who would listen?" He turned in the saddle. "Was our lovemaking so complete that it has addled your wits?"

"I can think of nothing but Longchamp. He is taking my husband from me." She did not attempt to hide the tears streaming down her face. "I love you, Simon Taillebroc, and you are leaving me. Because of that ape-faced Longchamp, I may never know your touch again; you may never see a child—"

He stopped on the track and turned his horse to face her. "Adeline, if there is away in God's world to come back to you, I'll find it. But I can't do what needs to be done unless I know you're safe—and hidden where even I couldn't find you, until the time is right."

Simon rode ahead again, picking his way through the boulders, and the aspens, to find the wide track around the moonlit lake. The moon's image shone in cold perfection from the gloss of ice upon the water and seemed to follow Adeline as she rode past that silver expanse.

That flawless surface held no trace of sleet or snow. Adeline renewed her prayers for snow to close the valley. For a fugitive, this still and cold air would spell death: open country through which men on fresh horses would travel fast; a bright moon to light the way to their quarry, and deep cold to slow or kill a solitary, exhausted outlaw.

She fell asleep in the saddle as they crossed the manor fields and woke with a start as Simon took her reins. "We're close," he said. "Can you stay awake until the gate? We'll hope they still have the bathing tub in our chamber and water on the fire."

Adeline rubbed her eyes and began to remember—

"Simon, we can't sleep here tonight."

"You'll be safe. I promise."

"No—it's not that. I told my father he should take back the lord's chamber and leave that drafty sleeping hut to the mice."

He shrugged. "Then we'll take the sleeping hut and deal with the mice."

"I told him we would sleep in the fortress tonight."

"Why? Did something frighten you?"

"We quarreled."

Simon laughed. "I have a changeling wife today. She picks quarrels with the most famous bandit in these mountains, rebukes her father's hospitality, and loses her maidenhood on the floor of a cave. What will my demure wife say tomorrow, when she returns and finds her life so changed?''

"She will say that she wouldn't change a thing."

"Nothing?"

"Well, a bed would have been good."

"We'll find one waiting for us in the fort. But first, we'll speak to your father if he has recovered from your temper."

"Simon, it was a serious thing. He refused to tell me how he leaves the valley. Despite all you did yesterday, he still won't trust you—or me—with that secret."

"I'll speak with him. He may keep his secrets in his—boots, for all I care. But he must get you clear of this place before trouble comes."

"Not tonight."

He hesitated, then spoke in the low, intimate voice she had heard for the first time today. "No, not tonight," he said.

Together they rode through the great wooden gates of Caerdoc's stockade.

CHAPTER
TWENTY-FOUR

They led their horses into the byre and left them tied near the door. Caerdoc's sleeping hut was dark; at the rim of the door, not even a small taper's glow could be seen.

Maida saw them from the hall and rushed out to them. "We were worried, once the sun set," she said. "Petronilla and Howyll wanted to ride out to look for you, but your father said they should leave newlywed lovers to themselves. Just now, Caerdoc began to think of a search."

Simon smiled and muttered an apology for worrying the household. He put his arm about Adeline's shoulders and followed Maida into the hall. They had been right to come to Caerdoc first: Had he sent out searchers on this moonlit night, they might have found the priest's body.

"Here they are," Caerdoc boomed. He offered his great cup to Simon; it held a bare inch of good brandy-wine in its beaten silver depths. "Now it's only the priest Ambrose missing." He waited for Simon to drink, then bid the serving maid fill it again. "Did you see him, on your ride up the valley?"

Simon had spent the last mile of road considering his answer for this question. "The priest? He haunts the garrison yard, speaking with my men, hearing their confessions. He has at least ten more to go."

Caerdoc laughed. "He'd do well to get himself back here before Cuthbert's mass for the Norman soldiers. Old Cuthbert swears he'll not do it if he must be alone in the chapel with your Normans."

Maida emerged from the sleeping chamber and spoke softly to Adeline. Simon strained to hear the words over Caerdoc's discourse on the need for brandy-wine as a winter staple.

Adeline touched Simon's hand where it rested on his shoulder. "Maida had prepared a bath, and offers it to me. I'll go now, and gather our things when I'm done."

"I'll be here," he said. "Be careful."

"The tub isn't deep enough to drown me."

He couldn't smile. "Be careful of questions."

Her smile didn't fade. "Of course." She was better at this than he could ever be. Even now, any soul at Caerdoc's table with a curious mind might notice his nervousness.

Caerdoc offered the newly brimming cup to Simon. It was not difficult to appear to drink deeply; to do less would have been an insult. "I'd like to ask your help," said Simon.

"Ah," the old man muttered. "Adeline said you might need it."

In the din that rose from the trestle tables, their own speech was as good as private. "Adeline needs it. Soon."

"What have you done?"

The old eyes were cunning, and focused upon Simon's face. He considered a distracting lie, but rejected the idea. Caerdoc would know he was concealing something. Simon cocked his head to a dark corner of the hall. Caerdoc picked up his cup and led the way.

"The priest Ambrose is dead," said Simon. "I killed him."

Caerdoc blinked once. "Why?"

"He tried to kill your daughter."

The drinking cup slanted out of Caerdoc's grasp.

Simon moved closer to steady the silver vessel. "There's not time to explain all of it, but I will tell you that he was linked to Longchamp and the danger to Adeline isn't over. She became a target when she came home, and her marriage to me increased the danger. I need you to get her out of here tomorrow, in secret. Take her to a kinsman first, then after a fortnight get her to the Marshal's new stronghold at Striguil. Will you do this? Get her out tonight, or in the morning?"

Caerdoc's knuckles were white about the stem of the drinking cup. "I'll do this," he said. "Not tonight, but when I can."

It would be unthinkable to strike his wife's father in his own hall, after drinking his brandywine. "Tomorrow then," repeated Simon. "It has to be tomorrow."

"Send her to me tomorrow, and I'll keep her safe until I can get her away."

"I'll leave her here tonight, if that would mean you'll get her out sooner."

"No. Not tonight. Take her to the fort."

Simon took the drinking cup from Caerdoc's loose grip and set it upon the rushes at his feet. "Listen to me, Caerdoc. She needs to go tomorrow. Without fail. If you can't do this, tell me how to get her out of the valley in secret. The roads from the pass will be watched. If you tell me another way out, I'll take an oath on my hope of salvation that I'll not reveal it, nor use it again."

Caerdoc shook his head. "You annoy me with your talk of secret ways. I'm not Merlin, Taillebroc. Your sentries are lazy. Don't blame me if I ride out under their noses and they fail to see it."

Simon placed a hand upon Caerdoc's shoulder, a gesture that would appear friendly to those who watched out of hearing, from the tables beside the hearth. "I would crush the breath from your body if I thought it would get Adeline out of this valley before Longchamp attacks. If she comes to harm through your indifference, I will return and send you to the hell you deserve."

From the sleeping chamber came the lilt of women's voices and the sound of water in the tub. Penric and Govan raced out of the chamber and collapsed giggling beside the fire.

"I'll brave any hell you can offer," said Caerdoc. "But I won't put my sons in danger."

"They haven't been threatened. Adeline is in danger. She could die—"

"Adeline is no fool. She will survive if any of us will, given half a chance. My sons are young. I must see to them first, and think of Adeline only when I know my boys are safe."

Simon picked up the drinking cup and placed it in Caerdoc's hand. "We all do what we must," he said. "For your own sake," said Simon, "do not fail her tomorrow."

Caerdoc's faced creased in puzzlement. "They said you were mad with anger when you killed the first priest. And today you have killed another. Yet you are here, threatening me in my own hall, with my men a spear's throw from your throat, and you keep your hand steady." He took the cup from Simon's hand, and drank of the brandywine. "Only the devil's spawn or a great warrior could do that, Simon of Taillebroc." Caerdoc's gaze moved to his wide chair and the two small sons who were climbing upon it. "Keep our truce," he said. "I made that oath, and I'll keep it. If you cleave to it as well, I'll do what I can about the rest." His hand rose in a vague gesture of peace—or farewell. And he walked to the head of his table, to his sons.

Simon turned from the sight of him.

Petronilla was at the chamber doorway, calling for Howyll.

Simon went past her to find Adeline tying their saddlebags closed. She was wearing clothes he had

not seen before: a fine woolen tunic and velvet surcoat, each dyed in the colors of summer. Her plaits
were newly woven with silk of the same deep rose as
her tunic, and about her slender hips she had knotted
a ceinture of silver links with cloth of scarlet woven
through. Her sodden cloak was hanging against the
wall, and in its place across her shoulders Adeline
had drawn a cloak of deep scarlet with cords of silk.
Upon the dark crimson and silver, the deep gold of
Adeline's shining braids invited his touch.

Adeline smiled. "Petronilla reminded me to open
the last of our saddlepacks. The lady Maude was generous with us."

He walked to her and touched her cheek. "It suits
your beauty," he said.

She was a vision of warmth and summer joy in this
wintering hall. Simon looked about the chamber and
saw that the pallet they had shared was against the
wall; Caerdoc's high bed frame stood in the center
of the floor, with rich linens and wall hangings piled
upon it. The master of the hall had decided to bring
his wife and sons out of the dark safety and shadows
of the old sleeping hut.

The world had shifted in so many ways since he
had left his bed that morning.

"You go up to the fortress now?" Howyll picked
up the last of the saddlebags.

Simon raised his head. "Yes, tonight."

Howyll looked beyond him to Adeline. "Did you
speak to the priest? For us—for Petronilla and me?"

Adeline reached for Simon's hand. "I saw him in
the weaving shed, and told him I'd vouch for Petronil-

la's freedom to wed." Her fingers closed about Simon's wrist. "It's really Cuthbert's place to speak the banns," she continued. "Have you told him?"

"Petronilla said she would. He's in a bad humor this day. Ambrose wouldn't come down from the fort today, and Cuthbert said the mass alone for the garrison men." Howyll lowered his voice. "If I didn't know better, I'd think I heard old Cuthbert out behind the chapel, complaining that Ambrose was spending his days hunting while the Normans' souls—begging your pardon, Lord Taillebroc—continued as benighted as before." Howyll rolled his eyes. "I'm hot to wed Petronilla, but I'll not go near Cuthbert until he's calm again." Howyll hesitated. "When you see the Norman priest, would you tell him we're eager to wed—Petronilla and I? We'll come up to see him tomorrow."

Simon took Adeline's hand between his own. "We'll remember, Howyll."

Simon took a torch to light their way despite the bright moonlight and rode at his wife's side until the path narrowed below the fortress. The loom of the torch gave life to the colors she wore and touched her hair in bright splendor.

"If you stare so," said Adeline, "you'll go off the path."

"I left the track months ago," said Simon. "But it led me here, and to you. I can't regret it."

"You have forgiven me for forcing you to wed?"

"With all my heart," he said. "When—"

"What?"

He swallowed hard. "When I find you in the spring, when I come back to you—will you wear these robes? I'll think of you, this winter long, as you look now. And I'll feel the warmth of you, and smell the scent of you."

She reached for his hand. "And I will dream of you, the winter long." Her mouth curved in a shy smile. "But tonight, we need not dream."

"This night," he said, "we need not sleep at all, my lady."

Above them, the guard called out, then opened the gates to them. Simon gave him their reins and caught Adeline in his arms. He picked up the torch where it lay blazing on the ground and called after the guard to bring the saddlebags.

The darkness of the ruined hall came alive as they entered with the sputtering brand to light them. He tossed the torch onto the hearthstone to set the dry wood alight. "My lady," he said, "I would be aflame sooner than that kindling, if I shut that door now. But I must bring Harald—"

She smiled, and looked beyond him. "Harald has found you, I think."

He turned to find Harald, brighter red than the firelight, attempting to make himself inconspicuous in the doorway.

"Your pardon, Taillebroc. There are two matters for you—"

Simon touched Adeline's arm. "Later," he whispered, "will I find you here, by the fire?"

"You'll find me at your side," she answered. "The

time for secrets between us has passed." She smiled
and beckoned to Harald. "Come sit with us."

The florid face turned to Simon. "My lord?"

"Speak freely, if you wish." Simon gestured to the
bench. "My lady wife is our ally."

Harald's pale eyes went from Simon, to Adeline,
and back to stare at his mad lord. "Taillebroc, these
are matters best left to men. May I walk with you in
the bailey and speak there?"

"Does it concern the archer Luke?"

"Yes, and one other—"

Adeline moved to the fire and began to warm her
hands above it. "Simon, you can't expect Harald to
trust me. You must have told him that I spied for
Longchamp."

Harald's eyes bulged at her words; he found the
bench and sat down in heavy astonishment.

"Simon, walk with Harald and speak in private."
She smiled into the bewildered face across the flames.
"Go on, I don't mind."

"No. There may be—there will be a time very soon
when Harald will be your only link to me, and to
Taillebroc. There must be trust between you."

At his mention of the coming months of separation,
a shadow came over her eyes. "Of course," she said.
And sat down opposite Harald.

Simon closed his eyes. "The priest Ambrose is
missing."

Harald sat up. "Yes. That's the first thing. He's
gone; they came from the manor to ask for him many
times today, but I couldn't find him among the garri-

son men. He had been hearing confession this morning, and I fear that he may have come to harm."

"He did," said Simon. "He lies dead beyond the lake, on the track up to the southern meadows."

"Merciful Christ—"

"I killed him." Simon rose and went to the largest of the saddlebags. "Where is the archer Luke?"

Harald passed a hand across his brow. "Up the sentry tower. It's his watch tonight."

Simon drew the bundle of crimson arrows from the leather bag. "I'm going up to him now." He placed a hand on Adeline's shoulder. "Harald will wait with you here."

"Simon, don't go alone."

He smiled. "I think Luke will soon understand that I'm the best friend he has."

Harald frowned. "We'll listen for trouble."

"Talk to my lady, old friend. Her well-being will be your only task from this day on."

The archer had seen him on the road and would expect Taillebroc to seek him out.

Simon used the inner stair to reach the sentry walk, and made enough noise in his approach that Longchamp's spy would not be startled and make a deadly mistake.

"Luke," he called. "We must talk." He had thought to pick up another torch from the guard at the gates and carried it well before him as he emerged into to the cold stillness atop the tower. He walked within an arm's length of the archer Luke and held the sheaf of crimson arrows before him in the torchlight.

"They're well made," said Simon. "Long, and balanced to fly far, with the smallest notches to hold the twine about your messages on the shaft."

For a long moment, the archer Luke stared at the arrows. "I am a soldier," he said at last. "The king's loyal subject and a soldier. Take me to Hereford, and I'll prove I'm no traitor."

"I know you are no traitor. But you had an enemy who would have made you a murderer." He tossed aside the arrows, save one. "This shaft," he said, "was to bear a different sort of message—that you had killed my lady wife."

Luke stepped back against the rail. "You lie."

"Where is Father Ambrose?"

The archer glanced down at the garrison house.

"He hasn't returned," said Simon. "He will not return. Ever."

He began to turn the arrow in the torchlight. "There is a thing you should learn about William Longchamp. He pays his spies well, but he doesn't keep them long. Those who come close to learning the shape of a scheme must disappear, one way or another. Longchamp sent Ambrose—whatever he was—to kill my wife and leave evidence enough to hang you. Ambrose kept the message-arrows and took them up to the hills today and lay in wait for my wife."

"I knew nothing—"

"This killing must have been important to Longchamp, and Ambrose was determined to finish his task. When he saw me running at him with sword in hand, he didn't flee. He turned back to take the shot. As he died, he didn't drop the bow." Simon paused. "What does Longchamp do, to make a man so reckless of his life that he will stand to be killed in order to do his master's bidding?"

Simon thrust the shaft of the arrow toward Luke. "This is the one that was to kill Caerdoc's daughter. She might have died up there; we would have found her with your arrow through her heart, and we would have come back to find you and decide whether to hack you into pieces or hang you from this tower. Or both."

"It's not true. I will not listen to your lies."

"Then wait until they find the body. Ambrose has been missed, and there will be a search. Then you will believe me. They'll find him with a single red arrow beside him. Will the garrison believe you were innocent of his death? Will Longchamp leave Ambrose's task undone?"

"Where is the priest?"

"I'll tell you when you swear to do one thing for me."

"What?"

Simon looked down to the valley floor, to Caerdoc's manor. "How did you compose the messages you sent? Did you write them?"

Luke hesitated.

"If you refuse to help me, I'll let them slaughter you any way they wish, for killing their Norman priest."

The archer let his arms fall loose at his sides. "I— I don't write. There were marks they taught me to

make—for people and what they did. Longchamp
didn't want writing."

"You made the marks on parchment?"

"On pieces of leather."

"Then find a piece of leather—from a skin you
have cut from before—and make the marks to tell
Longchamp that my wife is missing. Not dead. Missing. Can you do that?"

Luke moved aside. "If I make the marks, you'll kill
me and send the arrow yourself."

Simon shrugged. "I think you have ceased to be
Longchamp's creature this night. You have no choice
in this. Send the message yourself, in the usual way.
Add a mark to show that Ambrose is here in the valley;
Longchamp will have another messenger waiting to
find it. Then go up the track beyond the lake and
find Ambrose among the boulders in the aspen grove.
Bury him deep."

"If I do all this, what more will you want of me?"

"If you don't return here, get out of Wales and
stay clear of Longchamp. If you come back, I'll want
your oath of loyalty. If you ever return to Longchamp's service, I'll make sure you hang for
Ambrose's death." He pointed to the arrows spilled
across the sentry walk. "I have enough of them left
to put you under suspicion for three more deaths; if
I should fall, Caerdoc will do it for me. My goodwill
is your only hope of survival."

Luke looked down at the scattered shafts. "You
swear all that?"

"You have my oath."

Once again, the archer hesitated. "Then I'll tell

you that Longchamp is in Hereford. He sent word for your wife to get you to travel there. If she doesn't, Longchamp will come here for you, and there will be more bloodshed."

Simon shook his head. "He wouldn't have spared Adeline or her family. Does he imagine she believed him?"

Luke began to pick up the arrows at his feet. "Has she not asked you to leave for Hereford? She was to ask you to travel with her before the snow comes."

"No. She never spoke of Hereford."

Luke sighed. "I never trusted the woman."

Simon began to laugh. At the bottom of the stair, he stopped to wipe his streaming eyes and begin to imagine what his wife intended to do about Longchamp and the long road to Hereford.

CHAPTER
TWENTY-FIVE

"Simon is not mad, Harald. And I am not his enemy."

"My lady, I never said he was mad."

"I saw it in your face just now. You fear that I'll betray him to Longchamp."

"You worked with the archer, didn't you? And wed my lord Taillebroc to spy upon him?"

An eternity ago—in another world, she had. "I did," said Adeline. "Not for love of Longchamp, but in fear of him. I have given up that fear, Harald."

"Well, keep it close to hand. The man is crafty and evil."

"And he has good reason to want Simon dead."

Harald's eyes narrowed. "I wouldn't know about that."

"I do. Your lord told me about the treasury and the abbey crypt."

"Merciful Christ."

For an old armorer with muscled arms as thick as tuns of brandywine, Harald seemed a shy, soft-spoken man. Adeline watched the color drain from Harald's ruddy face as he learned that she held Taillebroc's dangerous secret, and saw him look at her with greater curiosity.

She decided to trust him with a secret of her own. "You see, now—Simon trusts me. He knew the worst of my dealings with Longchamp, yet he trusts me. Will you do so?"

Harald's mouth set in a narrow line. "I might."

"Then hear what troubles me now: Longchamp's last order was to get Simon out of the valley on the road to Hereford, where Longchamp will take him prisoner. If Simon doesn't go out that road, Longchamp will come into this valley and drag Simon away. Then he will massacre my father's people, for they might speak against him later. I don't know what he will do with the garrison. I believe he might do the same to these soldiers—to leave all witnesses dead."

Harald regarded her in silence.

"I won't lure him out there, and I won't let Longchamp come to slaughter my people or yours."

Harald picked up a stick of kindling and began to prod the bigger pieces of firewood to life. "What will you do? Claim he's dead and beneath the ground?"

Adeline considered the idea. "I didn't think of it," she said. "It won't work unless Simon disappears. He wouldn't agree."

"It's not like him to hide from trouble, but he'll have to do it this time." Harald fixed her with an exasperated stare. "As will you, my lady."

"Of course."

"What was your plan, if not to announce Taillebroc's death?"

The hint of suspicion had returned to Harald's gaze. Adeline forced a smile. "If we act together, your plan will work better than mine. Have you a sleeping potion in the garrison kitchen?"

A slow smile brightened Harald's face. "There should be something." He dropped his stick into the fire and stood up. "You'll drug him tonight, we carry him away, and announce in the morning that he's missing?"

"Yes. We'll hide him in one of the shepherds' huts. You will tell the garrison that you found him dead on the hillside, so that the men, including the archer Luke, tell the same story to Longchamp. And then," said Adeline, "you will stay with him and keep him quiet until Longchamp leaves."

"That should work," said Harald. He looked as if he believed it. "I'll go find the poppy juice for you."

Adeline sighed in relief. This would be easier than she had thought. Harald would help her get Simon safely away, and by the time he realized she had gone to deal with Longchamp, it would be too late for either of them to stop her.

She moved to Simon's strongboxes and found the ornate but serviceable dagger she had seen earlier. It was bigger than her eating knife, and much sharper.

She placed the knife beneath her small saddlebag. She was ready, now, to meet Simon's enemy.

*   *   *

"I think your lady wife is scheming to kill Longchamp herself."

Simon raised his head. "She told you that?"

Harald sat down below Taillebroc on the tower stair. "No, but the lady did tell me that she will drug you tonight, have me carry you away to a shepherd's hut, and announce that you are dead."

"She's too clever for that. She knows the garrison would expect to see the body." Simon looked up. "You agreed to help her, of course?"

Harald smiled. "I listened to her plan and said I'd get the poppy juice and wait to cart you away."

"Good. That will keep her from fretting." He sighed. "She must be desperate, to enlist a Taillebroc man to help her."

"She told me it was a way to save your life."

Simon heard a note of uncertainty in Harald's words. "Old friend, you know that if I lose her, I'd kill the man who helped her make that sacrifice."

"She loves you, Taillebroc. And she's clever enough to act alone, if she needs to."

"Then I'll have to make sure she's not free to do it." Simon stood and clapped Harald on the shoulder. "Go and get her a flask of honey and water. Tell her it's a sleeping potion, and promise to return when she wants you."

Harald heaved himself to his feet. "This promises to be a long night."

Simon smiled. "Not for you, I hope. Go back to

the garrison, and sleep well. My lady won't rise to call
you before dawn."

"She said—"

"She'll be late. I'll make sure of it."

Her hand shook as she poured the honey-borne
poppy juice into Simon's mead. Harald had warned
her not to use too much. The whole flask, he had
said, would fell a strong man and leave him sleeping
for more than a day. Simon, though strong as an ox,
had passed many sleepless nights watching over the
sentry changes in the fortress, and might be more
vulnerable to the potion as a result.

"You haven't told me what the archer said."

"He agrees, I think, that his future cannot be in
the chancellor's service. He may prove an ally yet."

"You told him about—"

"I told him where to find Ambrose; he'll leave
before dawn to find the place and bury him."

"Do you trust him to do that? He could take away
his own arrows and leave the body. You would be
blamed."

He looked over his shoulder and raised a brow. "I
believed his oath. He may prove as trustworthy as
anyone else in the fortress. They all have their
secrets."

Adeline turned away. In the morning, when Simon
awoke far from the fort and realized that she had
taken his fate into her hands, he would realize how
true his words had been.

Simon was stacking the firewood beside the hearth

and frowning up at the rafters. "If we had spent the winter here, I'd have raised a cover above the smoke hole, to keep the snow from killing the fire."

She walked to his side and offered him the cup.

He smiled at her and set the wine aside.

Adeline watched him go out beyond the door and return with another armful of wood. "Are you expecting a siege in here?"

"The weather is turning cold tonight."

She picked up the cup and offered it to him again. "You didn't seem to worry about the hearth fire, or your comfort for that matter, when I first came here."

He drank a sip of the mead and patted her tunic where it flared on the curve of her hip. "I didn't have a tender lady in my bed, and the north wind blowing." Simon looked down into the cup. "It's a good taste," he said. "This batch has herbs?"

Adeline waited a beat, then shrugged. "Maida said she sent her brew of mead and a tun of Frankish brandywine on the packhorse this afternoon. She's treating your garrison well, I think."

The fire was burning high and bright now, and the coverlets and pelts upon the bed were turned back to warm the soft linen stretched across the width. Simon had stopped stacking the wood and followed Adeline's gaze to the bed.

He drank again from the cup.

It was a pity that he would soon be too weary to stay awake, and the long night in the warm bed would be lost to all pleasures save sleep. Adeline felt crimson color rise to her cheeks as she remembered the desire she had felt for Simon in the high, windy cave above the valley. Now, in this warm chamber with the northern gusts no more than a whistling at the arrow loops, she and Simon might have shared a long night of firelight and passion.

She looked into Simon's dark gaze and felt her blood stir at the silent invitation in his eyes. She would do no harm if she delayed the potion for an hour—or two. Simon's expression told her that this was one night when he would stay close at her side.

Adeline crossed the chamber to take back the cup of sleep-laced mead.

"Here," said Simon. "Will you drink as well?"

She smiled and reached for the cup. "Must we drink at all, before we go to bed? My blood runs warm enough when I think of our time together in the cave."

He pressed the goblet into her hands and kissed the corner of her mouth. "Drink, my lady. We'll have nothing but kisses this night; you must rest and recover from all that we did."

Simon turned from her and went toward the door. "Where do you go?"

He picked up a bucket and held it high. "I'll fetch more water from the kitchens."

"There are two buckets beside the hearth—"

"The lads are late with our food. I'll fill this last one when I speak with them. Sit down, Adeline, and drink the mead. I'll not be long."

She slumped to the trestle bench and cursed Simon's sudden interest in provisions. If she didn't know better, she would imagine that he feared a long siege.

Adeline sighed and began to run a finger around the rim of the cup. Simon must be determined to leave her untouched this night; it was for that reason that he busied himself with water and firewood and kitchen matters.

Even if she survived tomorrow's bid to turn Long-champ away from the valley by lies or by the knife, Simon would be furious that she had deceived him. Much worse would be his discovery that she had persuaded the faithful Harald to join her in the deception. How many weeks—or months—would his anger persist?

Adeline rose from the table and found the ewer of mead and the other goblet, and poured a small measure of untainted honey wine into the empty cup, and filled Simon's goblet once again to the brim. She set them at opposite ends of the table, for she could not afford to make a mistake and drink the sleeping potion herself.

The door swung open with a great clap of timber as the wind caught it. Simon came through with a brimming bucket and motioned a kitchen lad to bring in a platter heavy with roasted meats and bread.

She looked from Simon to the crowded platter. "Are you that hungry?"

"Of course. We'll eat well and sleep well, and by tomorrow be ready to meet whatever the fates bring us."

It would take hours to consume that quantity of food. Adeline cast a longing glance at the bed. Soon, it would be too late to do anything but make sure that Simon would be in a deep slumber before Harald returned to carry him away.

"Would you bar the door?" she asked.

He looked from the table to the door and frowned. "The lads may have another platter to bring."

"Why this gluttony, Simon?"

Her husband approached the platter and began to examine the food. "Perhaps it's all here." Simon looked up and smiled. "I'll bar the door, then, if you wish."

He returned and picked up the wrong cup. Adeline reached for the other, pressed a lingering kiss to the rim, and offered it to her husband. Simon looked at the two goblets in mock confusion and raised Adeline's choice to his lips. And kissed it where she had done.

He pushed the full, drugged cup back to her. "Drink deeply, my love."

Adeline stepped away from the table and moved to the firelit space beside the bed; she extended her arms to Simon. "Come, husband, and love me well. I won't come to harm."

He looked at her over the rim of the cup and set it down.

"There is a limit to my good intentions," he murmured. "If you ask me again, I'll lose my resolve."

"I'm asking you," she said. And drew her surcoat from her shoulders. Her tunic was of fine wool; if she stood before the fire, the shadow of her chemise and the lines of her body would show through the subtle tracery of green.

He was at her side before she moved to the hearth

side, lifting her into his arms, bearing her with one
long stride to the waiting bed. Simon hesitated above
her. "Are you sure?"

"Yes. Oh yes."

With exquisite deliberation, he began to draw the
silken ribands from her plaits and to spread the curling tendrils into a radiant band to frame her face.
She saw the image before he spoke it. "A sunburst,"
he said.

She touched the tousled blackness about his face.
"And your darkness, my lord, gives my blood more
heat than the sun."

He caught her hand and brought it to his mouth
and kissed her on the pulse of her wrist. "You don't
need your tunic," he murmured.

"No."

"Then take it off."

He drew back and watched her, his eyes shining
deep gold in the firelight. When she had drawn the
robe from beneath her and held it before the thin
linen of her chemise, he extended his hand, and
waited for her to surrender the tunic.

Adeline sat up and drew her knees to her chin.
Only her chemise would remain to cover her body
from that golden gaze. She placed the green wool
upon his outstretched palm. "Do you need your clothing?" she asked him.

He tossed her tunic aside and smiled. "No, my lady.
You may take it off."

"You must."

"No. You must do it." His smile deepened. "It's
not fair, is it?"

"No."

"I'll make it fair. I promise."

She had seen him—all of him—many times in the days they had lived celibate in this chamber. Tonight, each smooth muscle, each sinew of his body was a revelation; he had shown her pleasure with his flesh, and she saw it anew.

He helped her to untie the ceinture above his hips, and brought her hands to draw down the chausses, then brought them up to touch his heavy sex. "Tell me what you want," he said.

"Everything," she breathed.

He pulled her to him, and touched her to bring her where he had taken her before; once again, she felt the world recede. There was only Simon in the place to which she had traveled, and only the firelight beyond the borders of their bed.

"Now," he said, and held her as she brought him within her. "Take me as you wish." He shifted beneath her and smiled at her breathless gasp. "Slowly," he murmured. "We have the night before us."

All about her, the crimson flickering grew bright; she closed her eyes, and found it brighter still. He rose to meet her, and gathered her tight against his chest as she reached a splendid crisis of light and heat and rushing.

When she opened her eyes, her head rested upon his shoulder; and across the room, like a cold beacon amid the glory of the firelight, was the silver cup from which she must bring him to drink.

"You weep?" he said. "I am an idiot to have done this."

"I weep from joy," she said.

There was an instant, then, in which she saw more than understanding in his gaze. He shut his eyes, and when he looked at her again, the moment was gone.

Simon kissed her mouth and rose from the bed. "Are you thirsty?"

"Yes," she said.

As he crossed to the trestle, the warm light of the hearth upon his body sent tears afresh into her eyes. She blinked them back, and when he returned with the two goblets, chose the shallow one. He sat beside her and drank of the other, then brought the ewer and poured more mead into her cup. Then she lay back and he remained beside her, stroking her face as she watched him.

He did not speak again. When she next opened her eyes, he was still sitting on the edge of the bed, watching the fire. She wondered how soon the poppy juice would draw him into deep slumber.

She yawned and set her goblet down upon the floor beside the bed. Until Harald came to summon her, she would sleep as well.

CHAPTER
TWENTY-SIX

She had dreamed that Simon was leaving her forever, that he had drawn the warm coverlet away from her temple and kissed her once before walking through the doorway into the windy sunlight.

The pounding of her heart woke Adeline and sent her scrambling from the tangled warmth of bedding. Simon was gone. It had been no dream that he had left her abed.

She ran across to the unbarred door and pushed it. It would not budge. Again she tried to push it, then threw herself against the panels.

Adeline slumped against the door, and saw the purpose of the firewood and the buckets of water and the platters of food that Simon had hauled into the chamber last night. He had her provisioned for a long imprisonment.

Beyond the solid timber she heard Simon's voice, then the whicker of a horse. "Simon," she cried. "I can't get out. Simon—" Hoofbeats sounded past the door, then receded. To her cries, there was no answer.

She darted to the north wall and wrenched open the shutter over the arrow loop. Her frantic cries brought two soldiers from out of the garrison house; they started across the bailey yard, then halted at the order of Harald's voice.

"Go back," he called. "Leave her and go back."

His voice was coming from the door itself. She crossed back, and beat upon the timber. "Let me out. He's gone, Harald. Simon is gone."

There was a scraping sound, then his voice again. "Don't harm yourself, my lady. The door won't open. Not this day."

"Where is Simon?"

"Gone. And I have sworn to keep you in that hall."

After a moment, he spoke again. "Strong words, my lady. Where did you learn them?"

"From your idiot lord Taillebroc. Go after him, Harald. If you won't let me go, then follow him and keep him from the road. Harald—how can you let him go?"

A muffled oath worse than any she had uttered was the answer. "He made his decision, and I will honor it."

"Then you are an idiot as well."

"I am, my lady. That I am. A loyal idiot."

She could hear the tears in his voice. "Go after him, and knock him senseless. I'll bear the blame."

"My lady, I cannot. I—" He broke off. When he

spoke again, he was shouting at the gatekeepers, far from the door.

Adeline looked up at the smoke hole above the hearthstone. Aside from the shuttered arrow slits, that square opening in the roof was her only way out of the hall. She pulled her dark green tunic from the clothing chest and drew it over the pale linen of her bliaut, then found her boots.

She toppled the firewood stack to find the sturdiest piece, then used it to push the hot ash and glowing coals on the hearthstone to one end. Small flames burned close to the edge; Adeline started to push the burning wood back again, but left it. If she couldn't get out through the smoke hole, she would set the floor afire and force Harald to open the door.

The clothing chest was too heavy to drag onto the hearthstone. Adeline abandoned that effort and turned to the trestle table. Frantic in her haste, she upset the remains of last night's meal and heaved the two trestle stands to either side of the hearth, and managed to get the board back up to rest upon them.

She went back to the clothing chest to get the dagger she had taken from Simon's strongbox, then went to the strongbox itself and took a handful of gold to thrust in her pocket. She might have to bribe her way through the gates if she found more than one guard.

The soot-crusted beams framing the smoke hole were just beyond her reach. Adeline climbed down from the trestle and ransacked the hall for a chest light enough to lift atop the board. In the end, she stacked the benches upon each other, and crowned the pile with the smallest of the coffers.

She made her way to the top of her unsteady structure and grasped a black beam with a gloved hand. Above her, a cold wind blew across the roof, sending soot and motes of dust stirring upon the old beams below. Adeline strained to grab a second beam.

The door to the hall sounded with a scraping thud, and began to open. Adeline stretched farther to reach the edge of the opening above her, and failed.

There were footsteps below her, and a hoarse voice. "Merciful God. Come down from there."

Adeline shifted her weight to one foot and tried again. The chest slipped from beneath her boot and clattered to the floor.

"Hang on."

She had imagined Simon's voice below her. Adeline craned her neck to look down.

"Now let go," said Simon.

Her grip faltered; she caught the beam again. She sucked in a short breath and looked once more. "You came back."

"I'll catch you. Let go now."

"I don't trust you."

He spread his arms wide. "Come now. I won't let you fall."

"Promise me you won't leave me."

"Madam, I am trying my best to recover you now." He mounted the table and kicked the benches aside. Adeline felt his arms about her knees and muttered a swift prayer. She released her hold on the beams and collapsed upon Simon's shoulder.

He lowered her to the rumpled bed. "Thank you," she said.

The hall was a shambles, the floor covered with splinters of the clothing chest and the remains of last night's meal. A corner of the trestle table was in flames. Simon heaved a sigh and upended the water bucket over the small fire, and kicked the blackened edge from the board. "How did you do all this in such a short time?"

"Why did you confine me here?"

"To keep you from harm."

"I could have burned to death."

"My lady, I can see you have tried." He went to the door and bellowed an order, and returned to look upon her. "I'll bring the water bucket."

"I bathed last night."

"For your face, Adeline. You'll frighten the sheep."

She pulled off her gloves and touched her cheek. Her fingers came away sooty. Her temples began to throb. "What sheep?" she asked.

He held out his hand. "Come," he said. "I don't know whether something I found just now has changed our future or not. But I thought you should tell me what you make of it."

"The sly way out of the valley?"

"I wish it were."

"Tell me."

Simon shook his head and found an unspilled bucket. He carried it to the single decent corner of the chamber and set it down. "I'll be outside. Come soon and"—he kissed her softly upon her mouth— "you might want another tunic."

She looked at her shoulder and saw that it was smeared with soot.

"Your brothers would be proud of you," he said, "but you shouldn't encourage their trips up the rafters."

"Yes," she said. "I won't let them see me in this state. Simon—is something wrong?"

"Come soon," he said. "We'll ride with Harald and half the garrison."

The ravens had moved from the north wall to perch in the trees below the fort, and protested in strident cries as the riders passed. From the valley floor came the sound of milling sheep and cattle.

"The sheep are out of the folds," said Adeline. "It's too late in the season to let them wander free."

Simon motioned Harald forward. "Take three men and ride up to the biggest of shepherds' huts. See who's there."

Adeline stared at her husband. "What do you expect?"

He pointed to the manor. "The stock is free. The cows are on the hill, and sheep are in the churchyard."

She turned her gaze to the manor itself. "Simon—there's no smoke—"

He put his hand on her shoulder. "There's no sign of violence. Not as far as I could tell."

They rode down to the deserted stockade.

The byre was empty of horses and harness. Adeline's heart began to pound. "They left on horseback, all who could. Even Penric's pony is gone."

"There are no horses among the cattle on the hill." Simon led the way to the hall to where the great door was rocking in the wind, its leather hinges sagging with each gust.

The long hearth pit was glowing with the last of the living embers. A raven rose from the crumbs of abandoned trenchers and flew up to a wall bracket and clung to the cold torch within its iron bands.

Adeline walked past the yellow-eyed bird into the doorway of the sleeping chamber. There, all was in readiness for Caerdoc's first night in his rightful place. The rich, shrouded bed stood square to the walls, its hangings little disturbed by the draft from the hall. Adeline felt Simon at her arm, and at his gesture held back to let him go first.

He entered the room and approached the bed; he turned to Adeline and shook his head. "There's no one here. The bedding is smooth. I doubt they slept here."

They went through the outbuildings. Looms stood burdened with half-finished work; the kitchen fires were banked and cooling below the cauldrons. Maida's chickens were gathered about a sack of grain left open in a corner of the manor yard. Outside the stockade, two oxen were standing at the chapel door. Within the small church, the altar was bare of plate; the reliquaries so recently presented to Cuthbert were gone.

Adeline led a curious cow from the chapel stoop as Simon wedged the door shut. "They loosed the cattle and the sheep to forage for themselves, and took their horses and what they could carry," she said. "And they did it all in the hours of darkness, after you and I left the hall."

Simon enfolded her in his arms. "It seems they had a plan, and time enough for an orderly flight."

"I hope they're safe, however they went."

"Where would they go—fifty souls, most on horseback, leaving their goods and cattle behind, with winter coming?"

"My father's cousin is a day's hard ride from here, in country rougher than this. Rhys is an old ally; he'd take them in."

Simon looked at the sky. Black, silver-framed clouds were passing high above the valley. "If the wind continues, we might have snow before sunset. Caerdoc and the others might have their tracks covered by the end of the day." He managed to keep his voice neutral; there was no trace, he hoped, of the anger he felt that Caerdoc had left his daughter behind without a farewell.

"He keeps his secrets well," said Adeline.

Simon's throat constricted in pain. "He must have left a message, or a sign for you. We'd find it, if we had the time. But we should be on our way before the weather arrives."

Adeline shook her head. "We would find no message. My father—" She looked up to the sky for a moment and continued. "My father knows that I'll be safe with you. He didn't need to tell me that he trusts you."

She laid her head on his shoulder. "Do you know what this means? My father has done us the favor of removing Longchamp's second threat: Without Welshmen to slaughter in the valley, there is nothing he can do to punish you or me for disappearing."

He smiled down at her. "Nothing at all."

Adeline closed her eyes in relief. "Simon, of all my life, there has been nothing to match this moment."

"Nothing? Last night, there was a moment. Or two—"

She shook her head. "Don't jest. We are one, Simon, and we will not be sundered."

The return of the errant cow cut short his caress. "Come," he said. "The beast can't be discouraged. Leave her to her devotions." He drew Adeline away through the churchyard, his arm about her waist. "I'll need to speak to the men of the garrison, and ask some of them to stay long enough for the Marshal to decide what to do with the fort. Its purpose was to watch over your good father; now that he's gone, we won't need the sentry tower."

"Your new tower proved useless in any case. I doubt that the valley people used the pass last night."

"That many people moving past the fort would have awakened even my worst sentry." He raised his head and looked back to the fortress. "It was Luke, last night, in the early evening. Harald sent a man to replace him at midnight. The new sentry said he heard nothing at all; the moon was bright, yet he saw no one on the road."

"The tales were true, then—my father found his secret way from the valley. Big enough for horsemen." Adeline looked up to the southern slope of the valley. "Do you remember yesterday in the cave—"

He drew her tighter against him, and whispered in her ear. "I remember, my lady. How could you doubt it?"

She drew back and pressed a single finger to his lips. "Don't make me forget this—Listen, Simon. Yesterday, in the cave, I smelled smoke."

"When?"

"After—"

"After we made love?"

She nodded. "I slept for a time, and awoke from a dream that we were back in the hall beside the fire. The smell of smoke lingered long after I awoke. You were down at the brook, then, and I went out to find you. By the time you came back, the smoke had disappeared and I had forgotten it."

Simon looked in the direction of the shepherds' hut. "Smoke from the shepherds' hut might have reached as high as our cave—"

"—but it was inside the cave, and when I rose to look for you the scent of it was gone. That wall of the valley has many small caves—"

"I know," he muttered. "I spent the last month rooting into all I could find. They were small—all of them."

"But there might be a passage behind them."

"For smoke, or for foxes. Or for a man to crawl on his belly. Nothing big enough for fifty souls to leave so quickly."

Adeline hesitated. "But the smoke came from behind the cave. If it was from the shepherds' hut—"

Simon closed his eyes, and remembered the old rebels gathered outside crude, high-linteled door of the hut, their well-worn weapons at their sides, living on Caerdoc's charity—

He began to laugh. "Of course. It had to be the shepherds' hut. The door was built high for a reason—to get the horses through."

Simon sat down upon the chapel stoop and drew Adeline down beside him. "The old fox was brilliant in this—His act of faith in the treaty—leaving the fortress and moving down to the indefensible manor—might have been nothing more than a plan to get his people close to the passage, in case of danger. Last night, they had only to ride up the hill to disappear."

A wild shriek and the sound of fast hoofbeats ended their speech. Simon pushed Adeline behind him and stood with sword in hand.

Harald rounded the stockade and set his mount toward Simon at a gallop. "Taillebroc. I've found it. I've got it—" He hauled the reins to stop the beast a few feet from Simon. "Come up and see. You won't believe it. The shepherds' hut—"

"Isn't a hut?"

"Damn it, Taillebroc. Listen. It's not a hut, not a proper one. It but hides the entrance to a cave. A big one. The old rebels are gone, the sheepfolds empty; those were no shepherds up there—they were guards to keep us out of the hovel."

He should have seen it before: the overlarge door, the armed men sitting idle before that door, the position of the hut against the base of the cliff.

Simon pushed aside the rude door and entered the hut. Two low benches pushed against the wall held crude bedding; against the back wall, two cowhides suspended from a low beam obscured the entrance to the cave.

Behind the hides, the portal was straight-sided and large enough for a man to lead his saddled mount into the larger cavern beyond. Simon touched the edges of the portal. "They cut through the stone here to allow passage into the big cavern. Before this work, it might have had small openings, like the ones in the other cave."

Adeline moved forward to look into the cavern. "They must have done it after I left for Normandy." She took the torch from Simon's hand and raised it high to illuminate the ceiling of the cavern. "It wouldn't be hard to follow them, once inside. The soot from their torches marks the way."

There was a cold, slow breeze coming from the branch blackened by Caerdoc's torches. Simon smiled. "It must go all the way through the cliffs. Your kinsman Rhys may not be as far away as you thought."

"Shall we follow them?"

Simon took the torch from her hands and walked the short distance to the narrowing of the way. "We'll go back and get food to carry with us, and I'll speak to the garrison. Then, if you wish, we'll follow Caerdoc's route through the caves. But on the other side," he said, "I'd like to ride south, to Striguil. I must report to William the Marshal before we decide anything more." He hesitated. "We might not be able to leave Striguil until spring. Do you mind?"

Adeline drew a long breath. "As I said, my father knows I'll be safe with you. If we give him another five years," she said, "I wonder what we'll find next time."

"Nothing would surprise me. I begin to believe his true name is Merlin, and I have wed a sorcerer's daughter."

Adeline looked beyond him, into the dark passage. "We'll pray he didn't leave a dragon to guard the way out."

CHAPTER TWENTY-SEVEN

Simon took a last look about the fortress hall. "I'm sorry to leave this place," he said. "I began here in deep trouble, and began to find peace, then found a wife—and love." He heaved the saddlebags to his shoulders. "One day, we'll return."

Adeline smiled and touched his arm. "Longchamp won't last forever. Even in Normandy, he was despised before he became chancellor. The people won't tolerate him."

"I pray he won't start a war among the king's vassals."

"He's a coward, I think. He might run before a threat. The gold he hid in your abbey is proof that he had begun to plan his escape as soon as he came to England."

Simon smiled. "If only King Richard had seen the

man as you did, we'd all be better off." He pointed to the small bag Adeline carried in her hands. "That thing you carry on your saddle—what is it?"

"You never looked?"

"Not yet."

"You said you thought I'd poison you with it."

"I said a number of stupid things."

She slipped the knot from one of the cracked leather laces, and opened one end. "It's a cloak, just as I said."

"Not a very big one."

"No." She looked up at the smoke hole and the grey sky beyond. "It was new. My mother gave it to me, and said to keep it for the cold."

He caught a subtle note of sadness in her voice. "Was that—before the boat?"

"Yes," she said. "She told me to keep it close to hand."

"And you kept it."

"Her things—the traveling chest, her rings, her other clothes, went to the nuns who buried her in Caen. This was only a child's cloak, so I was allowed to keep it."

"Tie it to your saddle, then, for good luck."

She tucked it under an arm and took his hand. "What did you tell the garrison?"

"Everything we learned today. They know I may not return, and that Luke will command them until the Marshal sends another warden."

"Luke?"

Simon smiled. "He's cured of his allegiance to Longchamp, and he's bright enough to deal with anything that comes through the pass." He hesitated. "I told the men that if your father doesn't return, they should inherit his sheep and cattle. Half of them are out now, gathering the stock."

"It's fair. Without tending, the animals wouldn't make it through the winter."

"And I told them that if they value their own lives, they should surrender the beasts to your father when he returns."

"They agreed?"

"To a man. Your father still has something of the other world about him, as far as the garrison is concerned. I told them about the passage through the cliffs, but they still seem to regard him as some kind of wizard. Now they mutter that he must have cut through the rock by magic." He sighed. "It must be in the air—my soldiers are more fanciful now than your Welshmen."

"And you, Simon, remain a hardheaded Norman?"

"I have to be. If I listened to these tales, I'd be frightened to bed the wizard's daughter, for fear I'd displease her and find myself made into a mule."

His wife smiled. "Not a mule, dear husband. You'd be a stallion, at the very least. But continue as you have done, and I'll gladly keep you as a man." She glanced back at the bed and the coverlets stacked upon the clothing chest. "Must we leave so soon?"

He set down the saddlebags and took her in his arms. Simon kissed her with swift abandon. "We must. But when we're far enough from the valley to count ourselves saved, we'll find a warm chamber and a bed and close the door upon the world until spring." He kissed her, then, and set her from him. "That, dear wife, is a promise I'll make good before three days are done."

Harald helped them close the door and wedge it shut against the rising wind. "The ravens are gone," he said.

Adeline frowned. "They were below the tower this morning when we rode down the hill."

Harald shook his head. "The men said they flew south over the valley after you left. They haven't returned."

Simon laughed. "They have learned to fear the ravens' displeasure as much as your people do. If the damned birds return, these men will be tossing them the garrison's best meat and begging them to stay."

They bid farewell to the men of the garrison and rode out the gates with Harald, carrying only two saddlebags each. Adeline had protested when Simon had tied the smaller of his bags to her saddle, for he had shown her that they bore a purse of gold and a small coffer of the jewels he had brought away from Taillebroc.

"My treasure," said Simon, "is all here on this palfrey's back, easy to defend."

Adeline frowned. "If there's trouble—"

"If there's trouble, and I have to deal with it, Harald will be with you."

He saw her attempt to hide the shudder that come over her. "You will be careful?"

"Life has become precious to me. I'll be careful. And there is no trouble."

He was wrong.

* * *

The wind was colder now, and the clouds it bore had darkened the day. Adeline pulled the hood of her cloak close about her as she rode past the stockade, and did not turn to look into the deserted place that had been the center of Caerdoc's domain. The snow for which she had prayed had begun to fall from the lowering clouds. Near the shepherds' hut, a downdraft from the cliffs drove the snow in crystalline gusts; through a rift in the clouds, the sun shone upon silver whorls of frost-smoke upon the earth.

Harald shouted something into the wind, and Simon turned to look behind them. He tossed his cloak back from his shoulders and touched the hilt of his sword.

Adeline turned in her saddle and saw that the snow was thin behind them, leaving a clear view of the pass.

And the dark-clad army pouring though it.

Harald grabbed her reins. Simon turned back for the space of a heartbeat. "Remember," he said. "You go for both of us."

She tried to snatch back the reins, then kicked her feet free of the stirrup. Harald's hand came down hard on her shoulder. "Don't force him to die knowing that you are within Longchamp's grasp. If you love him, lady, let him die believing that you are safe."

Adeline struck his face and clawed for the reins. "He must come with us. They don't see us yet. Stop him. Stop him."

Harald ducked, but still clung to her shoulder. "He

won't leave the garrison to be tortured. The men
know of the passage. It wouldn't be long before we
had pursuit. Come. Don't let him die for nothing.''

The wind increased, and turned north to drive its
burden of snow onto the valley floor. Simon had
disappeared into that glittering whiteness; the sound
of the stallion's hoofbeats were drowned in the wind's
white rush.

Adeline clung to the saddlebow as Harald spurred
his mount forward and forced her palfrey into a jar-
ring gallop up the last stretch of hill. As they reached
the hut, the wind increased, and the sun disappeared
behind a wall of blowing snow.

In the moment she saw the ring of wet, black
ground where the ashes of the campfire were melting
the snow, Adeline began to hope that they would
turn back from the caves for lack of torchlight. But
Simon had left a torch burning in the bracket deep
inside the hut, protected from the wind by the cowhide hangings. Stacked beneath the flaming brand
were three more torches.

Hot tears flowed upon her cheeks as she led her
mare through the doorway of the hut. Simon had
thought of everything that might have stopped them,
down to lack of fire, and left the escape route in
readiness. He had done everything but find a way to
preserve himself from Longchamp's raid.

''If only we had left a few moments earlier, he
wouldn't have seen the army,'' she said.

Harald wrenched the torch from its bracket and
thrust the others into his saddlebag. ''He wouldn't

have lived the winter, knowing that he had left those men to die."

Adeline wiped the tears from her face. "He didn't intend to go through with us, did he?"

Harald shook his head. "He had decided to wait here and follow when he was sure the pass was closed."

"The same snow would have stopped him from following us."

"My lady, he would have made it somehow. You can't stop him, once he has set his course." He peered at her in the torchlight. "Don't weep now, my lady. Wait until we're through the passage. We owe him that much, I think. Come, my lady. We have to go."

Simon rode down the hill and did not look back. The swirling wall of snow behind him cut off the sound of his wife's cries, and Harald's blandishments. He did not worry that Adeline would break free and follow; Harald was stubborn, and his lady would be kind enough to spare him the grief of seeing her trapped within Longchamp's power.

In all the months of his exile, Simon had not feared death at Longchamp's hands; he had lived in the expectation that one day he would meet that dark-liveried troop of the chancellor's guard and die at their hands. To avoid that fate, or to postpone it, had been no more than a game to him—a game he knew he must lose one day.

But now, with the memory of passion and the image of Adeline's beloved face before him, the end of his deadly game with Longchamp would come hard. He had lost Taillebroc, the company of his brother, and the familiar faces of his people; all this he had given up without bitterness. But he was maddened past reason by the thought that he would never again touch the wife whose joys he had only begun to know.

He stopped among the last stand of trees above the stockade and tried to put Adeline's grief from his mind. He heard her voice as if she were at his side: disbelief that he had left her; realization that he had never intended to leave his men prey to Longchamp's torture; and the pain of knowing that had the snows come only a day earlier, Longchamp would not have managed to bring his army through the pass.

He went through her thoughts as if she had spoken them to him, then bid her a silent farewell and closed his mind to Adeline and what might have been. At last, he began to register what he was seeing in the abandoned hall and bailey below him on the valley floor.

The fortress had been spared, for the moment. Longchamp and over one hundred horsemen had streamed through the pass and turned downhill to Caerdoc's stockade. Simon winced as he saw the chancellor's men begin to hack at the walls of the storehouses, searching for loot or hidden souls. A torch landed on the roof of the hall, to be knocked down a moment later at Longchamp's command. The chancellor must intend to settle in Caerdoc's great hall after dealing with Simon and the garrison. Simon smiled to himself as he imagined how Caerdoc would react to the news that Normans—this one in particular—had slept in his bed and drunk his brandywine.

A fair quarter of the riders detached themselves from the party in the stockade and rode up the hill toward the fortress. Simon gathered his reins and prepared to charge down the hill to show himself and stop the assault upon the fort.

The riders turned left, to pound across the fields in the direction of the lake and the high ground beyond. From his vantage point, Simon saw that the five men who had volunteered to catch the errant cattle were on the far side of the valley, traversing the exposed ridge to reach their fellows at the fortress. So far, Longchamp had found no living prey on the valley floor.

Longchamp himself was in Caerdoc's abandoned hall. Simon waited and watched the chancellor's guard dismount and lead their horses into the byre. A thread of smoke appeared from the roof of the hall, then grew into a windblown column above the stockade. The chancellor would be cold, and his spindly limbs numb from the hard ride into the valley.

Simon reached before him to stroke the neck of his stallion. Longchamp's need for comfort would give Simon another hour or two to live.

He considered trying to make his way across to the fortress, but decided that his men might live through the day if not tempted to defend him from the inevitable death at Longchamp's hands. With luck, he would be dead before they thought of riding out to help him, to waste their lives upon their doomed warden.

The snow was falling faster now, and had advanced

to the tree line where he waited. He saw a gift in the clarity before him and the opaque, silver tempest at his back. The past—Adeline's love, Harald's loyalty, were gone from hearing and from sight now. His fate—clear and cold, plain to view—was before him, and must now be his only concern.

The party of riders had reached the lake and circled it. They had gathered at the near shore and milled about as if deciding where next to search. They seemed not to see the cattle wandering in the aspen forest, abandoned by the men of the garrison in their furtive journey back to the fortress. The sheep were scattered about the high meadows, swarming, separating, then huddling again as the wall of snow advanced upon them.

Two of the riders pointed to the sheep, then turned back to the stockade. The untended, milling flocks had convinced Longchamp's scouts that there were no men on the slopes to question.

That would leave the garrison. As Simon had instructed them, the garrison guards had barred the gates when they had seen Longchamp's army coming through the pass, and lit the two great beacon fires in their cressets on the walls. Even with one hundred men at his command, Longchamp would not soon get past the stout walls of the fortress. With luck, the garrison might hold out long enough for William the Marshal to come to their aid, or witness the remains of their defense.

Once again, Simon gathered the reins. The scouting party would soon reach the stockade, and Longchamp would emerge from the small comfort of the hall to direct the riders to approach the oddly silent fortress. Before then, it would be time to ride down and make the sacrifice for which he had prepared.

The cold was biting into his back and numbing his fingers within his heavy gloves. Before long, there would be an end to discomfort and a remedy for the dilemma he had faced since that terrible night at Hodmersham. Simon patted his mount's neck one final time and resolved to dismount and goad the stallion to run from the confrontation before Longchamp reached him. The bay was a fine beast; Simon would not waste his life.

He drew his sword and held the clean, nicked blade shining in the winter light. He had sworn an oath to William the Marshal that he would not take Longchamp's life. But he would have to take as many other lives as he could before falling: If he walked weaponless into the ranks of Longchamp's guard, the wily chancellor would sense that he intended a sacrifice, and would begin to search for the reason.

Simon urged the bay forward and made his way down the hill. The wind was a rush of sound behind him, and the dark figures in the stockade below seemed unreal as they gestured and shouted beyond Simon's hearing. A gust obscured Simon's vision, then cleared to show that the guard was remounting and forming into a line.

He imagined the sounds of armed horsemen behind him. If he closed his eyes, he could imagine that he was once again on the hills above Le Mans, riding at the Marshal's side to cover the old king Henry's last retreat. Behind him, the sounds of arms and harness increased; in that moment, Simon began to wonder whether he had already passed into the hereafter, to find again his fallen comrades and ride with them into an eternal winter.

His last thought, before he climbed down from the saddle and set a hard elbow to the bay's flank, was of Adeline, and the warmth of her unbound hair before the firelight.

CHAPTER
TWENTY-EIGHT

His mount refused to bolt. Simon struck it again on its shining, well-curried flank and shouted a curse to frighten it away. The beast turned its head to look at Simon, then took a step to turn back uphill. The fine head came up; the bay whinnied and trotted away up the hill to disappear into the white wall of snow behind Simon.

Ahead, Longchamp's guard was hard to make out through the whirling eddies of snowflakes. Simon raised his sword and walked down the last few feet of slope above the great level field outside the stockade gates.

To shout at Longchamp's guard to come for him would seem suspicious and lead them to treat him as a decoy. The worsening weather had already discouraged an assault upon the fortress; it was certain, now, that the chancellor's men would not venture up the hill to discover Caerdoc's caves before Adeline and Harald were safely away.

Simon stood his ground, but did not rush forward to seek death. Before him, there was a shifting of place, and when the wind turned to clear the view, Simon saw that William Longchamp was among his guard, mounted upon a tall black steed, well behind the line of soldiers who faced Simon.

The black-garbed Longchamp moved an arm in sharp, slicing gesture. There were words half-borne upon the wind, and no meaning to either motion or speech.

Simon drew a gasping breath and bellowed across the short distance. "The fort is the Marshal's. Those men are under the Marshal's protection."

The wind resumed its first direction, and the sparkling fall of snow began once again. Ten of the guards moved forward, and halted close enough that their faces were half-visible through the weather; the huffing breath of the horses showed opaque white against the glittering snowfall. Once halted, the guards made no move to touch Simon.

The hunched, dark rider behind them moved to the back of their mounts and turned his horse broadside to the line. Between Simon and Longchamp there were ten mounted soldiers with swords at the ready. "Where are the others," came the petulant voice of the chancellor.

"Out hunting," said Simon.

One of the guards snorted. Then coughed, to disguise his imprudent laughter.

"And your wife, the bandit's daughter? Where is she?"

"Hunting."

"Take him."

At Longchamp's command, the two closest guards nudged their horses forward. Simon raised his sword and stepped aside. "Think again," he said to the guards. "I am the warden of that fortress, the Marshal's man. And I will kill the man who comes closer."

"Take him," repeated Longchamp. "Take him now."

Simon feinted a blow and ducked under the nearest guardsman's horse. He rolled clear and came to his feet a spear's length away from the second horse. The beast shied from Simon's bellowed curse.

Behind Simon, another horse whinnied.

They had flanked him, and surrounded him. This final fight was to be much shorter than he had imagined. The cold earth and deepening snow had chilled his feet within the sheepskin boots. Before long, he would become clumsy and miss a step. He flexed his numb fingers within the heavy gloves of good Taillebroc leather and remembered, in that instant, the day he had worn them new to see his father buried. He began to say his numbers in Latin; he would not think of Adeline in these next moments of struggle. Her image was waiting in the farthest corner of his mind, to be cherished when the fighting was no longer possible.

The horsemen behind him did not attack.

With deliberate and impossible precision, the guards before him nudged their horses to back away. To the right of the line, Simon saw his bay stallion canter past a group of horsemen. The guards saw them then; ten of Longchamp's men turned to face the advancing troop.

Simon turned his back on the guards and looked behind him. Through the whiteness, slicing through the thick curtain of snow, a deeply curved blade glittered as it wove a threatening pattern above his head. There was a flash of color at the hilt, and below it, a sleeve of wine-dark velvet.

"Who are you, who come from my stockade?"

Longchamp reined in his horse and turned to face that voice. "William Longchamp, chancellor to King Richard. Bishop of Ely."

The Saracen blade continued to work its shimmering tracery in the air. Caerdoc pointed it at the foremost guards. "And these men, are they sanctioned by William the Marshal to come onto my lands? My treaty shows that the Marshal is the only Norman lord who may send outsiders here to tend his fortress."

Longchamp's horse shied at the sound of Caerdoc's bellow. "I come to question the priestkiller Taillebroc."

Caerdoc laughed. "He killed the priest long ago. The Marshal freed him. Who are you to gainsay that decision?"

"I am King Richard's justiciar."

"And the Marshal has charge of these mountains. I'll not offend him."

"Taillebroc is a murderer, with new prey. I come to remove him before he kills again."

To the left of the line of guards, near to the corner of the stockade, another group of horsemen appeared as white shadows against the sparkle of windblown flakes.

"His only prey so far has been a few deer for my table. Know you something more?"

"Your daughter," called Longchamp. "Tell me where she rests."

"She doesn't rest," said Caerdoc. "She's hunting."

"Don't try my temper," called Longchamp. "I know your daughter is dead. I'm here to take her murderer to Hereford."

The extravagant gyrations of the Saracen sword ceased. "Did you ride from Hereford to make a fool of me? My daughter is still living—as strident as ever, in her wish to find her husband in this bad weather."

Caerdoc flourished the Saracen sword a final time, then spent some time sheathing it in the jeweled, curved scabbard. "My cousins Rhys and Madoc, and their household men have come here to speak with my new son, newly wed to my daughter Adeline."

The horsemen at either end of the guards' line came forward to crowd about Simon. A strange figure in a mustard-dark cape upon a spotted horse trotted forward with the bay's reins in his hand. "There, kinsman. Don't let him loose when you stop to deal with visitors, or you'll lose a good horse."

Caerdoc stood in the saddle. "We'll go into the hall and speak in there." He paused and looked again at the stockade. "By Saint Dewi's bones, there's a fire."

Longchamp made an angry gesture. "It was cold."

"Well," said Caerdoc, "Saint Dewi won't think much of that. We let the fire burn out, and the hearth get cold, once a year to honor him, then light it again before midnight. Now we'll have bad luck for the next year."

"Where are your women?" Longchamp demanded.

"Safe in my kinsman's house, weaving with their sisters." He rode forward and made a broad gesture. "You can't expect them to be here when we're honoring Saint Dewi with a fireless day."

The wind lulled, and through the thinning snowfall, the retinue of warriors behind Caerdoc and his fellow chieftains was revealed. Fifty mounted warriors in half armor were ranged in a half circle on the hill.

Longchamp's head turned to look along their line with a predatory grimace. "I have one hundred picked men to back my rightful demands," he said. "Tell your hill bandits to keep their swords down or suffer defeat."

Caerdoc made a careless gesture. "These men are seasoned warriors, and know not to raise their swords at every fool's insults." He glanced over his shoulder and shrugged at the snow-clad trees behind him. "But the others—not far behind me—are young wolves hungry for a taste of Norman blood. I forbade them to approach unless they hear iron on iron. If they do, no man here will stop them."

A sharp gust descended upon the line of silent Welshmen. Longchamp's gaze turned toward the snow blowing through the trees. "You lie," he said. "There are no more men behind you."

Caerdoc's gauntlet found the bejeweled hilt of the Saracen sword. "Tell me you speak in jest," he said. "Or my honor will demand your Norman blood."

For a long, silent moment, the Welsh chieftain and the black-robed chancellor regarded each other through the falling snow. From the woods came the whicker of a horse, and the jingle of bridle iron.

Longchamp's gaze turned once again to the ghostly woods, then back to Caerdoc's grim face. "It was but a jest," he said at last.

Adeline's father looked beyond Longchamp to the pass. "You see," he said, "the snow hasn't yet closed the way out of the valley. Best make your way through the pass now, before the snow worsens." He pointed to the stockade. "I have only my stock, and some grain, and a few sheep to get us through the winter. It's hard enough to feed the garrison, as I have sworn to do; if your guard is trapped in here for the winter, I cannot feed them."

Longchamp nudged his horse through the line to come face-to-face with Caerdoc. Simon mounted the bay and tarried near enough to hear them. The chancellor made another swift, chopping gesture. "I will remember this, Caerdoc."

Caerdoc's two kinsmen rode forward to his side and stared with him at the chancellor Longchamp. "I don't understand," said Caerdoc. "Please tell me."

"One day, you'll stop playing the fool. You and all your fellow brigands will understand that I never forget a slight."

"And I never forget a treaty. I have a treaty and the goodwill of the Marshal. That is all I need from the Normans. Now go," he said, "before the snow traps you here."

Longchamp turned his mount and moved back into

the line of his guard. He raised his fist to Caerdoc. "If any of you or your Norman kin pass beyond Hereford to the east, there will be the sheriff's men waiting to see you go no farther."

Caerdoc nudged his mount forward to stand beside Simon's bay. "Tell your brother the sheriff we want nothing from Hereford. But if pressed, we'll give him our steel."

Longchamp turned away and rode down the hill.

His guard remained in place until the chancellor had reached the stockade walls, then wheeled their mounts to follow.

Caerdoc made a sound of disgust. "How long will you Normans tolerate that carrion crow as chancellor?"

"As long as Richard Plantagenet is abroad in Palestine."

The old bandit shook his head. "There are too many fools among you Normans. One day, you'll lose these lands."

"Where is she?"

Caerdoc sighed. "Up at the passageway, with your Harald and my Howyll to keep her from coming down the hill."

"I'll go up to her when Longchamp's guard is clear of the valley."

Adeline's father nodded. "Go quickly, when you do."

Simon lowered his voice. "I thank you, Caerdoc. I owe you my life."

"If I had not stood by you, my daughter would have made my years a living hell." He gestured to his kinsmen. "Mark their faces, and remember them if war returns to these hills. I'll not have my daughter's husband raising his sword to men of my blood."

"I'll remember, if they keep their treaties with the Marshal."

"Fair enough."

Caerdoc's kinsmen and their followers waited motionless on the hillside as the chancellor and his guard formed a line and rode out of Caerdoc's stockade toward the pass. Behind them, only a low cloud of windblown smoke moved in the bailey yard.

The distant line of riders had reached the pass; behind them, the smoke from Caerdoc's hall had disappeared. Upon the watchtower above the hill, the men of Simon's garrison had gathered to watch the confrontation their warden had forbidden them to approach. Simon waved his arms above his head, and saw the gesture returned twentyfold.

Caerdoc shivered. "I'll go down and build the fire up. I'll fetch the women back tomorrow; they'll chide us if they find the mead pots frozen."

Simon smiled. "What was that talk of Saint Dewi and the cold hearth?"

Caerdoc shrugged his crimson cloak close about him. "Longchamp believed it. And Saint Dewi wouldn't mind." He looked over his shoulder. "Best not mention it to Cuthbert. It might give him ideas." He started down the hill, then turned back to Simon. "Tell my Adeline I'll follow you both to Striguil when spring comes. And bring her brothers to see her."

"I am in your debt," he called after Caerdoc.

The brigand chief raised the Saracen sword from his side and waved over his head in farewell.

The earth was covered with snow, and pocked with hoofprints vanishing beneath the hard-blowing sleet. With growing incredulity, Simon saw that the woods were empty: there had been no young, incorrigible warriors waiting for battle among the trees. Caerdoc, his cousins, and fewer than fifty armed men had deceived Longchamp and his guard into giving up their assault on the valley.

He spurred the bay into a swift trot through the snow-laden trees and crossed the white meadow to the hut. As he neared, he heard the sound of Adeline's voice and Howyll's words of caution. The door swung open, and his wife ran to him, and once again he found true summer in the path of winter's silver wind.

CHAPTER
TWENTY-NINE

Harald collapsed onto the hut's larger bench and mopped his face with his sleeve. "It was no use, Simon. Your lady wife wouldn't start through the passage without you. Just as well, for Caerdoc's warriors were coming through fast, two abreast, and we would have slowed them as they passed us."

"So we stayed here with her, and I missed the fighting," said Howyll. "How was the fighting?"

"There was none," said Simon. "My lady's father deceived the chancellor and his men, convinced them that there were twice as many Welshmen in the valley to oppose them."

Her father and his kinsmen had survived unharmed. Adeline heard the rest of their exchange with indifference. She sat upon Simon's lap, her head upon his breast, her arms clasped behind his neck. Never again would she let him go. Never—

Simon shifted beneath her and took her in his arms once again. "It's time to make our journey," he whispered. "Howyll says we're only hours from shelter; we should leave today."

With his words, the world had returned to something near to reality. Adeline stood up and went into the cavern to open her saddlebag and draw forth a leather bag. "Here," she said. "Howyll, this is Petronilla's dowry."

Howyll's blush glowed in the torchlight. "She has a dowry?"

"She has now."

Simon lowered his brows and looked into Howyll's face. "You intend to marry the maid?"

"Oh yes."

"Soon?"

"She has agreed, she has." Howyll's face flamed brighter still. "We'll have to speak again to Father Ambrose. Old Cuthbert won't hear of a wedding until the summer, and we can't wait."

Adeline looked down at her boots. How long would Ambrose lay in his unhallowed grave before the people of the valley began to suspect that he had perished?

Simon motioned to Harald, and passed him another bag of coin. "Old friend, will you see what this will do to sweeten Cuthbert's opinions of swift marriages?"

"I will," said Harald. "There's no harm done if Ambrose has gone on to Hereford. No need to go to a Norman priest when Cuthbert is close at hand."

His gaze went to Adeline, then to Simon. "There's no harm done," he repeated.

They heard Howyll's thanks with more emotion than the excited youth suspected, and each in turn clasped Harald in friendship and farewell.

The passage proved to be a simple matter; even without the soot marks above them, the way across the cavern and into the largest of its tributaries seemed obvious to Adeline. They walked slowly, torches in hand, leading the horses.

"I wonder, " said Simon, "why the way is worn smooth, as if well traveled. The portal in the hut was cut from the stone only a few years ago." He laughed; the sound of his mirth echoed around them in the passage.

She looked about her as the way narrowed. Far in the distance, beyond the loom of the torch, there was an indefinite glow of white. "For the horses," she said. "The work must have been done for the horses. Foot travelers might have come through earlier."

"From the time of Merlin?" Simon laughed again, and listened to the change in the echoes. "In truth, I have wed the daughter of a wizard."

As they neared the end of the passage, Simon doused the torches and thrust the half-burnt brands into a fissure in the wall. "I'll go first," he said, "and call to you if it's clear."

A stand of wind-twisted oaks stood sentinel a few feet below the opening of the cave. Adeline looked past Simon's shoulders and saw that the trees would hide the passage from sight in the summer. Now, the dark, complex branches and the snow they carried would hide the greater darkness behind them.

"God's blood," said Simon. "Go back."

"Not again," she said.

Adeline stepped back; she had seen a small part of the vista from the cave, and at first thought it was the ravens come to spy upon them outside the valley. But it was no raven that she had seen on the vast field of snow. It was a dark-clad rider making his way across the white, open space. Moving slowly. Stopping to look about, then riding on to stop again.

"How many?" she whispered.

"Only one that I can see," Simon answered. He gave her his reins and moved closer to the open air. Adeline stood with the horses and stroked the neck of the restive bay to keep him silent.

"Please," she whispered. "Please—" The great head turned to regard her, then reached with great delicacy to nibble the edge of her cloak. She stood unprotesting as the stallion mouthed the wool and dropped it. The beast snorted as he raised his head.

Adeline covered his nose with her hand, and looked back to where Simon crouched at the end of the cave.

The rider was closer now. Despite the wind, the tracks the scout had left were visible upon the white surface of the earth. He was methodical in his quest, and had crossed and recrossed the area, drawing nearer to the cave with each traverse.

Simon moved to the side of the opening, ready to spring upon the scout should he come close. He motioned for Adeline to move back, and pointed deep into the cave. His mouth formed the word she had sworn never again to obey. "Go," he hissed. "Go back."

If she obeyed and left the horses, the animals would make noise, whether or not they followed her. She shook her head and covered her lips with a finger.

Then it was too late.

The rider turned and began to ride directly toward the cave, close enough that they could hear the hooves of his mount crushing the new snow. Simon was motionless beside the opening, his hand resting flat upon the pommel of his sword. As the rider drew near, Simon's fingers flexed, then closed about the sword's hilt.

The sound of a whistle floated upon the wind.

Simon turned his gaze back to Adeline; she shook her head.

In the daylight beyond the cave, the rider drew his horse to a halt and raised his head. He, too, seemed to be straining to hear the whistle.

A more subtle whistling followed the flight of a single crimson arrow into the drifting snow behind the rider. The horseman turned his mount to face the red shaft where it lay on the white ground, then dismounted to pick up the arrow. He examined the shaft, then frowned as if betrayed.

The scout looked up at the ridge above the cave and began to shout a word of protest. The next shot silenced him with an arrow through his throat; with deadly precision, the second shot entered his heart even as he fell clutching the first.

Mercifully, the horses made no sound, nor tried to bolt despite the scent of blood upon the wind. The dead scout's horse shied as his rider fell dead, then stopped a short distance away to face away from the wind.

Simon had not moved during the silent killing outside the cave, and Adeline had stifled her breath for fear that they would attract Luke's deadly attention. She ransacked her memories of the land beyond the valley, but could not guess whether the hill above the oak trees would be too steep for Luke to descend.

Outside the cave, there was only silence, and the wind-borne whiteness that had already begun to cover the mortal wounds of Longchamp's scout.

Simon moved back to Adeline. "We can't wait for him to be missed," he whispered. "And we can't go back into the valley, for the dead man's comrades will come looking for him and find the cave. They might come through."

Adeline pointed to the body. "Soon, the snow will cover it. They may not find him."

"I'll have to go out. If I fall, leave the horses and run back through the passage."

"Wait—"

"There's no choice—"

"Hush. Listen."

The flute sounded again, as distant as before. But this time, there was a pattern to the whistling. Adeline clutched Simon's arm. "It's the tune he would use when he wanted to meet."

"I remember." Simon drew a deep breath. "What do you make of it?"

"I think he means to say we're clear to leave."

"Or he lures us out for his next arrows."

Adeline shook her head. "You spared his life, Simon. He may mean to spare yours."

Simon closed his eyes and passed a weary hand across his brow. "Is it possible that Luke chose the place by chance, and he doesn't know about the passage?"

As if in answer, the flute sounded again, with the same slow pattern of tones—rising, then descending into silence.

Simon drew the cloak from his shoulders, wadded it into a weighty mass, then threw it far from the edge of the cave. No shaft flew to pierce it. Once again, the flute sounded.

"If he's playing the flute," said Adeline, "he can't have his bow drawn."

Simon smiled. "I'll wager my life on it."

She managed to smile back. "I'll be beside you. If we're right, we should ride away before he changes his mind. And if we're wrong—"

"If we're wrong," said Simon, "ride back before he can draw again. Will you promise?"

"I have made too many such promises in these days past. I have said my prayers, and made my wishes upon the rowan tree. Simon, I'm ready to go."

"The rowan tree? What did you leave—" His gaze went to her palfrey, and to the saddlebow. "Your cloak—the bag with the cloak is gone."

Adeline handed him the reins and asked for a hand up into the saddle. "Yes, it's gone. Hanging upon the rowan tree, where it will do more good than it ever did in my keeping. Your life, Simon, should be long and fortunate, if the tree still holds its power."

"When—"

"When you rode down to face Longchamp alone, I took my offering to the rowan tree. It hasn't failed, Simon, in three hundred years."

He kissed her hand and mounted his horse. "Still, I'll go first." Simon crouched low on the bay's back and spurred the large horse out into the snowy field, reining him in a wide arc to avoid the scout's body. After an instant, Adeline followed his path.

Up above the cave, on a rocky ridge nearly obscured by the driving snow, they saw the archer Luke, his bow in his hand, that same arm raised in a gesture of farewell.

They raised their own hands in greeting and gratitude, and turned to ride south through the deepening snow.

Though they watched as they rode south, they saw no more horsemen that day, or the next.

The ravens followed them until they had sight of Madoc's far keep. When Adeline turned back, she saw the dark birds winging north, closing upon the blessed wall of white.